A BREATH APART

CHRISTINA LEE

Photographer: Leonardo Corredor

Cover models: Nick Champa and Pierre Amaury Bouvier

Cover Artist: Sleepy Fox Studio

Copyedits provided by Flat Earth Editing

Proofing provided by Lyrical Lines

Thanks also to Erin Clancy Lazzarini for providing additional eyes

PROLOGUE

SIX YEARS AGO

DEAR DIARY:

Stuff is so confusing lately.

I feel different from everyone else, like I'm living in an alternate reality.

No one at church or home seems to notice, but it's like my bones are too big for my skin, my breaths coming too fast for my heart to keep up.

It began at mixed-media camp this summer—probably before then, but that was the exact time my body started feeling strange. So maybe it's just hormones. Except they seem to be affecting me differently than my friends who are suddenly all girl crazy.

But not me. Not in the slightest.

There's this kid named Brennan Fischer who's a grade lower and lives in my neighborhood. I've never really hung out with him, not really, not even when we were on the same teams in the city baseball leagues.

So this camp was a mishmash of music, theater, and art, and he makes these really cool graffiti drawings that have me wondering all sorts of things about him. I'm still enjoying violin but it was way cooler when I got to perform during the theater production, and the art kids even made the set. It was so much fun and well, back to Brennan.

During rehearsals Brennan and I were substitutes for a couple of absent kids. So we hung out all day together mostly just standing around, but we laughed a lot and got to know each other. I found out he likes the same Marvel movies and watches stupid YouTube hack videos as much as me, so we had a ton to talk about.

There was this one part of the musical where we had to lock arms and dance together in the background of the set and though we were embarrassed because we were two guys, nobody paid us any attention. My whole body got like this pins and needles feeling when we clasped hands and had to stare into each other's eyes. Before we dissolved into nervous laughter.

And then there's that other thing that happened after the lead in the show threw up on stage following her solo number and well...I don't want to talk about it yet.

Point is, I find myself wanting to be around him any chance I get. And yeah, he'd make a really cool friend, but this feels like more. Like maybe I admire him too much or something. Like my chest gets really tight and full when I spot him across the room. Maybe I just want to be like him, but he sort of makes me nervous too. He's so quiet and shy, but his big brown eyes probably have seen a lot of the world. He told me a bit about life before he went to live with the Fischers and it made me want to... I don't exactly know, it's hard to explain. It's a feeling that terrifies me and fills me up at the same time.

What the heck is going on with me?

If he knew I was obsessing over him like this, he might run and hide. Everyone would. My father would lecture me, Mom would recite scripture, and my friends might call me a freaking weirdo!

So, I figure I have to get rid of this THING, whatever it is, before school starts and I see him in the halls.

I need to cast it from my body like it's a demon.

Get out, get out, get out.

Or at least have it make sense.

Make sense, make sense, make sense.

Please let everything finally make sense.
-Josh

1

THE SUMMER AFTER HIGH SCHOOL GRADUATION

As Brennan Fischer strode across the gravel, he glanced at the other cars dotting the lot. The drive-in double feature was *Cool Hand Luke* and *The Shawshank Redemption*. He wasn't sure what his dad was trying to accomplish with his prison movie combo—everything was so drab and gray—including his mood. But his parents had introduced a theme night where the blockbusters were placed on the back burner. The response thus far seemed lukewarm at best.

The moment he reached the bumper, and noticed who the clunker belonged to, he got that pins and needles feeling in his toes again. Fucking Todd Parker. One of the biggest assholes from the previous year's graduating class. Guess he was home from college for summer break.

The walkie-talkie on his hip crackled with a message from inside the concession area, but he barely noticed as he glanced around for Todd's teammates. The most pretentious of the athletes always seemed to hang in packs, but tonight Todd looked to be alone with a date.

His skin prickled as his gaze darted to the picnic tables up front where kids liked to hang out during the summer. Some of

Todd's teammates were definitely there, including one he hadn't seen since he went away to some private fancy college in the fall. A bubble of surprise arose inside him along with a spike of happiness as it always did when he saw Josh Daly.

Josh had played baseball with those guys, and a couple of them had even gotten full-ride scholarships. Josh's dad was assistant baseball coach at the high school, and he sounded pretty hard-core according to the stories he'd heard over the years —mostly from his best friend, Charlie, who definitely thrived on town gossip.

But their families only lived a block apart, and there were many days when he'd bike down Josh's street and see him playing an intense game of catch in the yard with his dad—the tension between them evident in the set of Josh's shoulders.

No wonder he wanted to get out of town.

When their eyes locked across the lot, Josh raised his hand in a wave, making the moths in Brennan's stomach buzz so fiercely, it was as if they'd been hibernating for months on end. Brennan's Elm Grove Drive-In Movie Theater T-shirt rode up his abdomen, but his fingers were too busy balancing the large tub of popcorn to yank it down as the extra buttered pieces spilled onto the gravel.

Damn, why does this guy fluster me so much?

Their lives had sometimes intersected over the years in organized sports or at the local arts center, so he figured he just looked up to Josh. He was talented, cool, and funny, and one summer they even did a camp together that Brennan still thought about to this day. That dance on stage. And then that *other* thing that made his whole body tremble so much that he declared it off-limits to think about.

Josh was a year older, and part of a group of athletes that liked to parade around the school like they owned the place, though he remained on the periphery. And maybe even felt obligated since his dad was a member of the coaching staff. But he was still always friendly in the halls whenever he saw Brennan, which made his stomach feel all strange until at least the next period.

The Chevy's window unrolled, breaking him out of his thoughts. Todd Parker reached across the girl sitting on the passenger side and practically ripped the popcorn tub out of Brennan's hand. "How about our drinks? We ordered large gulps."

Todd curled his lip as he looked him up and down, and Brennan could see the insult hanging off his lips just like it always did in the school hallway. *Faggot.*

The ground sloped like the carnival Tilt-a-Whirl, and his stomach turned and jerked.

Todd fucking Parker didn't know. He *couldn't* know.

He was only being an asshole. Todd called everyone that fucking word. It was the asshole's favorite blanket insult, and Brennan had wanted to throat-punch him so many times in the halls.

Too bad his parents didn't have a policy about serving dickheads.

Get a grip, Brennan.

He was being ridiculous. It wasn't as if anyone would notice what he'd finally admitted to himself. How it took him all of high school and beyond graduation to finally come to terms with some hard truths. How when he looked through the notebooks he doodled in on a regular basis, he saw himself so plainly it practically knocked the wind out of him.

But his questionable sexuality wasn't pasted on his forehead for everyone to see, for Christ's sake. Thank fuck for that. He was already toeing the line with his foster parents, scared of not doing his fair share now that he'd come of age. *Adoptive parents*, he reminded himself.

They had finally made it official during sophomore year, but he still had all the same fears. About not making any wrong moves that would get him kicked out and into a group home. Or

worse, placed with a family that treated him like shit or like he
was disposable. He'd had enough of those experiences to last him
a lifetime.

His parents made it clear that they were cool with him taking
classes at the community college until he figured out what the
hell he wanted to do with his life besides sketching in notebooks,
but somehow he couldn't shake the idea that they might still
never see him as their own. Which was why they didn't need to
know he might be questioning his sexuality. Not while he still
lived under their roof. Soon enough, he'd be striking out on his
own, and then he could finally do something about all the chaos
in his head. And seeing Josh Daly again was not going to make
his body cooperate, not while standing in front of this asshat's
car.

Brennan looked down at his feet as he clutched the roof of the
car as if his life depended on it, and brought his breathing to a
normal level. His insides felt shredded because he'd been
freaking out about every damned thing for weeks now.

Maybe this was his opportunity to finally feel good in his own
skin. To take it all in stride. He raised his head and looked Todd
in the eye. "Chill the hell out. I know what you ordered."

Even if this asshole knew one of his deepest secrets, the world
wouldn't come crashing down around him. His parents wouldn't
be disappointed in him or send him back to Social Services.

They couldn't anyway, jackass. You're an adult now.

Some days he still didn't feel like it.

The force of the passenger door knocked Brennan in the gut,
and he doubled over.

"Sorry, Brennan. Really gotta pee." When he finally zeroed in
on Todd Parker's date, he gasped. It was his sister's best friend,
Kylie. "Is there a line?"

"Not tonight." Brennan's cheeks colored as he turned toward
the building to walk with her. He willed himself not to look in
Josh's direction again.

"Be right back with your drinks." Brennan shot Todd a dirty look over his shoulder—the best he could muster until he got his wits about him.

Careful, asswipe. You never know what might end up in your cup.

He followed Kylie inside the concession area and steered her to the restroom, across from the kitchen. His foster sister, Sydney, looked up and grinned at her best friend as she rotated the hot dogs.

Adoptive sister.

Or how about just sister?

"Brennan," his dad called. "I've got orders up. I paged you on the walkie."

"Coming," he replied, strolling to the counter and lifting a questioning eyebrow at Sydney.

The popcorn machine was on the blink, so he was on his feet more than usual tonight. Customers came inside to place their orders, Mom handed them a number to hang out their window; then they retreated to their cars to watch the doubleheader.

The other times he needed to leave the safe confines of the concession area were to do a sweep for trash or to confront rowdy kids disturbing the peaceful atmosphere.

The rules were plainly written on the big screen before the start of every movie as well as on signposts in front and back:

Use the trash cans located at the end and middle of each row.

If using the picnic tables up front, please do not disturb others watching the show.

Don't block the walkway between cars.

No alcohol or drugs. *Yeah, right. Tell that one to a bunch of bored kids.*

No pets off leash outside of the car.

But people mostly complied with the rules and even when some got out of hand, they'd rarely had to call for security or kick people out.

People liked to spread out here in the warmer weather and Mom even encouraged it.

The usual crowd was mostly kids, who showed up for something to do, lame movie or not. There wasn't much else going on in the town of Elm Grove, located at the southernmost point of West Virginia. At least the ocean was only a few hours' drive southeast.

"You should let me and Brennan choose the movies for theme night sometime," Sydney said as she pushed the button on the popcorn machine.

She grinned at him as he grabbed a towel from his mom's shoulder and wiped the dirt off his palm. They had always been close, and even though she went from only child to having a foster brother in a few years' time, she'd adjusted pretty quickly.

"Fair enough, but the crowd's pretty decent tonight." Dad handed Brennan two large drinks in a holder, a hot dog, and a bag of Skittles. He pulled up his baggy Levis and wiped his brow. He always worked so hard. "Besides, when you take over the business someday, you can choose any movies you'd like."

"You already have trouble competing with IMAX, Dad." Brennan rearranged the Skittles bag to lie evenly with the hot dog. "I mean, even those places make their customers wait in line for their orders. They don't *serve* them."

"They're free to come inside and get their own food, but I think people appreciate the delivery," his dad said for about the hundredth time. "People like being in their cars almost as much as they like being in their own living rooms. I think drive-ins are going to come back in a big way."

"I hope you're right," Brennan said, if only to appease him. Drive-in theaters were already dinosaurs, but they'd been able to keep their business afloat for years in this town, especially since his parents invested in a used digital projector, the cost nearly putting them in debt. They also rented out the lot on weekends in the spring and summer months for the county flea market and for the large carnival in the fall, which definitely brought in extra revenue.

He knew how much his parents struggled to pay the bills and keep their heads above water, which was why he was fine with sticking close to home and helping out. He and his sister were cheap labor, after all. He also was secretly proud they would even consider allowing him to inherit the business. It meant they really did see him as their own. He didn't think he'd ever shake the feeling of never belonging to anyone.

Brennan headed out to hand Todd and Kylie their super-sized drinks, which were almost as big as his head, wishing he'd had the gumption to spit in it. Except he'd never do something like that. For one, that was totally disgusting and two, he didn't have the balls. As Kylie reached for the drinks, Todd grumbled, "If I taste anything funny, I'm ratting your ass out to your dad."

He rolled his eyes and smirked in Kylie's direction as her cheeks colored. At least he'd made Todd think spitting in his drink was a possibility. How Kylie could stand that asshole, he couldn't begin to guess. He wished he could give her some brotherly advice, but it probably wouldn't be taken too kindly. Sydney would only bitch at him for meddling.

As he passed by the picnic tables, Josh turned to glance in his direction, and Brennan's heart pounded in his throat. He noticed how his dark curls had grown even more unruly, but he was still lean, his green eyes and cheekbones striking.

Why the hell was he noticing all this stuff about Josh?

You know why, Brennan.

You remember other things about him too—like how his hands felt against your skin and his deep laughter resounded in your chest.

Still, he wished he could be less awkward and more vocal around the guy, and in general. His silence had more to do with nerves than anything else. So right then the best he could do with all his confusing feelings was lift his hand in a wave.

He concentrated on not tripping as he made his rounds. The guy totally unnerved him.

"I was thinking maybe you should stick to decades," his sister was saying as he returned to the concession stand. "Like '80s and '90s nights. In my pop-culture class this year, there were some movies that probably still live up to their hype."

"Not a bad idea, honey. We can discuss it over dinner this week." Brennan heard the sizzle of meat as Mom flipped the burgers on the grill. His dad gave her arm a squeeze, but she pulled away. Brennan's stomach knotted like the soft pretzels they sold. He hadn't heard a decent conversation between them in days. Or maybe even weeks. Not since the miscarriage. Losing another baby seemed to take the light out of Mom's eyes, and he felt helpless around her lately.

"Run your sister home, Brennan," Dad said, glancing at the clock as Sydney removed her red apron and hung it on the hook near the grill. "Cheerleading camp starts tomorrow."

"Lock all the doors and key in the alarm code," Mom said. "I'll be home soon."

"I know the routine," Sydney grumbled as she walked toward the exit with Brennan.

"Just do what Mom says." Brennan playfully knocked her shoulder, knowing he needed to appease his parents. Not only was Mom super protective but apparently, they'd been robbed after starting up their business, which prompted them to install a security system.

"Brennan, I need you right back here," Dad called after them. Their summer employee, Abbey, had called off tonight so Dad was extra overbearing, but Brennan got it. They had a business to run. No way they needed any bad reviews on Yelp or some other business page.

"I know," he replied before trailing outside behind Sydney. When he opened the driver's side door, Syd was already seated and buckled in.

"So, what the hell is up between Kylie and Todd?" Kylie had organized some sort of celibacy club at their high school for the past two years, so seeing her with Todd was a study in contrasts. He always acted like he was God's gift to women, spouting off how many girls he'd hooked up with over the years, so Brennan figured the bravado would definitely seep over into his college life. None of it made much sense, and he hoped he was wrong about Todd seeing her as some sort of conquest.

"Between you and me, he's an idiot. But she thinks he's hot," she said, and Brennan kept his expression neutral, even though he cringed inside. Sydney and Brennan were only eighteen months apart, and Kylie had been crushing on him since her freshman year. He never wanted to hurt her feelings, but he'd admit it sort of provided a cover for him. He could always fall back on the excuse that he'd never cross the line with one of his sister's friends—but he felt terrible about the duplicity. It kept him safely in the neutral zone. But he certainly didn't want her dating an asshole.

Brennan had asked girls to school dances and on a couple of dates his junior and senior years, but nothing ever felt right. Christ, he'd kept that part of himself buried for so many years, it was a wonder he was even admitting it to himself now. But fear had a way of crippling him to the point of immobility.

"How did they even get together?" Brennan asked as he turned onto their street.

Sydney shrugged. "Guess she saw him up at the Dairy Whip and he asked if she wanted to hang out."

He perked up at the words "Dairy Whip." Josh Daly had worked there the past few summers, and Brennan would volunteer to get ice cream for his family every now and again. His eyes would crinkle at the corners like he was happy to see him, and he had a way of looking at him that made Brennan feel exposed. His cheeks burned just remembering those striking green eyes that seemed to be searching for the underpinnings of truth—or connection. Or maybe it was only Brennan who yearned for that same link he'd felt with Josh that one summer. If Josh ever got wind of Brennan's fascination with him, he certainly didn't show it or attempt to punch his lights out, for that matter.

Brennan sometimes imagined Josh meeting a nice girl and settling down after college. He wondered why he could never picture that sort of thing for himself. Maybe he was meant to be alone—it was how he'd always survived, anyway.

"He's always been a dick, so I hope she doesn't get hurt."

And now a memory was flashing front and center but still fuzzy around the edge of his brain. End of Brennan's junior year, he'd heard about some skirmish between Todd and Josh in the locker room. Charlie'd said Todd had called him a name, and they had come to blows about it. *Faggot?* But Charlie always sensationalized shit, so he didn't really know.

"What's that funny look on your face?" Sydney asked as they pulled into the driveway.

"What are you talking about?" He needed to work on schooling his features better. He didn't want to give himself away, not before he had a chance to work it all through and figure out why he was so out of sorts lately.

"Okay, whatever. You've always got stuff brewing in that brain of yours. Anyway, Kylie knows about Todd's bad-boy reputation," she replied with a sigh. "It's only a movie, but I certainly would stay away from him with a ten-foot pole."

"Thank God for that," Brennan mumbled. His sister had only ever had a crush on one boy in school, and as she was about to head into her senior year, she seemed way more interested in her grades and hobbies, for which Brennan was grateful.

Listen to me sounding all protective and shit.

After making sure Sydney was safely inside with the alarm set, he returned to the drive-in. The second movie was well underway and the lot was quiet. Once back inside the concession area, his dad handed him the final cardboard tray with two hot dogs and another with nachos and cheese as the night wound down.

He glanced toward the picnic tables as he pushed open the door with his elbow and was disappointed to see that Josh was already gone. Might've still had that strict curfew. He wouldn't put it past his parents. But damn, now he wished he'd at least said two words to the guy before he took off.

After all, Josh Daly was the sole reason he'd begun questioning everything in his life.

Dear Diary:

Okay, that sounds lame so I'll probably start skipping the salutation part—or not, whatever. Anyway, I've begun the process of reading over my older entries since I've been home on summer break to see if there were any clues early on. And there definitely were. Most striking to me is that the truth has been festering inside me since the ninth grade. It took changing my environment and getting far away from the noise to help me finally see it.

And then I laid eyes on Brennan Fischer again, and it all came rushing back. My raging crush on him. I didn't know it then, but I know it now. Big time.

Do not act on your urges.

But what if I want to?

What if I want to be near Brennan Fischer, even if it's only going to be torture? Even if he'd never feel the same way in a million years' time?

What if I don't want to suppress these emotions inside me any longer, I just want to revel in them? Just live and breathe them, feel them, let them consume me for a change. I can deal with the aftermath later. Brennan doesn't have to know I feel this way, but damn it, I'll know and that's huge. I'll finally just let all these emotions live inside me. In real time. Instead of always suppressing them.

Let me just live, for fuck's sake. Be okay in my own skin the way I was never allowed to before. I no longer believe what I'm feeling inside is wrong—most days at least—and it took a fuckton of reading articles and googling YouTube videos to convince me of that. Thank God for headphones, because my roommate would've never kept my secret.

And hey, when I'm ready maybe I'll finally do something about it.

Because I don't want to feel so alone anymore.

-Josh

2

BRENNAN WOKE from a hazy dream where he was essentially running in place, unable to get to where he was going. Story of his life. His whole body thrummed as he sat up and stretched, noting it was already nine in the morning. Not a long enough night of sleep for him, having stayed to help out at the drive-in until past midnight. He'd also popped two Tums before bed, hoping it would help his stomach settle, but the only thing that worked was pulling out his notebook and colored pencils.

When he realized he had doodled Josh's likeness in graffiti-style art, it spooked him so much he nearly ripped out the page. But he kept it because his art was one of the only things that was his own. Private. How he worked through all the shit in his brain.

He reached for his phone on the nightstand and noticed a text from Charlie, notifying him he'd be over soon to pick him up. *Yeah, right.* Charlie was notoriously late. He'd been a regular in detention due to an abundance of tardy slips.

Brennan rolled out of bed and quickly fixed his sheets. He'd moved into the loft above the detached garage during his senior year. It gave him the privacy he craved without making him feel completely isolated from the family. And though it had a small sink and toilet, he still needed to share the shower on the second floor of the house with Sydney.

Once he washed up, Brennan slid into his swim trunks and a tee and smoothed down his mop of brown hair. It had a mind of its own, and he considered buzzing it all off this summer. Except he remembered the bald spot on the top of his head from pulling on it so much as a kid. He'd been one hell of a wreck, never knowing whether he would be moved around again. He'd almost never unpacked his ragtag suitcase given him by Social Services the first month at a new place.

Then there was the stress eating. Stuffing his face whenever he could, afraid he'd never get another hot meal. It was one of his biggest fears but no way he'd want to be his chubby, eight-year-old self again. "Fat-head," the kids at one of his schools called him. He cringed as his fingers traced over his waistband. He was not toned by any means, but hell if any type of workout excited him. Running food at the drive-in was exercise enough. Besides, he'd rather do something with his hands, like doodle in his notebook, which burned no calories at all. *FML.*

Brennan heard Charlie already yakking it up with his mother in the kitchen and if he didn't hurry, he'd eat all the breakfast his mom had cooked. He could already hear the frying pan crackling with what was most likely their usual staple of bacon and eggs, and he already salivated from the smell. Pocketing his wallet and phone from the bathroom counter, he hiked it down the steps two at a time.

"You about ready?" Charlie asked before stuffing his mouth with bacon.

"As soon as I eat something. Unless you already wolfed it all down," Brennan shook his head and smirked.

"There's plenty more, honey," his mom said, pointing to the center of the table, where a plate was stacked with eggs. Lately she'd been staying in her robe when she wasn't at the drive-in. Today it was the light-blue terry cloth one. Before she moved to the laundry room to put in a new load, he thanked her for breakfast and she smiled, but it didn't reach her eyes. He didn't know what he could do to help her feel better and when he tried to ask his father, he was told to give it some time.

It only set him on edge and made him try to stay more invisible, so he wouldn't add to her stress level. But even that wasn't working. She seemed to only be going through the motions and if things didn't improve soon, he didn't know what he might do.

Once Brennan poured himself a heaping cup of coffee to help alleviate his grogginess, they stuffed their faces in virtual silence. After he finished his first serving, he began loading more on his plate.

"A second helping?" Charlie asked with a raised eyebrow, and Brennan's cheeks heated up. "Your zipper's gonna protest."

Brennan stabbed the fork into his eggs and shoved them in his mouth to avoid cursing him out.

"I was only playin'." Charlie teasingly whacked his arm. That was the problem—he was always screwing around. "You're too uptight about staying in shape."

Then why do you always poke at my insecurity like a bruise? Christ, he was a shitty friend sometimes.

"You obviously know why," Brennan replied before taking a couple of bites and pushing his plate away. "Not an easy habit to break."

Charlie had been his first friend after he came to live with the Fischer family and one night in high school, when they'd sneaked beer from Charlie's older brother, he basically unloaded his life story on him in the midst of his first serious buzz. He totally appreciated the fact that Charlie was his friend during a crucial time when he was feeling pretty lost and alone. And they had plenty of fun times outside of school—before stuff like crushes and puberty and sexuality began to figure into almost everything. Lately he felt like he was outgrowing their friendship —if that was even a thing—or maybe he just didn't feel like he had much in common with him anymore. But he'd have to figure out a way to get past these frustrating feelings, especially since Charlie would also be staying in town to attend classes at the local university.

Once he cleared their plates and grabbed a couple of waters from the fridge, he pecked his mom on the cheek and was relieved when she offered him a genuine smile. "Have fun."

"We definitely will," Charlie said as Brennan followed him out to Charlie's red pickup. He noticed a toolbox and boots in the bed of the truck. In some ways, Charlie was as lost about his future as Brennan was, so at least they had that in common. Charlie had always gotten terrible grades, and he didn't feel like he was cut out for college. His parents were leaning hard on him about taking a construction job with his father's company, and this summer he was doing exactly that for extra cash, but it didn't seem like his heart was in it. More than likely, he needed to carve out his own path. Brennan hoped some things became clear to him soon as well. He loved art but he didn't know how that would translate into a career.

"You got any SPF, or should we stop for some?" Brennan asked as he climbed into the passenger side.

"All set," Charlie replied, backing out of the driveway. Five minutes later, Charlie pulled into the parking lot of Elm Grove Beach, where they were planning a morning of baking in the sun. The sand was already packed wall-to-wall with bodies, most likely because there wasn't a cloud in the sky and zero rain in the forecast. Plus, what else was there to do on a sunny summer day in Elm Grove?

"Same place by the lifeguard stand?" Brennan asked as he hauled the beach towels from the back seat.

"Yeah," Charlie said, reaching for the bag with the suntan lotion and volleyball. Brennan actually enjoyed most sports and would play them for fun. He just never enjoyed organized teams, where competition and winning became too intense for him after middle school.

Once they found a patch of sand to lay their towels down on, they spent the remainder of the morning sweating their balls off. He felt self-conscious about taking off his shirt, especially since his gut wasn't as trim as his friend's, but at least Charlie didn't call attention to his hang-up this time.

Laying around getting a tan was so not Brennan's thing, so once he finally got the nerve to strip off his shirt and apply sunscreen, he spent a good amount of time floating in the lake, getting into a dunking match with Charlie before joining a volleyball game with a few kids he recognized from the lower grades in high school.

Charlie was busy ogling the females in tiny bathing suits, and Brennan was glad he had dark shades on so he could school his responses and actually observe for himself. Truth was, none of the guys on the beach made his pulse pound like it did when he was anywhere near Josh Daly, so maybe that was something else altogether and he was only misguided.

Still, he had never really allowed himself to do that before—to really look at other guys—and certainly not during high school. It wasn't lost on Brennan that Charlie didn't even know how big of a deal this was for him. He was essentially sitting beside a friend who was possibly struggling to come to terms with the truest part of himself. Brennan wondered if Charlie would be disgusted with him, and the idea of losing his best friend over his erroneous thoughts made him want to pull away even more.

"Damn, did you ever realize that Jennifer Thorp has such a banging body?" Charlie asked with a nudge. He was looking toward the shore, where she was standing with another girl from their graduating class, both wearing string bikinis. "You wanna head over there and see what they're up to?"

Would Brennan ever be brave enough to approach someone

he found attractive, let alone to sit half-bare on a towel with that person? His stomach revolted just imagining it.

"I think I'm good," Brennan replied, and Charlie huffed out a frustrated breath. Brennan's gut roiled. He probably should've just pretended he was interested too and faked it all the way. He'd done it for years, but he just didn't feel like it anymore.

"What the hell is up with you lately?" he asked with a raised eyebrow.

"Lately?" Brennan countered. "What does that mean?"

"Dunno," Charlie ground out. "Suppose you've always been shy around girls. Guess nothing specific has changed."

He looked so downtrodden that it actually made Brennan feel momentarily guilty before frustration took hold again. "What the heck? It's not like you're the chick magnet. You talk a big game, but you've only ever dated a couple of girls."

Charlie's face fell and Brennan felt like shit, but it was unfair of Charlie to ride him about it so hard. "Girls always look at you first before they even give me a second glance. Always been that way. You're too fucking handsome for your own good."

Charlie had made similar statements over the years, but Brennan didn't ever take him seriously. Was that why he razzed him about his weight? Was he trying to knock him down a peg or something? Damn, Brennan was thinking the worst of his friend lately.

"I don't know about that," Brennan replied. "Besides, you're the one with the personality. At least you know how to talk to people and make jokes."

Bad jokes, sometimes hurtful jokes. But jokes nonetheless.

"Oh, just what girls are looking for, someone with a nice personality." He rolled his eyes.

"Well, they should," Brennan mumbled feeling foolish. Suddenly he sat up. "C'mon, we can go talk to them. I used to take art with Jennifer."

"Nah, forget it," Charlie said, his shoulders slumped. "I'm just being an ass."

Brennan wasn't going to argue with him there. But it also wasn't Charlie's fault that he had no idea what Brennan was going through, and he was too much of a chickenshit to ever tell him.

Dear Diary:

Guess old habits die hard. Lame greeting or not, you've gotten me through hard times, so no shame there. And I've been so restless that I need someone to unload on. Lucky you.

At least work is a neutral place away from the house and church because I'm just going through the motions trying to figure out every damned thing. On top of that, I have no idea what to do with my life. How does any nineteen-year-old know? Does it suddenly become apparent while you're taking your core college courses? My mom keeps pressing me about career options, and all I can tell her is that I don't know.

Did my parents always know? Mom is a nurse and Dad is a real estate agent—and a coach. Though you'd think they worked for the church because of how much time we spend there. Is this how they always envisioned their lives?

And how about my Dairy Whip manager—was he shooting for that position or did it just fall in his lap? Maybe these are questions I should be asking. Maybe I should've even asked Reverend Coleman when he pulled me aside after church on Sunday, except all I wanted was to get away as quickly as I could. It almost felt like he could see inside me and no way I wanted a lecture—or worse.

But now Dad is insisting I attend the young adult church group as well as help with the little league team that Holy Cross is sponsoring, as if it's some sort of conspiracy to finally get me to face myself.

Last night when I purposely took Maggie for a walk past Brennan

Fischer's house, I almost stopped and knocked. Almost. I could hear music blaring through the open window, and I willed Brennan to look in our direction. If he was even home.

I could just as easily have texted the other guys from my high school team to hang out. But something inside me has changed. My friendships feel superficial at best, and seeing Todd again after what happened between us before graduation was torturous.

The idea of talking to Brennan appeals to me more. Everything about the guy does. My mind regularly flashes through snapshots of memories from high school after life moved on post-camp. Like how he'd tutor kids after the last bell. Sometimes I'd walk by his table on the way to the locker room to change for practice and I'd feel his gaze on me. Or maybe I'd just pretend to because it made me feel like somebody could really see me.

How he would sometimes sit under the giant maple tree after school with a notebook writing or maybe drawing while waiting for a ride while I warmed up at second base. And how he seemed pretty patient and kind to his younger sister—and even his over-the-top best friend.

Normal things, sure. But things that always drew my eye.

And I promised myself I was going to live in the moment, didn't I? So here goes nothing.

-Josh

3

ON THE WAY home from the beach, it was Charlie's idea to stop at
Dairy Whip to help them cool off. Brennan's hands were clammy
the whole way there, even though he had the air vent blowing
directly on him.

"Isn't that Josh Daly?" Charlie asked, and Brennan stole a look
through the ice cream store's large picture window. Josh stood
behind the counter in his navy-blue uniform shirt, taking a
customer's order.

"Yeah, he was at the drive-in last night," Brennan replied
absently, attempting to get his pulse under control.

"Who with?" Charlie asked.

"Some of his teammates," Brennan shrugged. "You know, the
usual."

"Todd Parker?" Charlie arched an eyebrow.

"Todd was actually there with Kylie," Brennan grumbled.
"Hopefully they won't become a thing."

"No shit?" he looked just as stunned as Brennan had seeing
them together. "Well, isn't that interesting? Good old Todd, trying
to prove he's still God's gift. So typical."

There was an edge to Charlie's voice that made Brennan ask,

"What do you mean?" But Charlie was already getting out of the truck and heading toward the door.

A whoosh of cool air made Brennan instantly feel less heated as they stepped inside the store and waited at the end of the line. Brennan tried to study the board above Josh's head without seeming like he was looking him over. Fuck, he felt like a stalker.

What is it about this guy?

Josh totally made him nervous, even though he always looked forward to seeing him. He was super smart, talented, and always had the best comebacks. Brennan felt like an idiot around him most of the time. He guessed all that was just admiration. Besides other things. He squashed that feeling way down and padlocked it.

When they finally stepped up to the counter, Josh's wide grin was mesmerizing. "What's up?"

"Getting something to beat this heat," Charlie replied before Brennan could get a word out. His tongue was suddenly thick in his mouth.

"Spent the morning at the beach," Brennan stuttered. As if it wasn't obvious from their swim trunks and sweaty T-shirts. Brennan absently pushed the bangs out of his face as if it might help fix his unruly hair.

"Ah, so that explains the faint coconut scent," Josh replied, biting back a smile. "I would've never guessed."

"Smartass." Brennan chuckled, finally getting his wits about him. "Glad to see that fancy college didn't dampen your sense of humor."

Josh's eyes momentarily shuttered, and Brennan thought he'd said the exact wrong thing, but then a smile lined his lips. "Eh, it had its moments."

"Bet you don't get much studying done after partying with those college girls," Charlie added with a wolfish grin, and Brennan nearly rolled his eyes.

Sometimes he wished Charlie would just get a life. Or jump

off a tall bridge. He'd become so annoying the last few months. All he obsessed over was hot girls and fucking like rabbits, even though Brennan was pretty damned sure he never got any action. It was a topic they'd strictly stayed away from, probably for different reasons.

Besides, it wasn't like Brennan didn't obsess over things too. *Hello, Josh fucking Daly.*

"Guess you'll find out for yourself soon enough." Josh shrugged. "Where are you heading in the fall?"

It was the first time Brennan had seen Charlie look slightly uncomfortable. "Just sticking around here and taking classes at the community college."

"No shame in that," Josh said. "How about you, Brennan?"

"Same," he replied. "A couple of classes while I help out at the drive-in."

"Makes sense," he replied and almost looked wistful about it. Was he not enjoying his time away from home? Maybe Brennan had read him all wrong. Maybe going away to college wasn't all it was cracked up to be.

"How is playing ball at Solomon U?" Charlie asked with interest. He was a pretty big Major League Baseball fan, and they had attended a couple of minor league games this past spring. Charlie was also on the swim team and big into kayaking, and he'd already asked Brennan to join some water sports club with him, where they'd have to rent their gear for the summer. "How was your season?"

"Our record was 39-17, so not too bad." Josh was a third baseman and a pretty good batter as well, but he never seemed like a diehard player, and he wasn't sure if he could pinpoint why. He seemed dedicated and a team player, but Brennan had never seen the fire in his eyes like he did in other players. But what did he know? His father certainly seemed pleased, which could have its pitfalls, especially if he was as tough of a coach as he'd heard.

"Playoffs?" Charlie asked, leaning on the counter.

"Didn't qualify this year." He frowned, then glanced at Brennan. "You play any ball lately? Intramural league or anything?"

"Me?" Brennan asked, momentarily taken aback. It had been about four years since he'd even stepped foot on a field. But it was cool that Josh remembered. "Nah. Not something I was interested in pursuing."

"I hear you." He sighed and again Brennan was probably reading into it, but he seemed resigned or maybe regretful. "Still making art?"

Brennan's skin pebbled and he could feel Charlie's puzzled gaze on him.

"Yeah...well, no...not like that," he replied, meeting his gaze. "I still like to draw on my own."

"In that notebook that you won't let anyone see?' Charlie smirked. "Like it's some top-secret shit or something. One time I tried to touch the cover, and he almost had a panic attack."

Brennan's cheeks flushed. "Shut the hell up."

"I get it," Josh interjected. "Some things are just private."

"Yeah whatever, nothing is private in my house—my younger brother is always crashing into my room and touching stuff."

"Oh, I bet he gets an eyeful." Brennan cringed. Charlie's room was a pigsty, and his mom was always yelling at him to clean it.

Josh glanced behind him to his manager, who was busy making a sundae, and then cleared his throat.

"So, what can I get you?" he asked, all businesslike with his finger poised over the register.

"I'll have a large Butterfinger Tornado," Charlie said without another thought.

"And you, Brennan?" Josh's glittering green eyes focused in on Brennan, which only made him falter.

"Uh, just a large diet soda with lots of ice."

"Cool." He turned from the counter to prepare their orders.

Charlie lowered his voice, "Dude, I was only cracking on you about the food shit. Don't be a baby about it."

"Shut up," Brennan said under his breath. "Nothing to do with it. I'm thirsty, okay?"

But it had everything to do with it. And so did Josh. Brennan figured if Charlie thought he was looking out of shape, so would Josh.

Why the hell does it matter what Josh thinks?

"Here you go," Josh said, handing Brennan his soda. Brennan hesitated for a brief moment before grabbing the drink, because he noticed the lid wasn't clamped all the way down. His finger inched up to push it flush, making the grab awkward as his hand grazed over the top of Josh's fingers, which were surprisingly warm.

As warm as they'd been that one day at camp.

"Sorry about that," Josh murmured, his cheeks coloring.

"No problem." Brennan rotated the cup once, looking all the way around to be sure it was secure before taking a long swig. Josh watched him pointedly before twisting back around to make Charlie's Tornado, and his face felt like a lit match.

He didn't want Charlie giving him any shit for fumbling around, so he turned to look at the hand-packed ice cream pints inside the glass case along the wall.

Charlie reached across the counter for his ice cream, then rammed a huge spoonful into his mouth, savoring the sweet treat. Watching him, Brennan lamented not getting what he really wanted, all for vanity's sake. If Josh hadn't been working, he would have ordered the large Oreo Tornado and shoveled every last bite into his mouth. Christ, he was losing it.

"You're dripping ice cream down the front of your shirt," Josh pointed out. "We have paper bibs if you need one."

Brennan put his fist to his mouth, trying to hold in his laughter, but it was already too late. It was just the levity he needed from all his intense thoughts. Brennan always enjoyed Josh's refreshingly dry humor, and now he was basking in it.

Charlie reached for a napkin and dabbed at the front of

himself, while Josh smiled in Brennan's direction, making his stomach trip over itself. *Get a grip.*

"Funny," Charlie deadpanned as the customer behind them with two kids stepped up to the counter. He motioned to Brennan. "Ready to bolt?"

Brennan wanted to hang around longer, but he knew they couldn't. Josh was on the clock, and Charlie was acting impatient. Late and impatient, what a great combo for a best friend. A best friend becoming more of a pain in the ass by the minute. Though Brennan was sure Charlie didn't appreciate him having a laugh at his expense. Normally, Charlie brushed that shit off or even made fun on his own, but now he was just acting butt-hurt and strange.

"Yeah, sure. Catch you later," Brennan said as he followed Charlie out the door, making sure to only glance back once, but Josh was already busy ringing the customer up.

He slid into Charlie's truck, wondering what the hell was wrong with him. Why he desperately wanted to head inside and be near Josh a bit longer. Maybe he needed a newer friend and since they lived so close, it might even be possible for them to hang out sometime this summer. They had both graduated from the fishbowl known as high school and could do whatever the hell they wanted, for Christ's sake. Always could, he supposed, but now he felt way less under the microscope.

After he got home, he showered and changed, then spent time in his room sketching something new. *Some things are just private.*

What sorts of things did Josh have to hide?

Hungry, he headed down to the kitchen to grab a snack before dinner.

Kylie sat at the table with Sydney, poring over some Instagram photos. Once upon a time, Kylie would've tried to engage him in conversation, but her crush on him was long gone, and it was a relief. She was a sweet girl and a good friend to his sister.

Brennan overheard Kylie telling his sister that Todd talked an awful lot about himself all night and he wanted to say something, but thankfully his sister was pretty fierce all on her own. "If that's how you felt, don't see him again."

Kylie mumbled something about him being cute, but Brennan was stuck on remembering the comment Charlie made about Todd proving something. *So typical.*

"Stay true to yourself," Sydney was saying as he reached for an apple from the refrigerator. Just as he took a bite, the doorbell rang. He wiped the juice from his chin with his forearm just as he spotted Josh through the window.

"I've got it," he called to Sydney as if she were racing him to answer the bell, and he nearly tripped over his own two feet.

"Hey man, what's up?" he asked as he swung open the door. The Dalys' dog sniffed at his feet and he realized that Josh must've been out for a walk. He had changed out of his Dairy Whip shirt and was now wearing a plain white tee with a pair of gray sweats.

"Sorry to stop over like this," Josh said, his cheeks coloring. "I meant to ask you earlier, but then we got busy and you guys were already out the door…"

Brennan looked behind him to be sure they didn't have an audience before stepping out onto the porch and shutting the door behind him. Brennan's throat suddenly felt dry, as if whatever Josh was about to say was a big deal.

"What is it?" he asked as Josh shuffled back and forth on the balls of his feet. He wondered why he seemed nervous.

"My dad wants me to help coach this junior baseball team," he said. "And I figured since you used to play, you might be willing to help me out? Two games a week with short practices beforehand."

Ah, now his earlier question at Dairy Whip made more sense.

His head swirled. Why in the hell was he asking Brennan to help him coach a baseball team with a bunch of kids? "What about your teammates? Wouldn't they want to—"

"Nah," he replied. "Don't ask me to explain, not right now, but I just...I'd rather not ask any of them."

Brennan stared at him, wondering what in the hell that meant. Did it have anything to do with that incident at the end of school last year? But Josh had met up with them at the drive-in, which made it all the more confusing.

"Hey, listen, I didn't mean to spring this on you. It was stupid." He turned and tugged on the dog's leash to lead him down the stairs. "No worries and don't even feel obligated."

"Wait." Brennan felt the blood coursing through his veins. He had just said to himself earlier that he would love to hang out with Josh sometime, so what was the holdup? "Definitely, I'll do it. Just say when and where."

Relief flooded Josh's features and Brennan wondered if he'd ever get the real story. For now, he absolutely didn't want to put any pressure on Josh. He was flattered that he would even ask. "Thanks, man. I totally appreciate it."

Once he gave Brennan the details, they lingered a moment more, all shy glances and rosy cheeks. The air between them seemed to thicken, like it did for a drawn-out minute that one summer when they were backstage all alone, the world closing in around them.

"Guess I uh...better go. My mom, she'll be..."

"Yeah, of course," Brennan replied, lifting his hand in a wave. "Catch you later."

Brennan shut the door behind him and leaned against it, breathing hard. Maybe this time with Josh would help him understand his reaction better. Or only drive him madder.

———

Dear Diary:

I finally got up the nerve to ask Brennan if he'd help me coach the kids' team, so here goes nothing. Lying in my bed with everyone asleep, I feel calm about the decision. And okay, nervous too because it's Brennan Fischer. The way he looked when he saw me on his porch, all shy and shit. Same as at the Dairy Whip. He's always been overly self-aware. Constantly pulling at the hem of his shirt like he's not good enough.

And fuck if I don't want to just tell him how awesome he is. Of course, I can only go by that one summer, random fleeting looks, and conversations in the school halls over the last couple of years. But damn if I don't want to know more.

Because that camp experience defined everything, though I didn't realize it at the time. And in some ways, it feels like nothing and everything has changed all at once.

But really, it's me that's changed.

And thinking about this is way better than thinking about how much I must've ignored over the years. And I'm afraid my brother Jimmy might be doing the same. Not that he'd be questioning his sexuality anytime soon...or ever. But more so that our parents are strict and keep us so busy that it leaves little room to figure out stuff for ourselves. From school to church to sports—lather, rinse, repeat.

Truth is, I haven't felt connected to my parents in a long time, not since I was a kid—when I didn't know any better. That's not to say we haven't had our share of good times, but I feel like I've grown up in a perfectly formed bubble. And Jimmy has too.

And in some ways the university is just an extension of that bubble, at least where religion and "morality" are concerned. We were practically all made from the same cloth. Read the same bible verses, were told which to follow to the letter, or else.

And damn do I sound cynical. My parents and the church gave me structure, and plenty of kids grow up with way worse—or less. But I wish I was given the choice to figure some things out on my own. To be able to grow into the person I was meant to be without doubting myself every step of the way, terrified I'd be shunned or lose everything. And though I've made friendships in high school and college, I've never felt like I could totally be myself and let it all hang out without some form of repercussion.

So asking Brennan Fischer to spend time with me this summer coaching a baseball team was my little form of rebellion. It's me doing something just for me. Even if it hurts in the end.

-Josh

4

"I'VE GOT AN ORDER UP." Dad rang the annoying bell Aunt Mary got him for his birthday last month. Brennan had thought it was a gag gift, but then Dad brought it to the drive-in, saying it reminded him of some older TV show his grandparents watched called *Alice*.

"I'll get it," Abbey said, stepping to the counter and beating Brennan by seconds. She always worked summers and was fun to be around. But she had a competitive streak—especially with delivering orders the fastest. She'd been "out sick" the last couple of shifts, but Brennan figured she was just hanging with her friends who were all home from college too. Or the new guy she was dating. Except they had apparently been on and off for weeks, and Abbey said she didn't want to feel too tied down.

Brennan grabbed the nachos plate just inches from Abbey's grasp and swung his body around, momentarily ignoring the cheese dripping down the sides. He just wanted to win.

"Be careful you don't spill," Dad warned as Brennan stuck his tongue out at Abbey.

Abbey grabbed the Cokes and M&M's for slot number twenty

and raced out the door on his heels. "Last one back is a rotten egg," she yelled, and Brennan took off for slot number thirteen.

Abbey beat Brennan to the lobby because the customer wanted a refill on drinks, so he took a steadying breath and slowed down to be respectful of the elderly couple. He hated that he always toed the line, but he didn't know how to operate any other way, and Abbey sort of played on that. *You need to live a little*, she'd say, and he'd roll his eyes.

After another delivery that she undoubtedly got there faster, he walked his usual path on the outside of the last row of cars, weaving his way to the concession building until he was able to catch his breath. Abbey was going to make him lose his steam way early.

When a horn blasted in his ear, he looked up to find Abbey's boyfriend, Pete, with his head hanging out the driver's side window, a downtrodden look on his face. "Hey, can you send Abs out?"

"Yeah, sure," Brennan replied, wondering if they'd had another fight. He looked up at the big screen just as Jim Levenstein was about to enter his room with the hot girl in *American Pie*. It was '90s theme night—Sydney's idea—and so far the lot seemed fuller. If Charlie were already here, he'd be glued to the screen and cheering that guy on. After all, he acted like was just as hard up.

When Brennan walked back into the lobby, Abbey was reading the new menu his mom had created while waiting on his dad to ring up another order. He almost felt bad for Pete, who probably thought Abbey hung the moon. But he also wanted to tell him to stop trying so hard. If Abbey only wanted something casual, he should either go with the flow or date someone else. Not that he was an expert on relationships—far from it. But if he ever found someone he liked, he hoped they'd at least be on the same page.

"Hey Abbey," he whispered and motioned with his head. "Pete's parked outside. Just don't let my dad see you guys."

"What's he doing here?" she mumbled, laying the menu aside and heading out the door.

"I'll take the next order up," Brennan said just as his dad rang the maddening bell.

"Where did Abbey run off to?" his dad asked in an exasperated tone.

"Dunno, but let me get that." Dad didn't like when friends visited you on the job. Charlie never got the hint, and Dad was always trying to put him to work. But some nights were super slow and boring, and it helped to have a distraction. Business definitely picked up in the summer months and when kids were on break from school.

Brennan took the soda and bag of fries out of his dad's hands and grabbed four napkins before heading out. He held the door open for a couple looking for the restroom as his black Vans squeaked on the tile floor. That was when Brennan spotted Pete holding out a single red rose to Abbey. Yep, another fight. Dude needed to give it a rest. Even he knew that Abbey would find his offering corny.

Upon his return, he was distracted by Abbey's raised voice, and he glanced back just as she was thrusting the rose at him, petals scattering everywhere. Pete huffed, his face beet-red, his wheels screeching on the gravel as he took off toward the exit.

Abbey looked stunned but also something else. Relieved. He knew that feeling well. When he was just going through the motions in his few interactions with girls and knew things needed to end but didn't want to hurt anyone's feelings. It sucked big-time.

"You okay?" he asked stepping up beside her.

When she finally took her eyes off the bumper of his car, she turned her distracted gaze on him. "I didn't mean to hurt him."

"I know, Abs. Probably for the best. He'll be okay," Brennan said, throwing an arm around her shoulder. Her hair smelled like apples, and the familiar scent brought him comfort.

Turning her head, she planted a kiss on Brennan's cheek and warmth crept up his neck.

"What was that for?" Brennan asked in a confused tone.

"For always being super sweet," she replied with a sigh. "Pete deserves someone sweet too. And so do you."

He teetered uncomfortably on his feet, wishing he knew what to say right then as he heard tires crunching along the gravel behind them.

For the first time in a long while, Brennan was happy to be interrupted by his overzealous best friend. Charlie clapped him on the back a little too hard once he exited the car, his gaze on the screen. "I think I missed the good parts."

Brennan was surprised he didn't totally razz him right in front of Abbey, having caught him as he pulled out of the one-armed hug.

"Hey, Charlie." Abbey waved before heading inside and to Brennan's surprise, Charlie's cheeks colored. Interesting. In fact, now that he thought about it, he was always a bit tongue-tied around her.

"Dude, why didn't you go in for the big kill?" Charlie asked in a lowered voice as he watched Abbey slide through the door.

Brennan sighed because he knew what was coming next. His friend was such a contradiction of hormonal teenage angst and brash masculinity. If he'd just drop the act, he might actually do pretty well for himself.

"What do you mean?" he asked as Charlie popped a piece of cinnamon gum into his mouth before offering the pack to Brennan.

"The hug," he replied with a gleam in his eye. "The kiss on the cheek."

"She just broke up with her boyfriend." Brennan waved him off. "I was trying to be a good friend."

"She finally dumped him?" Charlie looked through the window at Abbey, who had taken up residence against the counter, staring into space. "That's the best time to move in, when they're most fragile."

"Who gave you that dumb advice? Your brother?" Brennan asked in an accusatory tone. His brother was a total player and always spouting off words of wisdom that were so full of misogyny, he was afraid his friend would only become more misguided.

"Damn, you're in a mood," Charlie scoffed. "What the hell is up with you?"

"Nothing is up with me." Right then, the great divide between them felt wider, and he didn't know how to find common ground. "Maybe try being yourself for a change. Drop the macho act."

"What the hell?" Charlie bit out. "Maybe you should quit riding me so hard over every little thing."

"Touché," Brennan replied as he stormed away, the dark cloud over his head following him inside.

Diary:

Dinners feel awkward lately, so I've been talking to my brother to fill in all the dead air. He told me all about his school year and baseball team, and I'm trying to spend more time with him so we stay connected. It'd been a hard transition for him when I left for college. He texted and called me a bunch at first, but my parents keep him busy with plenty of activities, so he adjusted pretty quickly. He's still so young and impressionable just like I was, and sometimes I wonder what's going on in that brain of his.

I also pulled out my laptop tonight and checked in on my favorite professor's blog—Mr. McDougal. Someday I might get up the nerve to tell him that he was the one who finally opened my eyes. All his posts about progressive Christianity in a world of biblical literalism gave me hope. And he got plenty of flak for it at Solomon U—was known as the liberal on campus, and it apparently almost cost him his job a couple of years ago when he wrote posts about patriarchy, racial bias, homosexuality, and called my generation the hope of the century.

And even though my parents see him as problematic, it's obvious most of the students on campus have been very curious about him. His classes fill up quickly despite all the sniggering behind his back, but I've read everything he's written online. And it made me wonder if I could fit in somewhere like, in between, if I was ever brave enough.

Anyway, I'm finally getting sleepy, which was my plan by bombarding my brain with a ton of reading so I didn't stay up all night with a bout of nerves. Because tomorrow, it's our second practice followed by our first game. And Brennan will be there because I asked him to help, even though the decision confused my dad. Screw that, I can ask who I want.

Until tomorrow. Sweet dreams.

-Josh

5

BRENNAN PRACTICALLY JUMPED out of bed that morning. He was supposed to meet Josh at the Gordon Park baseball field at ten a.m. sharp. The team had a short practice followed by their first scrimmage, which was usually how it worked for the junior league.

Brennan hadn't played baseball since middle school, not since it'd dawned on him how much time he was spending pacing the length of his bedroom before a big game, wondering how he might get out of it. He never used to dread it, not when he was little and various foster parents put him in city leagues. But then suddenly batting averages and records started to matter. To coaches and other kids. To parents and parents' friends. His stomach dropped, remembering how the parents in the stands would shout things at their kids and would get in heated debates with the coaches. That was when all the fun was zapped out of it for him. He'd always been extra-sensitive to conflict, and having any in his own family made his anxiety pique.

But he figured playing baseball again would be like riding a bike—especially with a group of kids under the age of ten.

When he arrived at the field, wearing his favorite black cap and carrying his lucky baseball mitt he'd dug out of a box in the basement, he spotted Josh and his dad setting up. His stomach buzzed with nervous excitement. Kind of like edginess and happiness rolled into one. Josh wore a gray T-shirt and black sweat shorts. And as he bent over to place an orange cone down for the out-of-bounds area near third base, his brown curls escaped beneath the blue baseball cap he wore with the Dairy Whip logo.

Josh spotted Brennan and waved him over. They already had a couple of kids in line for a batting exercise to begin. He jogged the rest of the way, figuring he was late if they were already practicing.

Josh slipped a red shirt over his head and handed him a similar-looking one that matched the rest of the team colors. It read Coach on the front and Holy Cross Community Church on the back.

"Might've forgotten to tell you that our church is sponsoring the team." Josh shrugged and rolled his eyes.

"That's cool," Brennan replied.

"Hey, Dad. This is Brennan Fischer," Josh said, and Brennan was sure that his dad would at least recognize the name since they lived in the same neighborhood and had gone to school together the last few years. Though they did not belong to the same church. His parents were raised Episcopalian and sometimes attended the church in the next town over when they weren't using their Sunday to whittle away at their to-do list for the drive-in, which took up the majority of their time.

"Hi, Mr. Daly." Brennan waved in his direction even though the man had barely looked up from his roster.

"Morning, *Brandon*," he mumbled and Brennan didn't correct his slipup, though he noticed how Josh winced. Brennan figured he might've been focused on choosing the lineup for the game. "Next time make sure you arrive a bit earlier."

"Oh. Um..." Brennan glanced at Josh who stared at the ground, his jaw ticking. "Josh told me—"

"*Dad*," Josh said through clenched teeth. "Practice starts at ten. Kids show up early. No big deal."

Mr. Daly walked away to speak to a parent standing on the sideline as if he didn't hear a word his son said. Josh balled his fists and said, "I could use some help behind the bag."

Thank goodness his dad left them alone, because they made a good team. They divided the kids into two groups. Josh positioned some on the field while Brennan lined them up in the batter's box and showed them how to swing all the way through the pitch.

The lesson was lost on most of them, except the hard-core kids who had natural ability. Brennan could spot those kids' parents a mile away, watching like a hawk, ready to have a full-on conversation with their child as soon as they were back in the car. *Keep your eye on the ball.*

Brennan's dad had used their rides home to compliment his batting or fielding, which was a relief. If he was honest, he loved those moments when it was just the two of them, stopping sometimes for a milkshake afterward. That was the beginning of him feeling like he was part of their family. But he'd been afraid of getting his hopes up, so he kept quiet and toed the line, praying they'd want to keep him around for longer.

Josh made practice entertaining by telling the kids they were swinging at zombies and that the bases were gravestones. Brennan loved that about him. He was fun to be around. A couple of the kids had full cases of the giggles and fell on the grass, holding their sides. Josh's father threw them a sidelong glance as he kicked at the dirt. Josh quietly told the kids to stand up. His dad was a real killjoy and from what he'd seen so far, he definitely fit the description of what he'd heard about him over the years. Tough and strict coach and parent.

The official game started at ten thirty and by then, Mr. Daly was long gone to Josh's brother's game. He was in charge of both teams, and it seemed like once he was satisfied Josh would coach the way he'd been taught, he was on his way. But his presence was still felt.

After seven quick innings the game was over, and they had lost by six runs. Brennan was drawn to a heavyset kid on the team, named Sean. After the game, he introduced himself to Sean's parents, told them Sean could be a real power hitter, and made a mental note to encourage him every chance he got.

Brennan noticed Josh listening in as he spoke to the boy's parents and his neck splotched red, wondering what he might think of him. He considered Josh might poke fun at him like Charlie would've done in a heartbeat, but somehow he doubted it. Even though Josh was funny and always had a comeback, he also seemed less tone deaf and even self-deprecating.

"That was nice of you," Josh said in a quiet voice when Brennan entered the dugout after collecting the bats. "Sean was a little huskier last season. Real shy. Came out of his shell a bit this year."

"I kind of know what that's like." Brennan resisted the urge to tug his shirt down after feeling it climb up when bending over to store the bases away.

"Seriously?" Josh trained his eyes on Brennan, making his palms sweat. "Didn't realize, I guess." He shook his head as if clearing away some random thought. "I was always the beanpole who could eat everything in sight and still not gain enough weight to make my father happy."

"What do you mean?" Brennan said, his eyes roving over his wiry biceps. Brennan always considered Josh to be in perfect shape. "He wanted you to be bigger?"

"Stronger, bigger, a powerhouse in sports," Josh said, rolling his eyes. "I tried for a while. Then I stopped putting so much pressure on myself to please him. In the end, there's always going to be something he won't approve of."

"Yeah, I hear you," Brennan said and felt the tethers of a connection forming between them even though Josh had no idea he was struggling with stuff too. "He okay with you now?" "Who the hell knows?" Josh said. "I just do all this shit to keep him off my back. For all I know, he pulled some strings or something to get me a partial scholarship at Solomon U." That stopped Brennan in his tracks. "Are you for real?" "Just ignore me. I'm only talking shit," he said with a sigh. "Point is, the expectations can be overwhelming." "Yeah, I bet." But at least Brennan's parents never pushed him to do anything. When he quit playing, he'd felt his dad's disappointment, even though he hadn't voiced it out loud. But as soon as he asked to join a camp at the art center the following summer, he realized they only wanted him to stay busy doing something he enjoyed. And that summer became his favorite in memory—for obvious reasons.

"But you shouldn't discount your talent on the field," Brennan said, and Josh actually blushed. "At least, from what I've seen..."

"Did you catch many games?" Josh asked, their eyes connecting and holding for a long beat, making sweat break out on Brennan's neck.

"Maybe one or two," he mumbled. No way he'd confess that he'd kept up with their schedule and Josh's record his senior year. It wasn't like he hated baseball just because he quit. And coaching these kids today was totally fun—and probably would be even if he wasn't doing it with Josh.

Plus, seeing Josh in those white uniform pa—*what the fuck was he saying?* He ruthlessly thrust the thought from his brain.

Josh grabbed the last bat from Brennan's grasp and arranged them in the bag. "Anyway, let's get out of here. I feel like I'm covered in snot and dust, and I need to shower before my shift."

"Tell me about it." Brennan slowed his pace walking to the car, savoring each step, prolonging this time with Josh. "Thanks again for asking me to help out."

"I'm glad you said yes," Josh replied and with one last look, he shut his trunk.

"Why did you, by the way?" Brennan added, his stomach tumbling over. "Ask me?"

Josh took his time answering as he chewed thoughtfully on his lower lip, and Brennan began regretting his impulse to ask in the first place.

"Remember those days at mixed-media camp when we made those colorful beaded necklaces, then wore them around the campfire while we ate s'mores and sang ridiculous songs?"

"How could I forget?" Brennan smiled wistfully at the memory. "And that day we were substitutes for the extras and goofed around backstage?"

"Yep," Josh replied. "And when Wendy puked after her first solo and we ran to the closet to get the bucket and mop."

Now Josh's cheeks dotted pink as he looked away.

"I still can't believe the door shut behind me and locked us inside."

Josh chuckled. "Holy crap, there were no windows and it was pitch-black."

Using the sound of Brennan's voice, Josh reached out and took baby steps until he touched Brennan's arm. "Found you."

Standing so close that their breaths were mingling, Brennan grew motionless.

"What if nobody comes for us?" Brennan asked but it wasn't like he was truly scared, just that they were so very near, he could feel the heat radiating off Josh's body.

"Someone will notice we're missing," Josh replied, moving his fingers up to Brennan's shoulders like he was his lifeline. Except his grip loosened, and his thumb was rubbing above the collar of Brennan's shirt as if to reassure him. But all it did was make him shiver. "Give me a second to catch my breath. Then we can find the door."

Except the second turned into a full minute where they stood way too close. Josh's thumb was sending gooseflesh across skin and his breath smelled like spearmint gum as it ghosted across his mouth.

"It was totally my fault for not propping the door open," Brennan mused as he watched Josh across the parking lot.

After they'd tag-teamed to the door, they'd pounded and yelled until someone let them out. Brennan wondered if any of that hushed nearness would've happened had the lights not been out. They'd avoided direct eye contact the rest of the day and neither brought it up again.

"Nah," Josh replied. "It was a good summer."

"The best," Brennan muttered, his cheeks heating.

They grinned across the space at each other before Josh cleared his throat. "Guess I regret not staying friends after that. But then school and sports got in the way, I suppose."

"Yeah," Brennan replied through parched lips. He could scarcely believe this conversation was even taking place. "So... what? This is what friends do? Coach a kids' team together?"

Josh smiled and it was so blinding that Brennan felt a stitch in his chest. "Yeah, maybe so. I just...I wouldn't mind getting to know you again. You were always a cool guy and now I'm home for the summer, and I want to hang out with whoever the hell I want to—and not out of obligation to team loyalty or whatever other bullshit—sorry, I don't want to sound cynical. It's just—"

"No, it's okay. I think I get it," Brennan mumbled. *Holy shit.* "I could always use a new friend."

"Same," Josh said and then raised his hand in a wave. "Catch you later."

It took him a whole minute to snap out of it as he watched Josh's car pull away.

Brennan already looked forward to the next practice. Baseball was looking sweet to him again.

Hey, Diary.

I couldn't stop smiling all through my shift at Dairy Whip.

When Brennan said he could use a new friend, I felt my heart clang against my rib cage. Hard. Damn, those words just spoke to me, and Brennan probably didn't even realize it.

And the way he took Sean under his wing reminded me what a compassionate person he was. Like that time at camp when he helped a girl with cerebral palsy finish her art project. He was kind and attentive. And really fucking adorable.

So it wasn't my imagination. I just always felt the right energy from him—one that seemed to complement my own. I don't think I'm reading into it. Well, not too much. I can't help if a little hope gets thrown in along the way.

And no wonder Brennan always yanks down the hem of his shirt. Next time, I want to reach for his fingers and pull them away from his stomach and tell him he's amazing just the way he is. Make him feel as carefree as he was that one summer.

Fuck, Brennan Fischer. What in the hell are you doing to me?

But who am I kidding—ever since the day we were locked in that closet together...I've never felt the same again.

-Josh

6

BRENNAN'S SOCIAL WORKER, Ms. Hurst, played with the miniature hourglass on her desk, rotating it from top to bottom, mesmerizing him. It had a magnetic base which made the sand form cool shapes and if her hands kept moving, Brennan was liable to fall into a trance and confess all his secrets. Not that she didn't know most of them already.

He'd had so many caseworkers change hands over the years, but Ms. Hurst knew him the longest. She had her own private practice, was recommended by the foster care department, and had been seeing him since he came to live with the Fischers. She knew he and his adoptive family would need transitional services once he became an adult and at this stage, he felt comfortable with her. She'd been with him nearly every step of the way. Even the night almost three years ago when his parents presented him his adoption papers on his sixteenth birthday. His pulse had sped up, and he'd doubled over, unable to get any words out through the blinding tears. Sydney had squealed, tackle-hugged him, and his social worker patted his back, telling him to breathe.

He was so grateful to his parents, whom he'd lived with since the seventh grade. The papers were mostly symbolic because he would come of age in only two years' time, but being officially adopted was everything. It was the exact reason he didn't want to fuck anything up. As it stood now, he was pretty certain his parents saw him as trustworthy and responsible, and he owed them so much—so there was no rocking the boat.

"How's your summer going?" Ms. Hurst asked, setting the hourglass down and breaking the spell.

Brennan considered the question, as a barrage of conflicting emotions took hold, one of them taking center stage. "Okay, I guess."

She'd had her head down, paging through her notes but now she looked up, focusing on him. "Why do you sound unsure?"

"I'm not," Brennan replied, adjusting himself in the seat. The backs of his legs always stuck to the faux black leather. "I just...it's strange to be finished with high school and enrolled in college."

"Are you all set with your courses?" She placed the notepad on her desk and picked up her pen as he tipped his chin in affirmation. He had to get the core requirements out of the way, so it wasn't difficult choosing the classes. "Any fears surrounding that?"

"Maybe just the usual," Brennan responded with a shrug. Would he truly be okay? What if he never resolved all the confusing shit going on inside him? "It's hard to see the future right now."

"Adulthood certainly doesn't come with a handbook," she replied with a smile. "It requires blind faith that you're heading in the right direction. Only thing you can do is try."

"Yeah." He settled back in the chair. "Suppose you're right."

She reached forward and patted his hand. "They're not going to leave you hanging, Brennan. They're good people."

Brennan nodded and swallowed past the lump in his throat. In his heart of hearts, he knew the truth, but fear was a potent thing and his social worker was certainly familiar with all his worries.

How he'd been afraid to be left alone or without food. How he could still hear his biological mother's soothing voice, envision her bleach-blonde hair, feel her delicate fingers—the only fleeting memories he had of her—and thank God for that because it would be way worse if he could recall all the other things. She'd been an addict and had overdosed in a crack house. No one else had stepped forward to claim him, so that was how he'd gotten his start in the foster care system at the age of five. He was pretty sure he'd blocked out other memories of his early childhood. They were possibly way too painful or maybe just that horrible, he didn't really know.

But he definitely wasn't ready to tell her about all his recent confusing feelings. He still wasn't sure what to make of them, and outside of reworking his last conversation with Josh *ad nauseam* in his head, he'd gotten nowhere except all sweaty and his chest sort of fluttery. Maybe the more time he spent with Josh, the better he'd be able to sort it all out.

"I mean, unless you're ready to strike out on your own?" she asked, breaking him out of his thoughts.

His shoulders immediately tensed. "What do you mean?"

She swirled her hand. "Do you want me to try and help you secure an apartment..."

Brennan's pulse pitched. "Did my parents say something to you?"

"No, not at all," she assured him. "The agreement when we last met was that they would be there for you as you transitioned into college. You'd sign up for classes and work at the drive-in. They thought it was the perfect arrangement. You are part of their family, Brennan. They want you there. Don't forget that."

Her voice became background noise as Brennan focused in on the sand in the hourglass. How it was settled right then, just waiting for some outside force to make it all scatter again. It was like some parallel for all his fears, and he needed to get a grip. He was an adult now and he'd figure shit out. He loved finally being part of a family, but even if he had to go it alone, he'd somehow make it work.

"Brennan, you with me?"

"Yep," he said, tearing his eyes away from the imagined sand formation. "So why bring the idea up now?"

She arched an eyebrow. "Because you seem preoccupied today. More than usual."

"Oh. Sorry." Damn, he didn't mean to perplex her, but he just couldn't seem to rein in his thoughts no matter how hard he tried.

"This is my job, Brennan." She gave him a pointed look. "So, I'm here to listen whenever you're ready to talk—about anything at all."

"Okay," Brennan replied with a sheepish grin. She knew him well enough to recognize when he was trying to work something out in his head—and to give him time.

She leaned forward. "How are your parents doing?"

Brennan was grateful for the change of subject, and that was one topic Brennan actually *wanted* to discuss. "Not really sure. Mom is still acting different."

Brennan's family had always been what other people would call close. They did everything together, including running their business. But there was something missing lately. Something that left a hollow space inside of him. They didn't dig deep and talk about what really mattered anymore. Not in the last few months. Brennan feared they were like a ticking time bomb just waiting for the right moment to explode.

She waved her hand. "Give an example of what you mean."

"Ever since she lost the baby, Mom's been moping around, mostly keeping to herself." Ms. Hurst simply nodded like it was totally understandable. He did hear his mom discussing pregnancy hormones over the phone with the doctor's office and he figured that, mixed with her gloomy mood, was probably contributing to how she'd been acting lately. "Sometimes I don't even know what to do or how to be around her. It's like walking on eggshells, and I don't want to upset her."

"Brennan, you are not invisible, no matter how much you try to act like you are," she said, and Brennan released a little gasp. "You are part of the Fischer family and you have a voice, an opinion."

He rubbed his eyes and sighed. "I know, but what if I say the wrong thing?"

What if she dropped him like she seemed to do with her own brother?

His Uncle Scott was gay, but his mom and dad never really talked about it. When he brought a "friend" to Christmas last year, his mom was polite and even sent home a plate of leftovers for both of them.

But they hadn't spoken since. Dad said it was private, between Mom and Uncle Scott, but Brennan had a sneaking suspicion bringing his friend along was the reason—he'd never introduced anyone to the family before, male or female. And the way his mom's eyes were tight at the corners and how she barely smiled through the meal tipped him off as well.

Brennan's breaths released in harsh waves as he recalled discreetly observing his uncle and boyfriend, how their hands would brush without looking too obvious. How hard it seemed for them to hold back affection—natural, ordinary affection— because it wasn't allowed. Not because anyone told them. Just because they *knew* not to do it in certain places.

He wondered how they even found each other. How any LGBTQ people ever found each other. Were there signs he was missing? No way he wanted to get punched in the face for simply being curious.

"It never hurts to be honest. To say you feel worried." Ms.

Hurst made a note in her calendar. "I'm going to make a home visit soon, and maybe we can do a family session."

"Yeah, okay," he said, blowing out a breath. She'd done a few family sessions over the years and had a decent relationship with his parents, so maybe having her there might break the ice a little. "I just don't want her to think I'm being unreasonable. I didn't even know Mom could still have a baby."

She cracked a smile that said, *Kids these days.* "Obviously she was still able to conceive. And nobody's ever too old to love."

Brennan hadn't considered the love part. He had only thought about the screaming infant part. And his parents were already stressed enough with their business. He couldn't imagine adding a baby into the mix.

"This isn't about you, Brennan. She loves you and Sydney, but you're older now. You don't need to be fed or coddled."

Hell yeah, they still did. Somehow he thought he'd always need it—that innate desire to be cared for and to belong somewhere.

But he got the point she was trying to make.

"Guess it would have been kind of cool to have a little person around again."

Except for the incessant crying and messy diapers. He'd had his fill in foster care.

"It helps to see it from another perspective." She scribbled something more in her notes before leveling her gaze on him. "So...tell me about your summer plans. Still hanging out with Charlie?"

"Uh huh," he replied absently.

Brennan almost told her how he'd been feeling so distant from his best friend lately, but those feelings were all mixed in with the other confusing ones. His senior year had been a whirlwind of classes, testing, and college prep, finally culminating in graduation.

Then Josh Daly came home, and suddenly he'd begun feeling off-kilter again—like there was something missing in his life—

but he was terrified of putting a name to any of it. All he knew was that he wanted to get to know Josh again like he did that one summer at camp. They'd just been kids, and now they were adults with that same magnetic energy zapping between them and soon enough, he'd be back at college.

"I'm helping this kid named Josh Daly coach a junior baseball team."

"Well, that sounds fun." She smiled. "How did that come about?"

Brennan rubbed his clammy hands together. "He's home from college and he just sort of sprang it on me the other day. I mean, he lives in my neighborhood, and we'd been involved in kid activities over the years. Baseball for a while and when I took some art classes, he took music lessons."

Mixed-media camp followed that same summer. And they'd talked, laughed, danced and—gotten close. But school and sports and being a grade apart interfered. Though he'd never forgotten how much fun they had together.

Josh had also played the violin, and Brennan had thought he was pretty darn good at it, but what the hell did he know about music? Sometimes he'd heard him practicing from his second-floor bedroom when he'd ridden by on his bike but that had been years ago. Now he wondered why he'd ever given it up.

"What made you say yes?" Ms. Hurst asked.

The question almost felt too intrusive and he didn't know how to respond, so he thought about it for a moment.

"I actually used to enjoy baseball," he finally replied. "Until it became too competitive."

She smiled. "I remember."

"So, I thought, why not? Besides, I..." he sputtered, his pulse speeding up.

She angled her head, studying him. "What?"

"Nothing. I just...well, I like Josh." There, he'd said it. That wasn't so difficult. "He's pretty cool, and I wouldn't mind getting to know him better."

She arched an eyebrow as if she could tell he'd struggled with the decision. "Sounds like a good plan. Hope it works out."

Dear Diary,

Texting with a couple of teammates from college felt too much like my high school days. The campus in general at Solomon University feels almost like a carbon copy of the church community I'm still part of, thanks to my parents.

I never questioned anything I was taught until the last couple of years.

What would Jesus do? He'd surely accept anyone, wouldn't he?

Dad pushed hard for me to attend his alma mater, and I readily signed the statement of faith that was required with college admission. It explicitly spells out that sexual relations are only to be between a man and woman and that abstinence is encouraged.

Do not act on any homosexual urges. It says that right there in the handbook—or at least some variation of that. You can be expelled and in fact, I heard a couple of kids were.

I attended the required chapel meetings both semesters, took the scripture classes, and even joined student groups. The messages about service to the faith community matched what I'd been taught my whole life.

But even if you party and hook up regularly, you'll be forgiven as long as you repent. Know what isn't easily forgiven? Being attracted to someone of the same sex.

Just ignore your sexuality and you're good to go for eternity.

Could I do that and still feel whole? I don't know anymore.

Not when I'm consumed by thoughts of Brennan Fischer. How his brown eyes are warm but pensive, and his smile makes my heart beat a little faster.

Will these thoughts send me to hell? So be it.

Fuck, fuck, fuck, did I really just write that?

There it is for all the world to see—but really just for your eyes, Diary.

Still, it feels liberating. Fucking scary, too.

-Josh

7

By the middle of the first movie, Brennan was already beat, having worked until after midnight the last two nights. Not that he'd have gone to sleep any earlier at home. But the busy nights of helping out at the drive-in along with incessantly thinking about a certain someone was making him crazy, and he didn't know how to stop. Other than to draw—that always seemed to center his head. Make his pulse slow down.

Brennan stood outside, hands in his pockets, watching the big screen. Tonight was Y2K movie theme night—aptly titled "The Year Brennan was Born" by his mom—and first up was *High Fidelity* with John Cusack. Brennan thought he was a cool actor and figured he was a lot like him—an average, decent person who flew under the radar. Nothing special. He swallowed the inadequate feeling that always cycled through his brain. It never did him any good.

When a familiar-looking blue Chevy pulled into slot number fifteen, Brennan glanced over to see if he recognized anyone. Not that their town was that small, but the drive-in had its regulars. The older set on seventies night, families on Disney night, and a mix of everything in between the other evenings.

Just as he suspected, it was Todd's clunker and he was with Kylie again. Truth be told, he sort of wanted to keep an eye on her. But he also wanted to avoid Todd like the plague. On that note, he hightailed it to the concession building.

"Hey, Syd," he called to her. "Kylie's here with Todd again."

"Yeah, I know," she said, slinging her backpack over her shoulder. "They came the other night too, when you were off."

Interesting, but ultimately none of his business. Besides, he knew everything about Todd he could possibly want to. Dudes like him were a dime a dozen.

"Order's up, Brennan," Dad said as he wiped sweat off his brow with his forearm. Thankfully, he'd laid off the bell the last few nights, giving them all a break. He had a feeling Mom had some terse words for him when he went overboard the other evening.

"Syd and I are leaving," Mom said, untying the red apron from her waist. Her eyes seemed puffier around the edges, so she must've had another rough night of sleep. Some mornings he'd come downstairs to a blaring infomercial and his mom curled fast asleep on the love seat. "She's got to be up early for cheer-leading."

"Don't you want to say hi to your friend?" Brennan said, a hopeful tone to his voice. "And take that order out with you?"

"I'll see her tomorrow at cheer. I'm tired," she said, following Mom out the exit before stopping in her tracks. "Wait a sec, are you trying to avoid them or something?"

"That obvious?" He rolled his eyes, then grabbed the food from the counter and spun toward the door. "Hopefully she's only seeing him because he's got some sort of redeeming qualities?"

"I think she's just having fun." She nudged his shoulder. "Something you should do more of."

"Yeah-yeah, I hear you," Brennan replied, following them outside.

When he stepped onto the gravel, he slowed his pace. He took the food to slot number seventeen, two cars down from Kylie and Todd and doubled back, avoiding eye contact with them. They might still place an order, but for now he could breathe a sigh of relief.

He still sort of felt guilty about Kylie even though he never did anything to make her believe she'd had a chance. The only reason any of it ever came up was because Charlie had razzed him in the school cafeteria about never liking anyone in front of their friends. So he randomly rattled off a couple of names of girls who were plenty attractive but ultimately were unattainable. Like the most popular cheerleader, who happened to be dating the quarterback—how clichéd. And right then, Brennan's gaze had swung to the double doors of the cafeteria, just as his sister passed by with Kylie.

"And there's no way I'd ever consider my sister's friends. Totally off limits." He'd never said he liked her or was even attracted to her, but it was enough to get Charlie off his back.

He could think whatever the hell he wanted.

Before he knew it, Kylie was suddenly looking in his direction as if it had become one of those self-fulfilling prophecies—and his sister was throwing him dirty looks until she questioned him one night and told him that she would be *mortified* and *under no circumstances should he ever think of her friend in that way.* He agreed with everything she said—*of course not!*—unable to admit he'd just spouted off that one day so that he didn't have to continually explain why he had no interest in girls whatsoever.

"Hey, you!" Brennan spun around and saw Abbey standing there. "Wow, you're lost in some deep thought."

"Hey, Abs. What are you doing here? You're not on the clock."

"My friends wanted to come tonight." She pointed to a maroon sedan parked a row over in slot twenty-nine. "Next is *10 Things I Hate About You* with Julia Stiles—one of the coolest films ever made."

"Don't forget Heath Ledger too—though I much prefer him

as the Joker in *The Dark Knight*," he replied, bummed that such talent had been expunged so young. "But yeah, *10 Things* definitely has some sort of religious cult following, which is obvious considering how full the lot is tonight."

Technically the movie came out before the calendar turned over to a new century, but close enough. Looked like their top pick was paying off.

When giggles erupted from the open windows of the maroon car, he looked past Abbey's shoulder and counted three friends who were singing and laughing their heads off.

"You guys been drinking?" He knew the answer before even having to ask.

"Maybe a little. It's Lin's twenty-first birthday, and we've been at a bar crawl doing this hilarious scavenger hunt thing." When Brennan cocked an eyebrow, she waved him off. "Never mind. And don't worry, we'll be sobered up by the end of the movie."

"Just be safe," Brennan said, having had more than one buzzed night with Charlie, usually after he'd gotten his brother to score beer. Except, he'd never dream of coming here, to his place of employment. What was Abbey thinking?

"Okay, Dad." She saluted him and then chewed on her lower lip. "Any chance I can talk you into something?"

Brennan looked through the window toward the kitchen to be sure Dad hadn't spotted Abbey—he didn't want any more trouble for her. But Brennan had to admit that since she ditched her boyfriend, she'd been coming to work on time, and was just as fun to be around.

He walked her over to the side of the building near a lone picnic table and well away from the front window. "What is it?"

She stared at the ground, her cheeks rosy. "One of the things on the scavenger hunt to-do list is to make out with someone cute."

Brennan's neck prickled as his gaze sprang to her friend's car.

Now it seemed as if Abbey's friends' gazes were glued to their windows as if watching a show.

His gut churned. "Abbey, I'm not going to—"

"You look like I'm about to maul you, silly." She took a step toward Brennan and he smelled her fruity perfume. "Just a quick smooch on the cheek to show them I gave it a good shot. And maybe it'll be enough to win. I got all the other things on the list —even the wooden doorstop from one of the bars in town."

Christ, there had been a similar type of game for a bachelor party he and Charlie had been invited to by his brother's friend. They weren't old enough to get into the strip club, and he could only imagine that might've been where one of them got the used condom idea he'd spotted on the list. Or the garter belt. He remembered how relieved he'd been to have to say good night, whereas Charlie was bummed.

Abbey looked at him with pleading puppy-dog eyes and he nearly laughed out loud before he shrugged in acquiescence. But he'd been in enough of these awkward situations with girls to know where this was headed. And he needed it to stop. At least he thought he did.

He liked Abbey and kissing *anyone* was nice. But not with an audience. And not with his parents just beyond that door. And not with a girl he wanted to remain friends with.

Before he could get any words out, her lips were against his cheek quick and smooth before she pulled away. When she glanced over her shoulder, the girls in the car were giving her the thumbs-down.

"Damn, I really wanted to win this competition," she whispered conspiratorially, and he could see that same driven gleam in her eye. "The grand prize is free drinks for the next month."

Brennan nearly rolled his eyes. He could totally see why all this would appeal to Abbey. She was way cooler to have around than he'd ever be. "Any chance you could just kiss me real quick on the lips? I'll stand stock still and won't even move."

She grew frozen as a statue and even closed her eyes. *Ah, what the hell.* It wasn't that big of a deal, so why was he pretending it was? He could taste her strawberry lip gloss when he leaned forward and gave her a lingering kiss on the lips—to make it count.

Because he wanted to help her out. And because he didn't want to insult her or have her think he didn't know the first thing about kissing. And maybe, just maybe he was sort of curious if he'd feel any differently this time.

But he knew immediately it was a mistake. Even though it felt sort of nice, it didn't feel like much else.

And that was when he knew. *When he really knew.* That he couldn't pretend for another year. Another month. Maybe even another week. Without losing a piece of himself.

When Brennan heard a gasp, he stepped back only to see Charlie push past him on his way through the concession door. He hadn't even heard him pull up. There was surprise in his eyes but also something that looked a lot like frustration. Which he didn't get at all. Hadn't he encouraged Brennan to go in for the kill or however the hell he'd put it the other day?

But maybe the kiss would buy him time. At least where his best friend was concerned.

When Abbey stumbled forward and leaned against Brennan, he placed his hands on her waist to hold her up. "You okay? I think you've had too much."

"I know. I'm sorry." She tucked her forehead against his chest. "Did I embarrass myself?"

She looked up at him, the whites of her eyes lined red. "Nah, you're fine, but maybe hold off for the rest of the night. Go have fun with your friends."

She grabbed for his arm. "Are *you* still my friend?"

"Of course," he replied with a smile as he was filled with regret.

It was only a kiss. It shouldn't mean anything. Except it stood for absolutely everything.

"Don't worry, I'll barely remember any of this in the morning." Abbey staggered toward her friend's car, giggling along the way as she raised her arms in victory.

When she swung open the door, she high-fived a couple of the girls and Brennan shook his head as he watched them. If only he could cut loose like that.

"Guess you finally took my advice," Charlie grumbled from behind him and when Brennan glanced back, he was sipping on a large gulp, a glum look on his face.

He should've gone with the lie and had Charlie believe that he might in fact be interested in a girl, but it felt all wrong in his stomach and besides, Charlie's mood made him wonder so many things about his friend that he couldn't organize his brain.

Brennan shrugged. "It was for some game she and her friends are playing tonight. Sort of like the one that one night for your brother's friend."

"Damn. Guess I always show up a minute too late," he griped, glancing over to the car where Abbey had gone to join her friends.

"Well, don't be pissed at me about your lousy timing," Brennan said with a nudge to Charlie's shoulder, trying to lighten the mood. When Charlie finally cracked a smile, he held the concession door open for him. "C'mon, I'll get my dad to spot you some popcorn with extra butter."

Diary,

I met my old teammates out tonight, which was fine. They used to be my friends after all. But it only confirmed everything I've been feeling about them. As usual, the conversation turned to sex and specifically Todd trying to hook up with the president of the celibacy club. I pretty much can guess the reason he's seeing that girl but no way I was going there.

Besides, from what I already gathered, she's been sticking to her guns, which made the guys razz him about it. Wrong thing to do where Todd was concerned, and when I said as much, a couple agreed that Todd should move on already. He was about to be a sophomore in college, for Christ's sake. But I bet he's no longer big man on campus at WVU—not like he was at Elm Grove High School. Welcome to the real world.

I just hope he doesn't do anything stupid. That's what happens when you feel like you have something to prove. Todd was watching me closely all night and it made my skin crawl. Ever since that locker room incident, I've made sure to keep my distance. He's always so afraid of his masculinity being called to the carpet. Asshole.

A whole year away at college and nothing's changed. A couple of the guys seem different, more grown-up I guess, and Paul is even in a serious relationship. But one thing still rings true—I hide an awful lot from the people I'm supposed to be friends with. I almost caved and pretended to have someone special away at college, but fuck that.

Would Brennan get it? If I told him I was struggling pretty hard, would he look at me differently? Or would he give me a shoulder to lean on? Guess only time will tell.

Fuck, this is going to be a long summer.

-Josh

8

BRENNAN HAD BEEN UP since four in the morning, anxious about so many damn things. He lay on his back, eyes trained on the ceiling, feeling like a boulder was sitting on his chest. Most troubling was the fact that he didn't feel anything when his lips had met Abbey's the other night. Sure, she was a friend and he didn't have any romantic inclinations, or sexual for that matter, but it was the same all the other times too—with girls.

It was nice being kissed period, better than his damned imagination, but it never seeped further—to his inner core, beneath his rib cage, where his deepest desires were locked away.

He knew for certain that he'd convinced himself that he could be attracted to women in general—if only he found the right one or some other convoluted reason his brain had created. Truth was, there was a different kind of stuttering in his chest every single time Josh entered his view. He felt so jumbled up inside that there was no way to unravel all the twisted places.

He lifted his pencil, flipped to a new page in his notebook, and drew an intricate maze of dark tunnels that felt as endless as they did dismal. But that didn't feel quite right either, so he added the barest hint of light at the top corner of the page with a yellow hue and breathed out in relief.

Hope had always gotten him through his bleakest times. When he'd cry himself to sleep and dream of his mother's hair and voice. He'd been through the wringer, so why he was so immobilized now he didn't quite understand. Except he sort of did.

His deepest desire had always been to belong. It was that visceral need that overwhelmed him the most. And if this thing going on with him turned out to be his truth, he might lose the closest people in his life. Maybe not completely, but it would certainly change the dynamics and that would still hurt like hell.

But this hurt too—bottling all of it up—and he thought he might explode if he wasn't able to let it all out one way or another. Drawing helped but only to a certain degree.

Brennan almost doodled a certain someone's name in the opposite corner of the page as he wondered how he might take in that information but refrained from being ridiculous as well as childish. Besides, the guy went to a Christian college, was active in his church, and he knew what his faith believed. He was no dummy, and he didn't want to imagine the look of disgust on his face.

His fascination with Josh was spilling over into every thought, every minute of his life, and he almost wished his summer break would've passed without any intrusion. He was going along just fine—at least that was what he'd told himself—until he laid eyes on the guy again. Maybe it was a bad idea to help him coach the junior team, but he also desperately wanted it as well.

And besides, it sounded like Josh needed a friend—and Brennan planned to push all this aside and be there for him if he needed him.

The sun filtered through the window, creating a pattern of stripes across his comforter. Since it was finally a reasonable hour, Brennan showered and dressed, trying to calm his thrumming pulse.

When he got to the practice spot, he pulled in beside Josh's shiny blue sedan, definitely a newer model than his vehicle. The brakes were grinding on his used Mazda SUV, and he knew he'd need service soon.

They were alone for the moment and worked in comfortable silence setting up the field. Brennan's lack of sleep wore on him as he scrutinized every look that passed between them.

"So, what've you been up to?" Brennan asked so he could quiet his overactive brain. If this was an unrequited crush on a dude, he needed to push through it and get to know the guy as a friend. Wasn't that what he'd just promised himself? Besides, no way he'd know what to do otherwise. He was too much of a coward to explore any other thoughts and feelings, afraid it would be like a dam bursting wide open. Better to keep it all tucked away in the deepest parts of himself.

"Mostly work." Josh shrugged. "Story of my summer."

"Tell me about it." Brennan was used to it by now. He'd been helping his parents since he was sixteen years old, the same age they put Sydney to work as well. Besides, the friends he had made through his earlier years in baseball and art classes seemed long gone by now. Except for Charlie. Good old Charlie. He felt guilty for being so aggravated with him lately. He had insecurities of his own—that much was obvious. "What other things were you hoping to do over your break?"

"Not sure. Though it was actually nice to see a movie the other night. I hadn't been to a theater in forever." Josh smirked when he noticed Brennan's expression. "Okay, that wouldn't be so much fun for *you*."

"I actually love movies." Brennan smiled. "It'd be cool to sit through an entire showing without having to run around."

Josh chuckled and Brennan zeroed in on the dimple in his

chin. It made his breath stutter. He turned away and cleared his throat.

"You ever show up on your day off with like a date or some-thing?" Josh asked with curiosity brimming in his gaze.

"Nope," he replied around a tight throat. "I don't really...."

What in the hell was he about to admit?

Josh shook his head and laughed. "Suppose it would be cringe-worthy to make out with a girl in front of your parents."

"Something like that, I guess." Brennan's cheeks colored. He'd kissed Abbey on a dare, but that was nothing compared to imag-ining the alternative. "They probably wouldn't mind since it's uh, been awhile. Or like...ever."

Brennan didn't know why he'd admitted it, but there it was.

He quirked an eyebrow. "Do they razz you about it?"

"Not like Charlie does," he replied, dropping the base harder than he'd intended.

"Still a poster boy for hormones?" Josh asked as he set up a cone by the third-base line.

They shared a grin, and Brennan felt guilty for ragging on his friend.

"How about you? Do you get teased about it—though I suppose I'm presuming a lot." He'd never seen Josh with many girls either, at least in high school, and now he was way too curi-ous. "I have no idea if you have a girlfriend in college or whatever."

Brennan's tongue felt thick in his mouth. He stared at Josh's soft-looking pale lips, which were slightly parted as he consid-ered his question. Why did he seem nervous? And why was it so important for Brennan to hear his answer? Maybe it would help him get over this thing—whatever it was.

You know what it is.

"Nah. Guess I'm the same...as you." Josh held his gaze and Brennan felt a punch in the gut that was so visceral, he nearly doubled over. It was as if Josh could see inside him to his very core. Though it really wasn't likely. *No fucking way.*

Brennan took a breath and let it out. Steadied himself. "What do you mean?"

Josh suddenly waved at someone over Brennan's shoulder. He let out the breath he'd been holding. *Damn it.* The kids and parents were already showing up at the field. He'd die for only a couple more minutes alone.

Brennan turned and spotted Sean walking across the grassy outfield with his dad. One of the kids on the team about the size of a beanpole ripped Sean's cap off his head and made a run for it. The kid threw it to another freckle-faced kid, and they played keep-away while Sean's father yakked it up with another parent. Sean puffed away, trying to get his cap back, all the while stealing glances at his dad, probably hoping for some help.

Brennan remembered being that kid and felt blinded by frustration. A gust of wind burst through the field and picked up Sean's cap, blowing it in Brennan's direction. He grabbed the cap off the dirt mound, just out of beanpole kid's reach.

"Listen," Brennan said, more forcefully than he'd intended. It came from some cavern deep inside him. "If I were you, I'd be glad Sean doesn't hold grudges. He's probably stronger than the both of you combined."

"That's 'cuz he's fat," the beanpole kid said under his breath. Freckle-face sniggered as Sean came up beside Brennan.

"Actually, it makes him a power hitter." Brennan handed the cap back to Sean, who looked incredulously at him. But he continued on like he was on a mission to set everything right. "Probably the best batter on this team. He could teach you a thing or two."

Sean's cheeks spotted red as the kids stole sidelong glances at him, hopefully seeing him in a different light. Brennan didn't know what'd come over him but damn, he hated when kids were needlessly mean to each other. Adults too. Too bad he couldn't be this bold in other parts of his life.

"Besides, you're a team. You're not supposed to be against each other." Brennan placed his hand on beanpole's shoulder and looked toward the stands where the parents were sitting grouped together. "If I see that happen again, I'll have to bench you."

When Brennan turned toward the dugout, Josh stood smirking at him—though there was a softness in his gaze he hadn't seen before, and it made his stomach feel unsettled.

"Too much?" Brennan shrugged, walking toward him. "Couldn't help it. Hey, where's your dad today?'

"Helping with our church fundraiser. Guess he thinks we can handle it ourselves." He eyed the parking lot as if looking for his car. "Sorry he called you 'Brandon' the other day; he can be such a—"

"No problem, it's a common mistake." Brennan wouldn't admit that it'd unnerved him. Made him feel like he did with the teachers at different schools who didn't take the time to learn his name—probably because he was too quiet or just too new. Besides, he always made sure to fade into the pale walls so that nobody guessed things about him. As if it was smudged across his cheeks, scribbled against his palms that he was a foster kid and didn't have a true home.

And it'd probably worked. Maybe a little too well. And after he quit the baseball team in middle school, his disappearing act was nearly complete. He'd still sit on the fringes, next to Josh and his old team buddies at lunch or during school events. But once you stopped being part of a team—their schedule, practices, gossip, it was harder to hold conversations and make plans. At least until off-season. And even then, most moved on to other team sports. Again, he was grateful that Charlie had kept him in the loop this entire time.

"Oh, my dad *knows* your name." Josh narrowed his eyes. "I've seen him do it too many times to count. Pulling his power trip. Thinks he always knows best."

"S'okay." He shrugged, not certain what else to say or do for that matter. Whereas he was bold when it came to Sean and the other kids, it was different from handling a rude adult. "I'd rather fly under the radar, anyway."

Brennan penciled Sean's name on the line-up sheet at spot number four, almost to prove that he could be the clean-up hitter. And then hoped he was right.

"Yeah, I noticed that about you." Josh scratched the top of his head, his wavy brown hair bouncing over his forehead as he studied him. "Don't like the spotlight much, huh?"

"Something like that." His cheeks heated. Absolutely like that. Brennan wondered how Josh was able to home in on that aspect of him. Maybe because Josh felt as if he were on the fringes too. At least that was how it'd always seemed when he'd spot him across the school hall or on the field. Maybe they had more in common than either realized.

After they lined the kids up in two separate rows, Brennan and Josh threw grounders side by side to help the kids practice fielding. "So how'd you end up friends with someone like Charlie?"

"He's not so bad," Brennan said, feeling the need to defend him even though Josh's question only seemed born of curiosity. "Back in seventh grade, I was a kid like Sean, and Charlie stuck up for me."

He'd had a major growth spurt in the eighth grade but still struggled somewhat when he looked in the mirror. He remembered the day as fresh as if it had happened yesterday. A kid calling his stomach a jelly roll and Charlie telling him to shut up. They'd been friends ever since. Though Charlie could never seem to stop pressing his fingers against the wound. Go figure.

"Ah, now it makes sense." Josh threw the grounder a little too far to the right and a parent retrieved it from behind the fence.

"Not that I've never hung with people who had different interests than me. Or personalities. We all have our reasons."

"True. But there have been fun times too over the years," Brennan said after giving a small kid the thumbs-up for throwing the ball straight at his glove. "Is that how it is with your former teammates?"

Brennan thought about how he'd seemed at the drive-in with all of them, but he hadn't noticed anything out of the ordinary. Though seeing Josh had been a shock to his system that night.

"Yeah, I guess," Josh said, rolling the ball softer now, making the kids run for it.

"Sorry, none of my business." Brennan didn't want to intrude but damn if he wasn't curious about the incident with Todd. About so many things, really.

Josh shifted on his feet as a look crossed his face—like bummed and pissed rolled together. "I don't know. Guess we outgrow people. Or whatever."

Holy shit, yes. It was like Josh was speaking Brennan's language. "Too true."

"Plus, some of them are jerks, and I'm no longer obligated to be a team player. It's okay to avoid them like the plague if that's what I choose to do." Josh's jaw ticked.

When their eyes met and lingered, Brennan nodded in agreement. Damn, now he was doubly curious. But they were building a friendship and along with that came trust. So maybe someday they'd get to the point where they could speak more openly about stuff.

Once the game started, he and Josh made a good coaching team. Sean got in a couple of decent hits with line drives up the middle, and they ended up winning the game by one run. The kids clapped each other's backs, the parents cheered in the stands, and the team seemed a bit more cohesive than the week before. By the time they cleaned up the equipment, Josh was hurrying off the field to get to his shift. After he shut his trunk with the bag of bats safely inside, he bade Brennan good-bye.

"Hey," Brennan suddenly said over the hood of his car. "What's your favorite movie anyway?"

"Dude, tough question." He twisted his lips as if in deep thought. "Guess it depends on the decade."

Brennan arched an eyebrow. "So pick a decade."

"All right." He rapped his knuckles on the hood. "The seventies would be *Jaws* and *Star Wars*, of course."

"Naturally," he agreed. Though there were plenty others like *The Godfather*, *Alien*, and *Rocky*, but that was for another conversation.

"The '80s were filled with the brat pack ala Molly Ringwald and gang." He looked off into the distance. "But I was actually a fan of *The Princess Bride*."

"Stop it," Brennan said without forethought, surprise registering on his face.

"What?" Josh asked, his eyes crinkled at the corners. "You making fun of me?"

Brennan shook his head. "No, I—"

Josh's eyes widened. "It's a favorite of yours too?"

"Yep." Brennan could feel his cheeks spotting with warmth.

Josh glanced at the time on his cell and his face sobered. "Damn it. Finish this conversation later?"

"As you wish," Brennan said, tongue in cheek, referring to one of the movie's famous lines, and Josh let out a hearty laugh as he slid inside his car.

And all the way home, Brennan's cheeks hurt from grinning.

As you wish.

As you fucking wish, Diary! I almost died and my heart beat out of my chest the entire way home to change for work.

Damn, if Brennan only knew our entire conversation actually made something register in my brain, and the realization hit me like a ton of bricks. How I'd watched that movie over and over because of Cary Elwes and how he'd look at Robin Wright. I'd get this tightness in my stomach imagining someone gazing at me that way. But let's be real, what I really wanted was for Cary to look at me just like that.

Fucking hell, how had I blocked all that out?

And the first time I got a similar sort of look, it was from a girl my junior year of high school after a night out. I felt sick to my stomach and everything felt off the entire evening. Her name was Ella, we were in church group together and had gone to each other's school dances. As I was walking her to the door she turned to me with that longing, I guess you could describe it, in her eyes and I just froze. I told myself she wasn't the right girl for me, and when I kissed her on the cheek the look of disappointment almost made me cave. But we'd been encouraged to abstain in church, so I could always fall back on that explanation.

But now I just want to shout it from the rooftops. I haven't had a relationship or "settled down with a nice girl" yet—because I'm not supposed to be with any of them.

None of them. And as God is my witness, I would rather die single than live a fucking lie.

-Josh

9

BRENNAN WIPED the crumbs off the picnic tables up front, thinking about Josh and why he was so drawn to him. Whenever he was around, it was as if a whole menagerie of instruments was being tuned inside his chest, most of all the drum section, and his mind couldn't comprehend anything over the booming. He knew what was happening beneath all that noise, like a lone cymbal striking out wanting to be heard, but was too scared to put a name to it.

He looked behind him at all the cars lined up on the gravel lot and sighed. It was going to be a long night, and Abbey wasn't due to come in for another hour. It had been back to normal between them, like she knew that kiss meant nothing, and Brennan was glad for it. He would have missed their easygoing banter. They picked up right where they had left off, competing to get food to the cars and Abbey always winning because his head was a mess.

Brennan stared up at the newest Marvel movie featuring an impressive cast of characters. When he was younger, Brennan used to pretend to have some sort of superpowers. Maybe to see his future so he wouldn't worry so much.

The cars would no doubt stay planted right where they were

to see the bonus scenes after the last of the credits had rolled. That was always his cue to go home. His mom liked for him to check on Sydney, but other times she left in his stead. Dad rarely took his leave early, no matter how much Brennan pleaded with him to let him lock up. The concession stand was already closed for the night, and his dad liked to wait until the final car had left the lot, long after he'd cleaned the grill. He'd make sure the gate at the entrance was secure from unwelcome overnight squatters or teens looking for a private place to party.

A blue Saab kicked up dust, driving at a considerable pace. *Dude, you're in a parking lot.* Brennan's dad had even placed a sign just beyond the ticket window that read SLOW YOUR SPEED. Stan, the retired gentleman who ran the booth, was already long gone since patrons rarely wanted to catch a movie that was nearly over.

The driver sported a baseball cap, and his mouth, while drawn tight, still moved a mile a minute. His hands gestured wildly, and Brennan hoped he'd use them to steer the car at any moment now. He pulled into space thirteen, and Brennan wondered if this would be his unlucky night.

There was a sticker on the driver's side front bumper that read, *What Would Jesus Do?* It lay crooked against the metal, as if placed there haphazardly, still hoping to convince someone of its reverence. Brennan imagined peeling it off very carefully and straightening it himself.

Damn, his brain worked in strange ways.

The woman in the passenger seat stared at the floor, but Brennan could see her nicely drawn red lips and hair-sprayed curls. He tried not to gawk, but they looked to be about his mom and dad's age, and he wondered what other parents' arguments sounded like—weren't they all about bills and schedules? He'd almost appreciate a good knock-down-drag-out fight between his parents; it would be better than all the silence between them now.

If it wasn't for his attention to detail, he would have combed of all the crumbs onto the gravel—but that didn't sit well with him, not at his family's place of business. Instead, he had to cup his hand and make sure they got into the garbage can on his way toward the concession building.

As he neared the driver's side door of slot number thirteen, he caught a better glimpse of the man and immediately knew why he seemed familiar. He wore a red Cardinals shirt, a Yankees baseball cap, and had a hook nose that tilted slightly to the right, maybe from one too many breaks. And now the words at the bottom of the second bumper sticker made total sense: Holy Cross Community Church.

Josh's dad.

And to make matters ten times more awkward, Brennan was pretty damned sure the woman in the passenger seat was not Josh's mom. He remembered seeing her at one of the games. She was slim, with short, black hair. The woman in Mr. Daly's car was platinum blonde, with an ample chest, and now he was lifting her chin with his thumb and she jerked back and batted his hand away. Christ, what in the fuck was going on? A lover's spat?

Brennan ducked and pretended to pick litter off the ground, afraid he'd be recognized. Although he was pretty darn sure his family's place of business never came up in the Dalys' dinner conversations. Heck, Mr. Daly barely looked his way when he was at the field.

Behind him, he heard the car rev up and the slow crunch of gravel, as Mr. Daly inched out of the slot—as if he'd just pulled into some random place of business to finish their supposed argument. Brennan turned and noticed the woman's tears streaming down her face as she stared straight ahead, and he wondered where they'd be headed next.

When he straightened on shaky legs, he heard raised voices coming from inside the concession building. Looking through the window, he saw that the space was empty, save for his mom and dad, their voices reverberating from the kitchen.

Brennan cracked the door an inch and heard his dad pleading with his mom to talk to him. His mom told him in plain English to leave her the *hell* alone.

Brennan swung the door open with force, startling both of his parents—as well as himself. His gut cramped and he ran on pure adrenaline. But he couldn't make any words form in his mouth. "I..."

"What's wrong, Son?" His father leaned over the counter.

What's wrong? Christ, seriously? You think me and Syd don't know what's happening with the two of you? His hands were shaking so badly, he braced them against his thighs.

"Just...never mind." He clenched his teeth so hard they hurt. Between his parents arguing and seeing Josh's dad, his stomach felt shredded.

"I'm just...gonna walk home." Tonight he'd ridden in with his dad because his car was in the shop, having the brake pads replaced. "I need to get some fresh air and like, get outta here."

Brennan flew out the door and jogged down the gravel lot toward the exit, counting to one hundred instead of the ten his social worker had taught him to do at an early age. It was freeing to break away. Everything felt like it was crumbling around him, but no matter how hard he tried, he couldn't line up or straighten all the pieces. If his parents couldn't work it out, they might just end up like Josh's family.

A couple of minutes later, Brennan heard a car hovering close behind, but he kept his eyes peeled straight ahead and kept going, despite the stitch in his chest. When the car sped up and then slowed next to him, he couldn't ignore his dad. "Brennan, get in the car."

"I-I'm sorry." Brennan slowed to a walk, huffing and puffing. "I'm sure I overreacted."

"Let's talk, Son." Hearing his dad call him that never got old. Fuck, he needed to get it together or he'd lose everything.

Breathe.

When he got into the car, he had a hard time looking his dad in the eye. He was embarrassed by how he'd responded to hearing them argue. But it had felt like fight-or-flight in that instance.

"I know things seem strange between your mom and me, but we'll work it out," His dad said as he pulled onto the road. "It's not the first time there's been a...struggle in our marriage."

That stopped Brennan short. He turned to look at his dad, his stomach constricting. "It's not?"

"Nope. All couples have their ups and downs," he replied with a shrug. "I don't want you to start worrying like you used to when you were younger."

Brennan hadn't even realized his dad noticed how uptight he'd get if he heard them disagree—though he supposed the social worker might've filled them in. He was so afraid of his family—the first one he ever had and truly loved—breaking up and him having to leave again. "Yeah, okay. It just feels so helpless to see the two of you—"

"I know, but things have a way of coming to a head." His dad's voice sounded melancholy as he pulled down their street. "You'll see someday."

Brennan crossed his arms. "Nah, I probably won't."

He didn't even mean to say the words out loud. This was definitely not the right time.

"Of course, you will." His dad's forehead creased. "Why would you say that?"

"Because I don't even like any...girls." Brennan needed to stop himself before he said it all. *Not the right time, damn it.*

"But you will." His dad cracked a smile. "I was a late bloomer, too."

Maybe that was his problem, but Brennan knew he was only

fooling himself. It was almost too easy to cling to the comfortable lie. Except it wasn't always comfortable. Lately it felt more like an itchy sweater against his sensitive skin.

Once his dad pulled into their driveway and shifted the car to park, he turned to face him. "Did something happen tonight, Brennan?"

He felt the stinging of tears behind his eyes. What the hell was wrong with him?

Did he even have the guts to be honest? He felt like he was totally losing it.

He was terrified of what his dad might think of him. He'd been holding on to the secret for so long—since that one summer. And how being locked in that closet with Josh felt so intimate that he wondered if he was the only one who'd experienced it. And then the first time he saw Josh in the school hall afterward, he'd felt a stirring in his chest that had become pretty regular now.

Brennan felt pinpricks on his neck as other memories suddenly surfaced. Like how much he looked forward to Mr. Wells's history class. Not because of the subject, but because Mr. Wells was way cool. Did he have a crush on him? His throat felt tight, like he couldn't inhale a decent breath, almost like that first time he laid eyes on Josh in the middle of field practice after school. The clingy shorts and sweaty tee. He thought he might pass out from overwhelming...what? Lust? Attraction? Fuck, he could not take his eyes off the guy.

When his dad repeated his question, it became background noise while Brennan thought about how he'd always hoped Mr. Wells would ask *him* for help after class like he did other kids. And if he was being completely honest with himself, he also fantasized about his teacher resting his strong hand on his shoulder and leaning in to make eye contact. *Christ.*

Not yet. Too soon.

There were other more important things prominent in his

brain. Foremost, his parents and then the other thing that just happened at the drive-in. It felt like it'd been a dream.

"Um...yeah, maybe." He took a deep breath. "I just...I'm sort of bummed that I just saw my friend's dad with a woman who was definitely not his mom—and I couldn't make sense of what I was seeing."

His father inhaled sharply. "Maybe it was a family friend or relative. Even a coworker. Maybe Charlie's dad..."

"It wasn't Charlie's father." Brennan stole a glance at his father. "And I don't think I should say anything until I really know—I could be way off base. It just threw me is all."

"No, you're right." Now his dad squeezed his shoulder. "But I can see how uncomfortable that would've been. They weren't, uh —" His father winced.

"Ugh, no." Thank God. *Gross.* "It looked like a disagreement and then straight after I heard you and mom..."

"Ah, I see," his father replied with some regret in his voice.

"Yeah." Brennan stared at a gum wrapper on the floor of his dad's car. "But it's not like *you* would ever—"

"Never." There was so much conviction in his father's voice that Brennan's gaze sprang up to meets his. "Your mother is the love of my life, and I plan on growing old with her."

Brennan batted the wrapper around with his foot. He was afraid of asking the other question rattling around in his head. *Mom feels the same, right?*

Instead, he asked the safer question. "Why were you guys trying to have a new baby, anyway?"

"We weren't trying, it just happened." He sighed. "We were so excited. You and Syd are the best things that ever happened to us. But then she miscarried, and I don't know...things went haywire after that. It's normal for women to experience some...sadness from all the hormones. But she's also made an appointment with someone who might help."

Brennan let out a light gasp as relief flooded him. He was glad to hear she was seeing a professional, and he hoped things got back to normal soon. Maybe she'd even patch things up with Uncle Scott again. If she did that, maybe there was hope for him after all.

Except nothing would ever quite be normal again. He'd have to figure out to navigate life with all these new changes.

"And just so we're clear, I was heartbroken too..." his father added. "So just give us some time to work through it all."

"I'm sorry, Dad. I didn't realize that you guys were having such a hard time."

"You're not a kid anymore, so I figured you'd want it straight, right?"

He grinned. "Right. Thanks."

But he also wished he could remain oblivious too. Ms. Hurst was right. Adulthood definitely did not come with a handbook. And it certainly looked nothing like the brochure. He smirked to himself, thinking that was something Josh would say.

"I'm glad we talked, Son."

"Me, too." Except something important was missing from this conversation. Or rather, *someone*. And if Mom didn't come around soon, Brennan was afraid she'd drift even further away at a time when he needed her most.

Diary:

I'm in my room with my brother tucked into my side because my parents have company downstairs, and I could tell he was feeling sort of lonely, so I asked if he wanted to hang out and watch a movie. But then he fell asleep midway through and I'm totally cool if he stays with me until morning. It's feels comforting to me too.

I wish I could take him away from all this someday, but I'm making big assumptions. He might even follow in my father's foot-steps. He's already more naturally athletic than I ever was, but I hate to think how much more pressure is being placed on him as a result.

And now the voices downstairs are raised, and I can mostly hear my father, which is nothing new. He's typically successful at winning arguments or bulldozing right over you to make a point or get the result he wants. He was the same as a coach and obviously as a parent.

But in this case, since my parents are sort of considered elders in the church, they do a bunch of counseling. Obviously not the kind that you need a degree for but the kind that "helps" people stay in the church and on their path to heaven.

Major eye roll. But for all his faults, my dad is always helping one person or another. He'll invite people over, like tonight, or go wherever he's needed. Last night he was apparently helping the church secretary, according to Mom when I noticed he had skipped dinner. When I asked why she wasn't helping, she just shrugged and glanced at Jimmy. It's the way it's always been, and I guess I'm just noticing it all a lot more now.

And maybe preparing myself. Because pretty soon something between us will be coming to a head. And I have a feeling it's not going to be pretty. Nothing is sitting right with me anymore, and today's church group was almost brutal. It's like I'm hiding in plain sight and no one—not one fucking person—sees me. Really sees me.

-Josh

10

BRENNAN HAD the urge to skip baseball that morning, but every excuse he came up with sounded lame. Besides, he wanted to help Josh. To *see* Josh. It was Josh's father that'd fucked everything up for him. He knew Mr. Daly wouldn't remember Brennan from the drive-in—he hoped—but maybe today Brennan would let it slip that his family owned the place. So he wouldn't think of randomly showing up again.

Brennan walked toward the field from the parking lot, his bag slung over his shoulder. He spotted Josh, a lone figure on the pitcher's mound. His heart climbed its way to his throat. Josh stared off into the space of his own thoughts and looked so peaceful. So confident and sure of himself. The very thing Brennan was not.

Brennan stopped near the empty concession stand to admire that about him. Like he was a bubble of perfection. Smart, funny, cute, and sweet. He choked on the idea of ever ruining that for him.

He wondered if Josh knew his father spent time with other women besides his mother. He didn't want to be the bearer of bad news. The one to shake his confidence. Isn't that what happened to kids? They found stuff out about their parents—significant stuff, like a drug overdose—and their whole world crashed down around them. Or maybe it was like tiny cracks in a perfect glass mural, which splintered and shattered over time.

Like silence and a miscarriage. No, his family was much stronger than that; his dad had even said as much. And he vowed not to add to their problems. Not before he could strike out on his own and make some sort of life for himself.

Besides, Josh already knew his father was a prick—he bristled around him quite a bit—and he wondered when it began unraveling for them. The idea made him sad. That maybe there had been a time Josh could pinpoint in his childhood that was pure happiness. Or maybe it was a matter of people having layers. His biological mom might've had a drug problem, but that didn't mean she didn't love him. Same with his adoptive mom—everyone struggled with one thing or another. And Mr. Daly seemed pretty rigid as a parent, but who was Brennan to question anything about him? Damn, if only he hadn't seen him last night.

He wished he could just sweep it all under the rug, but now he felt like he was keeping a secret—a new one which would more than likely be more damaging to all involved—if he was right about his suspicions. He hoped like hell he was totally off-base.

Maybe he'd get lucky and what he saw between Josh's father and the woman was totally blown out of proportion. Or possibly them ending things. Maybe Mr. Daly realized the error of his ways and would ask his wife to attend couples counseling or to speak to the minister at their church, for that matter.

He could definitely use a dose of something like enlightenment or confidence in his own life, that was for certain.

Josh slowly turned his gaze toward the parking lot, almost like he knew Brennan was watching him. Their eyes locked. A single, long, unblinking look. And Brennan felt that loud and solo drumbeat in his chest.

He wished he could read into the depths of his eyes. What was he thinking? If he was creeped out to have found Brennan scrutinizing him, he didn't readily show it. Brennan was taking a giant leap in his assumptions about practically everything. Jesus, he was a piece of work. Besides, it was more wishful thinking than anything else. So when Josh arched an accusing eyebrow, Brennan looked away first.

He commanded his legs to move toward the field, all while concocting an excuse for why he'd been watching him. He felt queasy, wondering if Josh would want to pound him or tell him to stop coming to help coach. When he finally reached Josh, his lips turned to stone. He was terrified to have Josh mad at him, to lose their burgeoning friendship.

"What were you doing over there?" Josh's eyes were dark as emeralds, but glossy like the sunlight filtered through them.

"I was just...I thought I had forgotten some of my gear. So I stopped and did a mental checklist."

"Really," Josh said, his lips contorted to keep from laughing. "You make checklists a lot?"

Brennan felt caught. If he admitted that yes, he did, it was almost like admitting to his ridiculous compulsions. If he said no, it looked like a lie.

"Sometimes." His blood coursed through his veins. "What's the big deal?"

"No big deal at all," Josh said. He gave him one last pene-trating look, turned, and headed toward the dugout. Brennan stood breathing in and out. He watched the parking lot fill, and parents and kids exited cars with bats and gloves in hand.

Brennan felt a hand clap his shoulder and was shocked by the sting of it. "How's it going over here?"

When Brennan looked back, he saw it was Mr. Daly.

Mr. Daly offered a tight-lipped smile, almost like it hurt him to grin any wider. "Brennan, right?"

"Yes sir," Brennan responded with a clenched jaw. At least he got it right this time.

What the hell was this about? Had Mr. Daly recognized him from the drive-in?

"Thanks for helping Josh run the team," he said. "Maybe Josh can convince you to join his young adult group at our church."

"Yeah, um...." He stammered but thankfully Mr. Daly was already turning to speak to another parent.

Brennan had only stepped foot inside a church a few times in his life—for holidays, weddings, and funerals. His parents never really preached about God or a higher being. And they certainly didn't go around with "What Would Jesus Do?" bumper stickers on their cars. Not that there was anything wrong with that. His adoptive grandparents were certainly devout, and that'd been just fine with him.

But Mr. Daly always seemed to have an arrogant edge to him, and it made Brennan wonder if he was one of those believers who refused to be accepting of those different from him. Though Josh certainly didn't seem to hold the same rigid standards but how the hell would he know? Up to this point, any notions he'd ever concocted about the guy had only been from their handful of interactions over the years. But normally his intuition about people was right.

If only he'd learn to listen to it more.

Mr. Daly walked toward Josh's younger brother and mother waiting by the bleachers. Josh's brother held his glove rigid to his side and pulled his cap farther down on his forehead. Brennan thought he seemed nervous, maybe about his game.

"Sorry about that. He's always trying to get people to join our church. It's what we're supposed to do, but it's never sat right with me." Josh handed Brennan the bases and rolled his eyes. "At least he finally caught on to your name."

Brennan couldn't tear his eyes from his dad as he greeted his wife and kid. Josh's brother couldn't be more than eleven. If he knew his dad was getting busy on the side, his whole world might come crumbling down.

Mr. Daly gave his wife a peck on the cheek and she smiled. But her smile didn't seem to reach her eyes, or maybe Brennan was reading way too much into it. Maybe she was tired because she was busy or just from being a mom and juggling schedules. It could've been anything. She absently rubbed the gold cross around her neck as she spoke to him, and he patted her arm in a caring way.

Brennan decided against mentioning the drive-in incident to Josh. Instead, he'd find out more about his family and make an informed decision later. He could've been completely off about what he thought he saw, and then he'd definitely make a huge mess of everything.

Instead, he'd get to know Josh better. The very thing he hoped for.

While warming up the first baseman, Brennan noticed someone waving by the fence. *Charlie.* He had his running shoes on and looked sweaty.

"Hey, just jogging through the park. So, this is where you coach?" he remarked when Brennan headed over to greet him. Brennan couldn't help wondering whether he'd come to check up on his friendship with Josh, or some other stupid shit. Because he didn't remember ever mentioning the field name to him.

"Been running a different route?" Brennan quirked an eyebrow.

"Not really." Charlie kicked at a stone, looking a little lost and Brennan wondered if he'd embarrassed him. "Just felt like a change today."

"I thought you were joining that kayaking team at Cone River and would be busy every morning."

"Nah," Charlie said. "Was hoping you'd do it with me, remember?"

Brennan felt a new kind of tension between them. A push and

pull. Like Charlie was trying to hang on, while Brennan was trying to break away. Not far away, just...*away*. At least until he could work out all the stuff in his brain.

But he wasn't totally solid about his reasons. Maybe he should be seeking his best friend's advice instead. Except, the idea of telling him about his feelings for Josh or that he saw Josh's father at the drive-in made warm bile crawl up his throat.

"I've got too much on my plate already," Brennan said. It felt like he was growing away from Charlie. Toward the sun. And Charlie was a weed, strangling him.

Okay, that was overly dramatic.

"Yeah, I figured," Charlie said like he kind of knew it too. But couldn't figure out what to do about it. And neither could Brennan.

"Need you to coach third base," Josh shouted before waving at Charlie.

"Gotta go," Brennan said, turning toward the field in relief. "But maybe we could—"

Before he could make some sort of lame plan, Charlie was already jogging toward the path.

Holy shit, Diary!

Tonight was the first time I legit fantasized about Brennan. Okay, that's a lie. I definitely have before in different ways. But tonight... tonight I thought about how he was watching me from a distance on the field and when our eyes met, it was like a line of electric energy zapped between us. And I don't even think he realizes how fucking adorable he looked in that moment. How his cheeks had colored and how his tongue licked at his soft bottom lip. And I got hard.

I fucking got hard. It's like my body is betraying me—or signaling me.

Mayday! Mayday!

You are in fact attracted to guys and might need to do something about it.

And initially I felt shame because masturbation has always been discouraged in the church. But then I reminded myself that I was going to embrace this aspect of myself. I was going to follow it through to see where it leads me. And remembering that, I finally relaxed....and just let go.

I pushed down my underwear and finally looked at my junk standing all hard and proud. I've only ever rubbed one off quickly—and of course quietly—in the dark. And then I used my hand to get myself off to Brennan fucking Fischer. I even imagined him using his hands on me in that closet when it was only the two of us. His mouth too. And it was fucking heaven.

Don't get me wrong, I've gotten hard plenty of times over the years—wet dreams and all that comes with hormones and teenage angsty bullshit, but I'd always brushed it off as part of human nature and never really concentrated on WHY I was so turned-on.

But now...now I'm forcing myself to think about it. And it felt so good to just let loose and allow my fantasies to take me into oblivion where all I felt for a few blissful moments was pleasure instead of pain. And you know what? It felt right. The rightness of it made me tremble. Because goddamn it, I was born this way. This is not a choice. My body showed me that today.

Of course as soon as I cleaned myself up, the awful shame immediately crept back in—especially that I'd fantasized about a friend who was unattainable.

The same kind of shame that colored Brennan's cheeks when I'd caught him standing near the concession stand staring at me or through me, more than likely. He was embarrassed and tugged down on the hem of his shirt like he always did. Trying to hide himself and become invisible. But he could never be invisible to me.

He's like the sun on a warm summer day, and the draw is almost visceral.

And you know what? Screw it. Release is natural—despite what's been hammered into my head. And not only used for the purpose of procreation. Give me a break.

If anything, I'm way behind all my friends. I'm a fucking virgin at almost twenty years old, and I will not be ashamed of actually feeling something other than confused and numb.

Am I embarrassed it was Brennan I fantasized about —the guy I have to see pretty regular all summer? The guy I now consider a friend? A little. But it can't be helped.

I have a raging crush on the guy a few years in the making, and all I can count on is that it will pass. Maybe there'll be a guy like Brennan that comes into my life someday. A guy as cool and sweet and gorgeous as him. And maybe then I'll be brave enough to come out to him.

And to them. All of them. Or maybe it'll be before that when I've literally had enough. Maybe I'll finally do it just FOR ME.

All I know is that I can never go back to the way things were. I am forever changed.

-Josh

11

BRENNAN PROPPED himself on the edge of a picnic table next to Abbey and looked up at the big screen. An animated movie with dragons was nearing its end, and if you didn't know it was family night, the low squeals and buzz of excitement on the lot would surely give it away. Kids always added an extra dimension to the theater atmosphere, almost gave it a life of its own, and it was the first time he'd seen a genuine smile from his mom behind the register tonight. She'd even reached out to pat an infant's head and retrieve a fallen pacifier for the parent. Behind the smile he spotted a hint of hurt, and it made him want to hug her. But he certainly didn't want to call attention to any of it; it was what he did best—remained in the shadows.

The air was muggy and the cool breeze felt nice against his face. Brennan kept the walkie slung on his hip, and it crackled every time the wind kicked up. But there was currently a lull in orders, and it felt nice to take a chill pill for five minutes outside the concession-stand doors.

Kylie was here with Todd again, but tonight they had brought out a blanket and were sitting on the hood of his car and far enough apart that they just looked like acquaintances. *Had Kylie friend-zoned him?* Damn, that would make his night. When Brennan had served them earlier in the evening, Todd had inquired about him helping Josh coach baseball.

"Who knew you two were even friends?" he scoffed.

Brennan thought it was an odd enough statement, almost like he was jealous he hadn't been asked, but he shrugged and replied in a more civilized tone than he wanted to. "We've known each other for years. What's it to you anyway?"

When Todd mumbled something under his breath, Brennan looked right at Kylie with an arched eyebrow, and she had enough gumption to blush before he walked away. He totally didn't get the attraction. Probably something about a misunderstood bad boy with a tender heart or something stupid like that you'd normally see in one of those cheesy Hallmark movies. But he had to remember it wasn't any of his business, and more than likely Todd was all bark and no bite. *Fucking blowhard.*

"Okay, here's the scene I was telling you about." Abbey's voice bubbled with excitement. For being so badass, she was also innocent in a lot of ways. In the show, the female Viking punched the male love interest in the arm, then kissed him hard, and it was such an Abbey move that Brennan understood why it was her favorite part.

After they shared a grin, Brennan briefly sobered, remembering the family dinner conversation last night. "I was suggesting '80s movies to my parents. One was *The Princess Bride,* but can you think of other decent ones?"

No way he'd confess why he'd made the suggestion. But he had this vision of inviting Josh up to the theater on the night of the showing. It was stupid really, but he'd gone ahead and followed through with the idea anyway.

"I'd suggest *Sixteen Candles* if it wasn't for my rewatch a couple of years ago," Abbey said with a sigh. "Too much misogyny with a toe dipped in rape culture too."

"Yikes. How much you want to bet it was that whole generation of movies?" Brennan replied after considering it. And now he wondered about his own favorites from the era that he hadn't considered in a few years. His parents would remind them how much times had changed.

"Oh, I'd lose that bet in a hot minute." Abbey nudged him with her shoulder. "I'm glad we can still be buds after I made a total fool of myself the other night."

"You didn't make a *total* fool of yourself," Brennan said, and she play-punched his shoulder, which was lucky because he knew she could hit a whole lot harder.

"Thanks a lot," she replied. "Geez, you can at least tell me it wasn't so bad."

"Of course, it wasn't so bad." Brennan looked her in the eye, his cheeks heating up. "Any guy would be *lucky* to kiss you."

"Anyone but you?" Abbey grinned playfully. "You could've looked a little less *deer in headlights* and more *oh, this could be fun.*"

"Sorry," he murmured. Story of his dating life. "Five minutes later and Charlie would've been a much better choice."

"Charlie?" she said as if considering him for the first time. "That could've been interesting."

He cocked an eyebrow. "Yeah? Well, he might show up here at some point, so maybe you can go for round two."

"Ass," she said with a laugh, but he could've sworn he saw a twinkle in her eye. Except there was always that hint of playfulness when it came to discussions about hooking up. Maybe she and Charlie could become friends with benefits.

Charlie would love that idea. In fact, Brennan felt so guilty about their conversation the other day at the field that he texted Charlie and invited him to hang out soon. He took longer than usual to respond, and Brennan thought that had been purposeful.

"And what about you?" she replied. "Who are you crushing on these days?"

Brennan felt a thud in his chest, like a lone beat. He shook his head and looked away.

"C'mon, you can tell me." Abbey tapped her feet to the music in the movie.

Brennan spotted gum and candy wrappers dropped near the garbage can by the last row of cars but stayed put. Told himself he'd get to it soon; he didn't have to flee his friend no matter how uncomfortable the question was. "No one."

"Not one person makes you feel mushy inside?"

"Dunno," Brennan admitted, looking down at his lap. "Maybe I don't exactly get what you mean."

"Like, your chest aches when you see them and your stomach is all fluttery," she explained, and Brennan's chest beat with a lone drum solo. Fuck. "You mean to tell me you never felt that way about anyone?"

Brennan shrugged. He thought of saying he once did about some girl or another, but he was finished with those lies.

When he heard the familiar clearing of a throat, his head sprang up.

Josh was walking toward the concession area with an arm slung around his kid brother. When the hell did they arrive? Brennan straightened, so completely flummoxed at seeing him that his knees nearly gave out. Josh's dark hair was all tussled liked he'd been wrestling with his brother and his lips were plump and red, as if the blood had rushed to the surface from biting on them.

"Josh, what are you..." he stammered. "Well, I mean *duh*, you brought your brother to a kids' movie, obviously."

"Yeah," he replied with a nod in their direction. "Thought we could use some brother time together."

Brennan wanted to ask more but didn't want to be too intrusive into his family life. He thought of Josh's father speeding into the late movie the other night and his stomach revolted. Fuck, what if that had been tonight?

Josh leaned forward conspiratorially. "Plus, don't tell anyone, but this is my favorite kids' movie franchise."

"Mine too." When Abbey elbowed him, he snapped out of it.

"Oh uh, Josh...this is my coworker, Abbey."

"Hey, how's it going?" Abbey said and he knew that look; she was sizing Josh up, and it made him feel uncomfortable. She had only moved to the area a couple of years ago and had attended high school in another suburb, so she didn't know the locals as well as he did.

He was feeling all protective, maybe even possessive of Josh, which was ridiculous because the guy didn't seem to even notice. And even if he did, what could Brennan possibly do about it? The two of them would probably be cute together. He tried to bat the idea from his brain.

"I've got to get this little guy some snacks before he starts eating the gravel or something," Josh said with a smirk as their eyes met and held for a drawn-out moment that made the moths kick up in his stomach. "So, um...catch you later?"

"You got it," he replied numbly.

Josh's brother grumbled about being called *little* as they pushed through the concession stand door, and Brennan stood there like some creep staring after them, his mind a whirlwind of thoughts, his body tingling with a strange awareness.

That was when he noticed the ending credits of the movie and a line forming near the concession stand door as families stepped inside to either use the restroom or place an order at the counter.

"We better get inside," Brennan said absently before he noticed Abbey looking strangely at him. "What?"

She glanced through the door to the counter, her gaze seeming to land on Josh and his brother. "Talk about a crush."

The words slid from Abbey's lips so effortlessly, it made Brennan gasp.

"What?" he sputtered, the air feeling trapped in his throat. "What the hell are you talking about?"

"God, don't have a cow, Brennan." Was it that obvious? Or maybe she wasn't even referring to him and Josh. Inhale. Exhale. Before you pass out. "Maybe I'm wrong, but the way that guy was looking at you...it was sweet, really. But I could be totally off base."

"I...huh?" Brennan could barely even register what she was saying as he took a wide step back to give himself enough room to breathe. To deny. To process.

He had the sudden urge to run—far away. From Abbey's scrutiny and his cyclone of confusing feelings.

"I should've never opened my mouth," she said, stepping closer with a hint of regret in her eyes. "But please stop acting so appalled. Like there's something wrong with same-sex attraction. Or any attraction, really. Sheesh, Brennan. I thought you were cool with—"

"Fuck, Abbey," he gritted out. He needed a minute to think, goddamn it. "You just caught me off guard is all."

Relief flooded her face. They had always seen eye to eye on most topics—especially when it came down to human rights. "Yeah, I didn't think you'd be so uptight about it. Besides, I'm probably way off base. But it's definitely cute to see you all flustered like that."

"Screw you," he replied with a strained laugh. "Josh, he...he's the guy I'm helping coach this summer."

"Oh, that probably explains why you guys seemed so... adorably awkward yet, *chummy*," she replied, looking Brennan over. "Didn't you mention something about his church sponsoring the team?"

She narrowed her eyes as she stared through the window to the counter again, and Brennan couldn't help wondering what in the hell she thought she saw. How could she possibly think there was anything more between them than friendship? What the hell was he missing?

"For the record, I don't believe sexuality is a choice. You're born the way you were meant to be. Period."

"O...kay," Brennan sputtered. "Why are you telling me all this?"

Abbey leaned over to make eye contact with Brennan. "Because we're friends...and friends have your back no matter what, right?"

"R...right." Was there something he was supposed to be reading into her comment?

When his dad's bell rang and the walkie crackled on his hip, he snapped into action, following Abbey inside and trying to fix the popcorn machine, which was on the blink again. But tonight he seemed to have the magic touch and once it began working, his mom clapped him on the shoulder, and he trailed Abbey outside with a delivery. Thankfully she seemed too preoccupied to make it into a competition.

After a few trips across the gravel, he was able to sink into the familiar routine and push aside that strange and uncomfortable interaction between him and Abbey. On his way to the concession stand, he noticed the tail end of some terse words between Todd and Josh. They were standing near the bumper of Josh's car, and his teeth were clenched as his hand pushed roughly at Todd's shoulder. *Holy shit.* What the heck was that about?

He didn't want to stare, so he pushed his legs to keep going and when he next glanced out the large concession stand window, Todd had gone back to his perch beside Kylie on the hood of his car, his jaw ticking as he practically glared at the screen.

When Abbey handed off a medium tub of popcorn and Skittles, then reached for her own order of hot dogs and sodas, he followed her outside once again. He didn't realize until he got closer that she had given him Josh's order in slot twenty-five.

What in the hell? She had obviously done that on purpose.

Brennan's pulse pitched as he made his way to the driver's side door to hand off the order. Josh smiled as he passed the tub to his brother on the passenger side, and Jimmy dug right in, his gaze on the screen as the second movie was well into the first hour.

When he handed off the large soda, their hands caught around the perimeter of the cup for a fleeting moment, making Brennan's heart thump hard against his chest.

"Wow, you guys got busy," Josh's cheeks were dotted red as he ripped open the bag of Skittles and popped a couple into his mouth.

"Just like your hectic nights at Dairy Whip, yeah?" he replied, considering how the line was sometimes out the door on their muggiest nights.

"Sure, but I just stand still and punch shit into a register. You're working up a sweat." Josh's gaze zeroed in on Brennan's damp bangs. The heat felt like sludge and for sure, he'd been hauling ass practically all night. He hoped he didn't smell funky and almost considered stepping back but stayed put, not wanting to bring attention to it.

When he offered the pack of candy to Brennan, he lifted his hand to beg him off, but he wasn't sure why. "Not much of a sweet tooth?"

"Probably too much of one," Brennan replied in a show of honesty, but he kept his hands to his sides. He would *not* pull on his shirt.

Josh stared at him for a moment before his eyes widened briefly, and he wondered what exactly he'd homed in on about him. "What flavor Tornado would you get if we were at Dairy Whip right now?"

Brennan felt like he'd totally given himself away and more than likely, Josh remembered how he'd only ordered a soda that one day he and Charlie showed up after the beach. Still, he didn't hesitate. "Oreo, all the way."

When Josh smiled like that, a wide and toothy grin that showed off his dimples—it made his breath hitch. Damn, he was cute. Brennan looked at the screen before he gave himself away, and he wondered if that was what Abbey had seen between them. Brennan staring at Josh a little too long and hard. "Oreo is a good one. I'm more a fan of heath or just plain vanilla."

"Vanilla, huh?" Brennan said with a smirk. "Is this where I make fun of you for being too *straight*?"

Josh's face faltered briefly as a small gasp left his lips and his cheeks dotted red. Brennan was confused because Josh would normally run with something like that and have a good comeback ready to lob at him. But now there was just silence between them and awkward throat-clearing. Suddenly everything that Abbey had said to him was amplified, and he was more confused than ever.

He tried thinking of something, anything, to change the subject and the first thing that jumped out at him ended up being the exact wrong thing to say. "So...everything okay between you and Todd?"

Now Brennan could cut the tension with a knife.

"Ugh," he said, tilting his head against the seat. "Another time, maybe?"

"Sorry," Brennan muttered feeling incredibly stupid that he'd even asked.

"No, don't be," Josh replied. "Just a strange night."

"Yeah, I hear you." Brennan took a deep breath. "Well, I gotta get back to work. Catch you later."

Straight. Such a strange portrayal of someone's sexuality, Diary.
If I'm not straight, does that mean I'm bent or like, twisted?

I hate the connotation.

Queer is no better but I've been reading up on everything LGBTQ online, and my generation is trying to own the word again. I'm not sure it fits me but I'm a newb, so what the hell do I know? At this point, I can't even admit that I'm not straight to anyone other than myself.

Does Brennan have any inkling? Could he possibly guess from that brief awkward moment between us when he delivered our food? And what if he does? He didn't seem revolted—if anything, he just looked stunned or embarrassed. Unless it just hadn't sunk in yet and he decided to stay the hell away the rest of the summer. But I could also be reading into his behavior. Things definitely seem uncomfortable between us sometimes. But other times it feels so natural, like we've been friends forever and I could talk to him about anything.

Can I tell him, though? It's practically spilling out of me, I need to tell someone.

I need to confess all of it. Okay, maybe not all of it, but enough of it to alleviate this pressure in my chest. Maybe then the panic will finally recede.

I'll admit I took Jimmy to the drive-in on purpose. I wanted to do something fun, just the two of us and after playing a round of Putt-Putt golf, I thought he'd like hanging out and watching a couple of movies. Plus, Jimmy loves buttered popcorn and the drive-in rates up there as some of the best I've had.

I wasn't even sure if Brennan was working but then I saw him sitting on the picnic table with...Abbey, I think her name was. And they looked so chummy, I initially felt jealous. She was touching his arm and I wished that I could so easily reach out and touch him too. But that isn't what this is supposed to be, so I need to get over it already. Or at least I should, by the summer's end.

Damn, this shit is getting complicated.

-Josh

12

By late afternoon on Monday, Brennan was restless in a way that drawing didn't resolve. The drive-in was closed, his parents were running errands, and Sydney was in her room, most likely on the phone with Kylie.

It was the one night of the week they tried to eat dinner as a family, and he and Sydney decided to give their mom the night off from cooking. Earlier in the afternoon, he'd peeled and sliced the vegetables for his mom's potato salad recipe Sydney had recently mastered. Once his parents got home, he'd cook some burgers and hot dogs to give his dad a break from the grill.

He threw aside his sketchpad and strode down the stairs, reaching for the basketball from where it was stored along the garage wall. Heading outside, he took a couple of rusty shots at the basket before it dawned on him that he hadn't messed around in the yard like this in a few months. He'd played a lot with his dad or Sydney when the basket was new, but then the novelty wore off and life had gotten busier. He was never interested in joining a team, but he knew the basics pretty well and his layups never missed. Unless he was thrown off—like he was now when something caught the corner of his eye.

Glancing down the driveway toward the street, he saw Josh walking past the house with his dog. Josh looked equally surprised and lifted his hand in a wave, a small smile lining his lips. Brennan instinctually looked down at his too-tight-and-stained Iron Man T-shirt that he'd changed into after his shower. *Damn it.* That was what he got for lazing around the house.

"Hey, you." Brennan walked toward the sidewalk, resisting the urge to tug at the hem of his shirt even though he could feel it riding up over the waistline of his cut-off jean shorts. At this point, Josh knew what his body looked like, and what the hell did it even matter between friends?

At least he wouldn't needle him about it like Charlie did.

Except when he'd met his best friend at a graduation party they'd both been invited to on Saturday, Charlie seemed overly cautious and Brennan felt super guilty about the awkwardness that acted as a barrier between them. He was sure it was all his fault, and he wasn't certain what to do about it.

The uncomfortableness lessened a few degrees when he'd followed Charlie's lead by stopping at different groups of mainly girls to catch up on their summer or ask about future plans. And once Brennan took some sips of the beer he'd been offered, he'd loosened up quite a bit too. Brennan thought Charlie probably got at least one phone number out of the deal.

He knew Charlie's family couldn't afford an elaborate party to celebrate him earning his diploma, and Brennan had opted out of any type of gathering in favor of an end of the summer trip to one of his favorite camping spots at Big Bear. It might do them all good to be together before Sydney's senior year and his fall schedule of classes.

"Hey yourself," Josh replied, but his attention was over Brennan's shoulder to the backyard. "Is there an actual room above your garage? Guess I hadn't noticed before."

Brennan glanced toward the sturdy structure that was more

of a loft than anything, but he felt cozy there for now. "Yeah, that's where I sleep."

"Seriously?" he replied, leveling his eyes on Brennan. "That would be cool. Just far enough away but close as well."

"Exactly. I figure it's the best arrangement since I'll be sticking around for college." He laughed uneasily. "It's probably why they haven't thrown me out yet."

"That something you're concerned about? Because I'll tell you, sometimes I'd almost welcome the idea of—" His words suddenly died on his lips as he studied Brennan, and a strange kind of stillness settled between them. "Sorry, I didn't mean to poke at any sensitive spots."

Brennan felt a twinge in his stomach. "What makes you think I'm sensitive about it?"

"Because you told me. That day we hung out as extras backstage at camp," he replied. "I shouldn't have brought it up—none of my business."

It was like Brennan had fallen under a spell that day. Under Josh's spell, to be more accurate. They both had friends and families and responsibilities but that day, it was just the two of them talking and laughing without a care in the world, so it made sense he would share more of himself. Josh had too, about his dad being a tough coach and them belonging to the church.

"S'okay," Brennan replied as he bent down to pat his dog on the head. "What exactly did I say?"

"That the Fischers were your foster family and you hoped..." Josh's cheeks flushed as Brennan held his breath. "You hoped you'd be able to stick around for longer than a couple of years."

Brennan inhaled sharply. He'd been so vulnerable, waiting for the hammer to fall again, and obviously it was still a sore spot to this day. He tried to stutter out a response, but he couldn't get his mouth to move. Besides, his wish had come true, and he wasn't ashamed of wanting a family of his own, for fuck's sake.

"That's always stuck with me, you know?" Josh explained,

trying to meet his eyes. "My family is too damned much sometimes, but at least I—"

"How are they too much?" Brennan lobbed his own question
at Josh. Turnabout was fair play.

"Dunno exactly." Josh blew out a harsh breath. "Too strict.
Too rigid. It's just lately I've been questioning everything. Even
my beliefs."

When Josh leveled his penetrating gaze on Brennan, he didn't
flinch. Instead, he felt that same tether of connection binding
them together again. "Me too."

Josh nodded, glancing down to Brennan's sneakers, then up
to his eyes, and Brennan burned with curiosity, wondering
exactly what he was thinking and whether he liked what
he saw.

He didn't know why it mattered so much, but it really fucking
did.

Brennan stared at Josh's soft mouth and considered how it
might feel against the tips of his fingers. He'd been so damned
conflicted for so long but when he looked at Josh, all he felt was a
pure kind of longing. To know him, get closer to him, even...*holy
fuck.* That line certainly couldn't be crossed unless...the hairs on
the back of his neck stood on end as Josh bit his lip, seeming to
struggle with something as well.

Brennan felt like he might crawl out of his skin if he didn't
take some sort of action, and he certainly didn't want Josh to
leave—not yet.

So he motioned with his thumb behind him. "Want to see it?
The loft?"

"That would be awesome." Josh picked Maggie up and
followed him through the side door to the garage and up the
stairs to the loft.

As soon as Brennan stepped inside his space with Josh on his
heels, it suddenly occurred to him that Josh would be seeing
exactly how he lived. Crap. There was a bed, couch, desk, and a

small fridge and though everything was in its rightful place, he wasn't always very neat with his things.

"Don't look at that pile of laundry on the floor—or my unmade bed."

Josh chuckled. "I promise I won't. But gotta tell you, you might have me beat."

Brennan cringed as Josh's gaze swung around the room, and he wondered what made him think this was a good idea. "This is really great. I might be jealous."

"Yeah, not too shabby," he replied. "But you have a dorm room, so..."

"And a roommate, don't forget—who might be messier than you."

When Brennan's cheeks burned, Josh pushed playfully at his shoulder. "I'm only messing with you."

As Josh took in the wall art and knickknacks, Brennan considered what clues it might tell him. Could he see a former foster kid who still kept things clumped together in easy to reach places in order to leave at a moment's notice? In fact, as Josh's eyes made his way to his overflowing bookshelf, he felt embarrassed by the amount of stuffed toys he still kept. He'd left one too many treasured animals behind, and he couldn't seem to part with them as an adult.

"They were the only thing I could cling to when I moved around so much," he said, feeling the need to explain himself. "They brought me comfort, and I didn't want to just toss them."

"Makes sense. Which is your favorite?" he asked and Brennan wondered if the surprise was evident in his features.

He glanced over the stuffed toys, from the black cat to the video game characters like Mario, and almost feigned ignorance. But Josh was so attentive, it felt like maybe Brennan could share it with him and he wouldn't laugh—even Charlie had told him to pack them all away.

Decision made, he reached for the gray elephant. He had

always been attracted to the large mammals on the zoo trips with different schools, and when he was allowed to actually buy a stuffed one from the gift shop, he'd slept with it every night.

Josh stroked his fingers across the elephant's worn ears and tusks as Brennan held in a shiver because it felt as if he were an extension of the elephant. And maybe he was. "Does he have a name?"

"Peanut." His cheeks colored. "Lame, I know."

"Not lame at all. Sweet, actually." When the corners of Josh's eyes crinkled in a smile, Brennan's stomach flipped over.

As Maggie sniffed around the floor, probably looking for any leftover crumbs—and Brennan wouldn't be surprised if she found some—Josh moved around the room as if cataloguing everything. They brushed against each other a couple of times in the small space, which almost seemed deliberate and definitely made gooseflesh rise on Brennan's arms and legs. But if Josh noticed, he was good at disguising it.

Now he took in the artwork on Brennan's walls. He had some prints by Banksy who was a famous street artist, and Josh zeroed in on his most dramatic piece of a person holding a sign that read, I Want Change.

There were also movie posters that his parents had given him from the drive-in over the years, like an iconic '70s *Star Wars* one as well as The *Godfather,* and Brennan realized that Josh was pretty much seeing a snapshot of his life with the Fischers.

Now Josh pointed at a four-by-six print his mother had framed. "You made that at camp."

It was Brennan's name in graffiti art and his favorite work at the time. He was drawn to the style because it was organic and gritty and less refined than other formats. It felt like it fit him—a scruffy foster kid who was probably closer to living on the streets than people realized. It was the reason he held on to everything so stringently.

"You were good," he remarked as he studied it closely and Brennan was glad he couldn't see him blush.

"You were too," Brennan replied. "Do you still play the violin?"

He averted his eyes and mumbled. "No—guess life got busy."

Brennan sighed. "How does that happen? The things you wanted to do as a child get all mixed up with real life, I guess."

"Yeah, something like that." Josh's eyes snagged on his messy bedspread. "Is this the famous notebook Charlie was making fun of?"

Josh didn't pick it up, which he appreciated. "Yeah, I draw some. It helps relax me."

"I hear you." Josh glanced in his direction. "I do some journaling. It helps to get it down and off my chest."

Now Brennan wondered what he wrote about. None of his business.

"Suppose we have something in common."

"A few things, I think." Josh picked Maggie up again and rubbed her chin.

Brennan figured that was his cue to leave.

"Anyway, I'll walk you out," he said, and Josh followed him down the stairs.

When they stepped onto the driveway, Brennan spotted the basketball he had discarded earlier. "Maybe sometime we can shoot some hoops?"

"How about now?" Josh's smile held a tinge of relief. Unless that was Brennan's imagination. But maybe he wasn't ready to be on his way, either. "I'll just run Maggie home. Be back in a few minutes."

As Brennan waited, he took some deep breaths along with some lame shots as he paced the length of the driveway. After another minute, he went inside to grab a couple of waters from the fridge. Twisting one open, he took a long swig to quench his thirst as well as tame his nervous energy. Jesus, he was around

Josh twice a week at baseball games, so why did this seem different? More personal? This is what friends did, and they had
agreed to hang out more.

"What are you up to?" Sydney asked as she bounded down
the stairs and reached for the family-sized pack of Twizzlers from
the pantry. Her sweet tooth was almost as bad as Brennan's.
When she offered him the half-eaten package, he waved her
off. "Josh is coming over to shoot some hoops."

"Awesome. Didn't you guys used to be friends when you did
that camp?" she asked, and Brennan nodded. "Glad you
reconnected."

"Yeah, uh, me too," he replied, then fled out the door to avoid
any more probing commentary about it.

When Brennan reached the driveway, Josh was strolling up
the walk, one hand in his gray sweat shorts pocket, the other
clutching his phone. His shirt clung to his muscular shoulders
and for the first time, Brennan noticed the height difference
between them.

"How tall are you, man?" He asked as he reached for the ball
from where it was abandoned near the rose bushes.

"Five eleven," Josh said as Brennan bounced him the ball.
"How about you?"

"Five nine," he replied, and he could see Josh sizing him
up too.

Perspiration beaded his neck from the hot sun, and Brennan
now regretted not changing into a fresh shirt. He considered
telling Josh he'd be right back out but that would look pretty
dumb after the fact. Besides, they'd get sweaty shooting hoops,
anyway. He'd just have to suck it up. And *in.*

"Want to play HORSE?" Brennan asked. Perfect game for him.
Rules. Order. He wouldn't need to think too hard in front of the
guy that made him most flustered.

"Sounds good," Josh said, taking a practice shot. It rolled
around the rim before going in. "Want to wager on it?"

"Sure." Brennan grinned, his stomach dipping. "What do you want to play for?"

Brennan could have sworn Josh's eyes lingered on his lips for a full second before he replied. "Um, how about free food?"

Brennan let out the breath he was holding. Maybe it'd only been wishful thinking. Besides, he was too much of a chicken to do anything about his assumptions anyway.

Brennan took a practice shot and was way off. Story of his life.

"So then...you'd owe me something from Dairy Whip, or I'd owe you from the drive-in?"

"Exactly," Josh replied. "And it looks like I'm going to be visiting you, based on that shot."

"I've got my game face on now," Brennan deadpanned and Josh chuckled.

They dribbled and shot from various locations around the basket hoop all while making small talk about their baseball team, college courses they'd have in common, as well as their jobs. Brennan tried to ask more questions about his family, his father in particular, but the only thing Josh mentioned was how involved in sports and church they all were—their entire lives apparently, and how it was beginning to wear on Josh. That fit with his statement about him questioning everything in his life.

The more time went by, the more Brennan wondered if what he'd seen that night at the drive-in with his dad had been his imagination. He was no further along in knowing how to handle the topic or whether he should at all. When Josh mentioned that his parents were having some church friends over tonight and that he was for once glad he had church group to attend, Brennan arched a questioning eyebrow.

"My parents...well, mostly my dad...counsel people a lot." He used air quotes and rolled his eyes. "Like if someone is struggling with their faith or has fallen on hard times, he sort of takes them under his wing or something. I don't even fucking know."

Brennan almost asked if they had a platinum-blonde member

of their church, but that would only sound ridiculous. Besides, what Josh explained seemed to fit what he'd witnessed. Someone was upset and his dad was trying to console them. Right? But when Josh opened up a little more and confessed that his dad was pretty strict and that Josh went with the flow just so he didn't catch any flak, he thought maybe Josh had lots to hide, too. At least on the feelings front. Brennan didn't know if he would fare as well under their roof and was again grateful that his parents had given him the kind of family he'd always craved.

He opened his mouth a couple of times to tell Josh what he'd seen of his father at the drive-in but more and more, he wondered if it was any of his business after all.

Before Brennan knew it, they had played two rounds of HORSE and were dead even. He threw Josh a water before guzzling some from his own bottle.

"Let's play one more game for a tie-breaker," Josh suggested.

"You're on," Brennan said, not even waiting for Josh to get into position. "Or we can play one-on-one."

He bounced right past him into a layup for a basket. Jesus, it felt good to just let loose after all that built-up tension.

"Oh, I see how it is," Josh replied as he grabbed the rebound and dribbled toward midcourt. "You like to play dirty."

As Josh dribbled the ball toward Brennan, he raised his hands in a defensive stance. Josh took a weak shot and they both jumped up for the rebound, heads close, breath heavy. When the ball went out of bounds, they both raced for it, tripping and laughing along the way.

Josh grabbed hold of the hem of Brennan's shirt in an attempt to get to the ball first.

"Cheater," Brennan shouted reaching toward the grass. When he spun around with the ball Josh stood just a whisper away. So close that Brennan could see the dark stubble growing on his chin.

Losing his balance on the uneven pavement, he stumbled

backward. Josh's hand shot out to steady him but it was no use; gravity brought them both down on the grass.

When Josh fell on top of him, he attempted to cushion his fall using his forearms as well as his knees, landing on either side of his hips, but the entire length of their bodies still came in contact.

Their chests and hips were flush, and *holy hot damn*. Brennan stopped breathing and became very still—the sensation of their bodies so closely aligned bombarding him at once. How Josh was smooth skin over hard muscle.

When Josh looked into his eyes with a modicum of surprise laced with something else he couldn't read, Brennan's face lit up a thousand degrees.

He could feel Josh's breaths against his cheek, smell his spearmint gum, as he tried to untangle himself and even when he finally did, Brennan still lay there in shock. His dick had plumped in his shorts and fucking hell, he was mortified. It was the first time it'd happened in front of Josh instead of from just thinking about him. There. He'd admitted it.

Thankfully Josh didn't look down at him or even act like he'd noticed.

Instead, he yanked the ball up with him, turned, and shot a basket, all in the space of a heartbeat.

Brennan sat up on his elbows, panting shallowly. "All yours. Your food wish is my command." He pulled the hem of his shirt down as an afterthought because it surely had ridden up throughout the game and especially during their fall.

Josh breathed heavily and paced back and forth in his driveway. He lifted his shirt partway to wipe the sweat off his face. Brennan caught sight of his flat abdomen and the trail of dark hair below his belly button and willed his dick to cooperate. He tore off a blade of grass and began winding it around his finger to occupy his mind.

Josh stood in front of Brennan and ran his fingers through his sweaty hair. "So, *anything* I want, huh?"

Brennan squeezed his eyes shut and tried to collect himself. His heart ping-ponged painfully around his chest. He knew Josh was just asking about food, but *damn*. The way his lips mouthed those five little words, Brennan's imagination would be running wild for the rest of the night.

"Brennan..." Josh took a step forward, his eyebrows meeting in the center of his forehead. "Hey. You okay?"

Now Brennan just felt like a hard-up fool. He needed to get his shit together. Thankfully, his dick had finally flagged.

"Yep." Brennan stood and wiped his sweaty palms on his shorts, afraid he'd be rock hard again if he thought about it for much longer. Josh watched him closely. "We make a mean double cheeseburger at the drive-in."

"Nice," Josh replied with a grin. "Then you need to pay up soon."

And just when something really dumb was about to come out of his mouth that bordered on flirty—a skill he wasn't very practiced at and probably wouldn't fly very well in this situation—he heard the motor of his parents' car as they pulled into the driveway. A few minutes earlier, and they would've spotted their crash landing. Thank God for timing.

Not that they were doing anything wrong. Now if they could read Brennan's thoughts, that would be a completely different matter.

"Mom, Dad, you remember Josh Daly," he said once they exited the car.

"Yes, of course," his mom replied, and his father reached out to shake Josh's hand.

"We decided on a bucket of chicken," Mom said, pulling a large bag from the familiar fast-food place from the back seat.

"Sounds good," Brennan replied. It would also go well with Sydney's potato salad. "I'm starved."

When his mom smiled, he noticed how she looked a bit lighter today and hoped that only meant good news. "Would you like to stay for dinner, Josh?" his father asked, and Brennan's stomach dipped. *Holy shit.* Why the idea of Josh hanging around affected him so much he didn't know, but it warmed him in a different way than when they'd invited Charlie.

"I'll have to take a rain check," Josh said. "I have this church group thing."

The disappointment that settled in Brennan's chest seemed to match Josh's eyes. But he wasn't sure if it was about his church function—after what he'd shared earlier—or because he'd hoped to hang out longer.

Josh waved his good-byes and Brennan watched as he made his way down the driveway, thinking about that cheeseburger he owed him and when exactly he'd pay up. When he turned to head inside, he noticed how his mom was closely watching him from the kitchen window, and that similar sort of fear and shame settled in his stomach. Same story, different day.

Holy fucking hell, Diary.

We were only a breath apart.

One single breath apart.

One inch closer and I would know. I'd know everything.

Good or bad, heartbreak or hope—it would make it all that much clearer.

And that look in Brennan's eyes, could it be my imagination?

A breath apart. I thought about it all through church group, and I was so distracted I didn't even hear what the reverend asked me about our baseball league.

And when I came home I was so restless that I dusted off my violin and tuned it. I could only strum a couple of strings because it was too late, and I'd wake Jimmy up. But damn, I haven't had that urge in ages —hadn't even considered it until Brennan mentioned it.

To let my emotions play out of my fingers.

Not since that day at camp. My hands on his shoulders in the pitch dark, my thumb tracing the hollow of his throat, his pulse thrumming under his skin.

We were a breath apart then too.

If I concentrate hard enough I can still smell him—like coconut oil and sweat mixed together.

He smelled like summer.

I'm going to shut my eyes and pretend because that's all I can do.

Pretend that maybe, somehow, we can be more than a breath apart.

--Josh

13

As soon as Sydney was buckled in for cheer camp, Brennan cranked the stereo way up, hoping to drown out any conversation. He had so many thoughts swirling through his brain since that one-on-one game with Josh that he was having a hard time settling on any one thing.

"What the heck?" Sydney said, turning the knob to a lower volume.

"I'm in the mood to listen to music." If Brennan were being honest, he wasn't even aware of what song was playing, so lost was he in his own head.

"Then wait till you get home and blast your stereo," she snapped at him.

Brennan rolled his eyes and tapped with the melody on the steering wheel.

Sydney had never been a morning person and was always a grouch until well after breakfast, so he should've known better than to push her buttons. But he couldn't seem to help himself.

His sister crossed his arms. "What is up with you lately?"

"What do you mean?" Brennan said, humming to the tune. It wasn't that he was in a bad mood—probably the opposite—but his skin felt like raw edges, like he didn't know what to do with all the sensations coursing through him at once.

She looked out the window at the passing scenery. "I don't know. Seems like you've got a ton of stuff on your mind lately."

Brennan's fingers stopped moving. His sister's voice sounded strange. "That obvious?"

"Yeah," Sydney said. And then she stole a sidelong glance his way. "You're distracted too. You even left your notebook in the bathroom this morning."

"Shit, did I?" Brennan nearly missed the stop sign, he was so taken aback. He stepped on the brake, hard. Syd's hands flew to the dashboard to brace herself. "You didn't look at it, though, did you?"

"Whoa, take it easy," she scoffed. "I know how you are about your precious notebook. I took it to the garage and put it on the stairs to your room."

It was like the universe was conspiring against him—forcing him to figure stuff out before he was ready. And he definitely *wasn't* ready. At least he didn't *think* so. "Sorry, you just took me by surprise."

"Does any of this have to do with that kiss from Abbey?" She made a gagging gesture with her finger. "Seriously, Brennan? You are so lucky Dad didn't catch you guys."

"Abbey came with a bunch of friends and they were playing some sort of game," Brennan explained. It felt like the car was filling up with water and he'd be submerged at any moment, drowning in his own half-truths. "You know how Abbey is. And no, I don't feel that way about her."

"I just hope it doesn't ruin your friendship," Sydney said, worry in her eyes. She was always stressed about stuff like that with her own group of friends and sometimes he worried about peer pressure when it came to school parties she attended—he obviously knew what went on at some of them. But he also knew that Sydney was strong in her convictions, so he needed to cut her some slack.

"It's cool. We talked it through. It'll be okay," Brennan responded. That, of course, was one of his own fears as well. Plus it would've been so awkward working with her if they hadn't gotten on the same page about it.

"Who told you about that anyway?" he asked as he turned down the street toward the high school. The cheer squad would be sharing the field with the football team and majorettes like always.

"Kylie," she replied with a smirk, and Brennan remembered she was there that night with Todd. *God.* He thought of Todd's terse words with Josh. What in the hell? But he definitely wouldn't push it. If Josh wanted to tell him someday, he'd be all ears.

Brennan rolled his eyes. "What's going on with her and what's-his-face anyway?"

"You know his name," she said in an exasperated tone. "And I'm not really sure. It sounds like they're more friends than anything."

Wasn't that surprising? Kylie's celibacy principles probably came into play, but there were other things they could be getting busy with—according to an overheard conversation between my sister and her best friend. It was more than he wanted to know, quite honestly.

He truly hoped Todd wasn't trying to wear her down to try to prove something to his macho self. If Brennan got wind of that type of behavior, he'd have some words for him. And maybe even a fist. But if what Sydney was saying was the truth, then why was Todd hanging in there? Not that he knew about the guy's dating life or how many girls he was seeing on his summer break home, but it certainly was puzzling. Kylie was a sweet girl, so maybe he actually enjoyed her company and they had fun together. Go figure.

He knew all about that.

"Wait a minute...why do you keep asking? Does your mood have to do with Kylie?" she asked in an alarmed voice. "I mean, I know you used her as an excuse before, but are you interested in something with—"

"Hell no," Brennan replied a bit too forcefully.

"Oh, thank God," she replied, visibly relieved, her hand plastered to her chest. "That would be way awkward."

"Totally. And what do you mean, an excuse?" Sydney was way more aware than he thought she was. Suppose his invisibility cloak didn't work on his own sister. "I've never pretended anything when it came to—"

"But you didn't correct it either," she said with a cluck of her tongue, and he could no longer deny it. The familiar guilt came roiling back in his gut. "You know how Charlie likes to tease you and play things up. You obviously just wanted to be left alone about not liking any girls."

"I...*fuck*," She had him here. Brennan couldn't help the panic swirling inside of him. He felt like shit for not being brave enough to own up to anything. But at the time he didn't even recognize what the hell was going on inside him. But now...he thought about feeling Josh's breath on his cheek and thrust it from his thoughts. No way he wanted to get overheated while sitting beside his sister. It was enough that it'd happened last night in bed and he ended up with a raging boner, making for a restless night of sleep.

"It's okay, Brennan." Sydney reached for his shoulder across the front seat, sympathy in her eyes. "You're my brother and I love you. I don't want to see you uncomfortable about anything. I'd rather you felt free to be yourself, especially now that you graduated high school."

"I *am* myself." Brennan felt the lie creep up his neck onto his cheeks before he muttered, "*Mostly.*"

He pulled into a space in the parking lot of the high school.

He got Sydney there about five minutes early for camp, but she didn't make a motion to leave the car. "I'll always be here for you if you want to talk. You know that, right?"

"Yeah, I know that, Syd." His heart squeezed tight. Even if everything went to shit, he instinctually knew she'd be in his corner. "Thanks."

He reached over and gave her a one-armed hug.

"Syd?" he asked just as she reached for the door handle. Her body stilled as she turned to look at him. "Why do you think Mom and Uncle Scott don't talk anymore?"

Her eyebrows knit together. "Guess I hadn't even thought about it like that. Just thought maybe he was busy and would come around soon enough."

"Remember last year at Christmas?' he asked. "I think it started that night, whatever it is. They barely made eye contact."

"He brought his friend," she said, her head slanted as if thinking it through. "He was his boyfriend, right? Uncle Scott is gay?"

"Well yeah, that much is obvious." Brennan's voice came out all small and shaky as if admitting his uncle was gay was somehow testing it out for himself as well. "Do you think that has something to do with it?"

Brennan was asking about his worst fears come to life, but referring to someone else entirely. It hit home for him nonetheless.

Things were bad enough with Mom's long silences—he wouldn't want to go the rest of his life without hearing the melody of her voice. Her hysterical laughter that always ended in a snort. Or how she hummed boy-band tunes off-key while making dinner.

His chest felt tight as a screw.

She scrunched up her nose. "What do you mean?"

"Is that why there's so much tension between them?" Brennan could barely catch his breath. "Because he's..."

"Because he's gay?" Sydney asked, snapping her head toward him. "Is that really what you think?"

"Dunno. What else could explain it?" Brennan said in a frustrated voice.

"Why not just ask her?" Sydney replied like it was as simple as that—maybe for her. "Bring it up at dinner one night."

"Because Mom and Dad aren't doing so well right now in the relationship department." His hands flew up in exasperation. "No way I want to rock the boat. Haven't you noticed that they barely talk?"

Sydney gasped, her eyes widening at the thought. "Things have definitely been weird lately and now that you mention it, I heard an argument between them the other day."

Brennan's jaw clenched. "What was it about?"

"Dad asked her to talk to him and she waved him off." Syd's tone was hushed, her cheeks reddening. "Do you think they're getting a divorce? Kylie's parents are divorced, and she hates having her stuff divided between two houses and only seeing her dad on weekends."

Now he'd done it, needlessly worrying his kid sister. He needed to stop thinking about himself and be a better brother. "No, of course not. This is Mom and Dad we're talking about. They'll definitely work it through."

"I hope you're right." Sydney grabbed his hand and squeezed his fingers so hard, she almost cut off his circulation. "I'd miss our family."

"Everything's going to be fine, Syd." He carefully pulled his hand from her grasp. "I shouldn't have said anything."

"Yeah, okay," she replied, reaching for the door handle. "You won't be leaving anytime soon, will you?"

"Not if I have anything to do with it," he said, swallowing past the lump in his throat. "Now go have fun with your friends."

I'm not sure I can take anymore, Diary.

It feels like I'm slowly withering inside. Last night at church group all the gossip was about a teen girl who was caught in a compromising position—as the church elders called it—at the park on the jungle gym with another girl.

According to the son of the Reverend, the situation is being "handled" and the idea of it makes my stomach turn. The girl would be getting "counseling" to help rid her of impure thoughts and actions. Yeah right. I've heard that before. Like it's possible for someone to rid their body of what is intrinsically part of them.

As I looked around the room at all the disgusted faces, I had the sudden urge to reach out to the girl and offer her comfort, support—tell her that I understand completely and to hang in there.

Why is there so much shame around it? Why the hell is it shameful to want to hold someone, touch them, and kiss them? Isn't it simply a show of affection—and getting your needs met?

And now it's hitting me like a ton of bricks. I'm an adult. I can make decisions of my own. It will absolutely be to the detriment of my family, church, and school community, but I can still freely choose to walk away and live my life.

Fuck. And then the same fear starts creeping back inside, gripping my insides and squeezing them so tight I can barely breathe.

I also understand why people stay put, hide who they are—until it's safer. To lose everything in your life has to be worth it.

And I can almost taste that freedom. Like a bird who's lived in a cage their entire life until someone finally throws the door open. Or maybe you just steal the key.

Regardless, one push of the door and you're fucking free.

But then you walk to the threshold of the opening and look down. In order to actually make it, you have to fall from grace. Even crash and burn before you can stand up on weakened legs and rebuild yourself from the ground up.

So maybe the secret to all this is to begin with a single step forward. To choose one person in your life you trust. Trust enough to tell. To relieve you of some of the burden. One person who might see you just as you are and might stand by you regardless, and I think I know who that person might be. But fuck if I'm not completely terrified. Nearly frozen solid with fear.

So maybe in the morning I'll wake to a new day. A day where I feel brave enough.

-Josh

14

AFTER THEIR BASEBALL game that morning, where they were slaughtered 10-2, Josh asked Brennan if he wanted to tag along to watch his brother's team at the other field.

Brennan was surprised by the request, but he agreed without giving it a second thought. Anything to keep hanging out with Josh. They recapped the game with the parents, making sure to steer away from some of the hardcore requests—*Can Sammy be moved up in the roster?*—something he and Josh agreed upon because parents got way too invested and totally took the fun out of it for the kids. When Sean's dad waved him over, he thanked him for helping his son have a more positive outlook in general, and that warmed Brennan's heart.

"You're pretty good at this coaching thing," Josh remarked as they rounded up all the bats and bases and walked them to the trunk of Josh's car in the mostly empty lot.

"So are you," Brennan replied, a familiar buzzing settling in his stomach from the compliment. "Maybe you'll follow in your father's footsteps?"

"Hell no," he replied a bit tersely, and Brennan was surprised by the vitriol, but given their recent conversations he supposed it was expected. "I've actually been considering quitting altogether at the college level."

"Seriously?" Brennan asked once he shut the trunk. He knew that Josh hadn't seemed too enthusiastic in general when asked about his team's stats, but he could never put his finger on why—besides what he said about the expectations being overwhelming. "But don't you have, like, a partial scholarship?"

His shoulders deflated. "That's the thing. I sort of feel stuck. Between that and my parents footing the rest of the bill, I suppose I need to just suck it up for three more years."

"Damn, that's tough," Brennan replied, not having considered that Josh might be that miserable at his fancy private college. Everything was relative, he supposed, and getting to know Josh in this way was definitely eye-opening and pretty damned cool as well. He was glad to be a sounding board any time he needed the support.

"No, it's okay. Thanks for letting me bitch about it," he replied before pointing across the road to the path through the trees. "I suppose we could drive to the field, but I sort of want to walk."

"As long as there's shade, I'm all in," Brennan replied.

Besides, this was what friends did, right?

They walked the trail side by side, moving apart for cyclists and joggers every couple of minutes, while enjoying the cool air under the canopy of elms and maples. "I almost forgot how pretty it is back here. It's been awhile."

"The park is probably the best part of this shitty town." Josh said, and they chuckled. "Did you guys used to hang out here to drink or smoke weed?"

Brennan looked down at his feet. "I've always worked every weekend and have never wanted to do anything to get myself kicked out of the Fischers' house. I know it sounds pretty lame but I'm just keeping it real."

In fact, the only time he would attend a party was when Charlie begged him to make an appearance somewhere. Mostly it was in someone's yard or an empty field in the park at night. But the grounds were patrolled by rangers, and Brennan was always nervous about getting a ticket and disappointing his parents. Charlie always ragged on him about it but never pushed him too much.

"Nah, makes a lot of sense actually. It was about self-preservation, right?" Josh asked and Brennan nodded. "Maybe we're just two sides of one coin." *Damn, he gets me.*

When they almost got run over by a pack of cyclists, Josh nudged him onto the grass away from the paved trail. "Let's walk along the creek bed; I bet it's even cooler."

He followed Josh through a copse of trees, toward the edge of the stream, where they picked up rocks and tried mostly unsuccessfully to skip them across the water.

"For me high school was all church, work, and sports," Josh said in a sobering voice. "So, in a way, I never really let loose either. Not that I wanted to—not in the way everyone else seemed to, if you know what I mean."

Brennan arched an eyebrow. "You mean like hooking up and stuff?"

"Yeah, that's what I mean," he replied and before Brennan could process that, Josh was tabbing out of his sneakers. "C'mon let's go hog *wild* and wade in the water."

Brennan laughed and followed suit, pushing his sneakers aside and stepping toward the shore. "We're a couple of party animals."

When his feet hit the water, it was initially cold, but then he sighed in relief because it felt so refreshing. He made sure not to move too quickly to avoid biting it on the slippery rocks. He was sweaty and covered in dirt from the field, so he scooped up some water and doused his forearms as well as the back of his neck, thinking about what Josh had just confessed to him.

"So, are you saying you haven't been with anyone?" Brennan's cheeks colored. He was probably crossing a line, but he couldn't help being interested. Besides, it was the kind of conversation he might've had with Charlie, and he definitely considered Josh a friend. "Maybe I shouldn't have asked. Was just curious is all."

Josh crouched down to search for some flat rocks beneath the water. "Well, abstinence *is* taught in our church—and specifically in youth group. You know—gotta wait until marriage."

Josh snorted as his rock skidded across the top of the water.

Brennan thought about his sister's friend Kylie and how her abstinence was born of a different philosophy—a stance against the casual sex that happens in high school, which was why her friendship with Todd was an interesting development. But maybe he was making too many assumptions.

"Are you telling me everyone's been good at ignoring their hormones?" Brennan smirked. "Man, Charlie would probably go off the rails."

"Plenty of them do. But not to worry, all will be forgiven as soon as you repent and fall back in line with the church's teachings again," he said in a mocking tone.

Brennan was certainly getting an earful, and he didn't know what to make of it. Some of it sounded along the lines of what he'd remembered in their own church sermons about everyone being a sinner, which essentially boiled down to being human and making missteps, but Josh's voice definitely had an edge of something different to it. Although maybe he was only making fun to blow off steam, while still being fiercely protective of his beliefs. Besides, he would guess belonging to a religion helped plenty of people feel grounded...or something like that.

"But to answer your question about whether or not I've been with anyone," Josh said and Brennan held his breath, though he didn't even know why. He was being ridiculous. "I've definitely dated a couple of girls, but we never had sex."

"Same." The confession flew out of his mouth before he had a chance to take it back.

Josh's eyebrows rose. "Seriously?"

"Well, yeah," Brennan replied, his cheeks warm from more than the blazing sun. "Why does that surprise you?"

"I don't know...I mean," he mumbled as his neck splotched red. "You're certainly not hard to look at, so I figured you'd have ample opportunity..."

Brennan felt pinpricks all over his body, even on his scalp. Josh Daly thought Brennan was attractive—in one way or another. Is that what he just admitted?

"I, um...thanks?" he replied through a parched throat. "Guess there was never anyone I felt that way about."

"No one, huh?" He looked at Brennan from beneath his lashes and he nearly melted on the spot. *Holy fuck*, the guy just did it for him. Made him all mushy inside—to use Abbey's description. Guess Josh was his bona fide crush.

"So guess that means I haven't truly lived." Brennan shrugged. "I'm like an old soul in the body of an eighteen-year-old."

"Or just an old man." Josh grinned. "Suppose that makes two of us."

Brennan took too wide of a step and nearly toppled over. His arms sprang out to steady himself. "Hurry, pass me my cane before I fall and break my hip on these fucking slippery rocks."

Josh's fingers braced Brennan's shoulders from behind, and he pretended to push him into the deeper end of the creek before steadying him with sturdy hands.

"Oh, I'll get you for that," Brennan said with a laugh, then stilled as he reveled in Josh's hands on him, the heat of his body behind him. Their hips were nearly touching, and he could feel Josh's soft breaths against his nape, almost like in the darkened closet, except that time had been face-to-face. Had Josh been facing him now, Brennan wouldn't be able to meet his eyes, so just as he'd suspected before, the lack of light had lent to his bravery.

When he leaned forward to whisper in his ear, Brennan shivered. "Guess you'd have to catch me first."

In one move, Josh tottered to the shore, toed into his sneakers by the edge of the creek, and ran toward the path.

"Cheater," Brennan shouted as he struggled into his shoes and then took off in an attempt to catch up with Josh. The way Josh's face lit up when he glanced over his shoulder and saw Brennan gaining on him was everything. And when he finally caught hold of Josh's arm, it felt so good to laugh from deep in his belly. Fuck, he liked spending time with Josh Daly.

They slowed down to a walk as they caught their breaths in companionable silence.

Josh slid his phone out of his pocket to glance at the time. "Damn, we better get going to Jimmy's game, so I don't disappoint him."

Josh's concern for his brother's feelings warmed Brennan's stomach.

When they got to the game, the stands were half-full as Josh glanced around for his mother. She lifted her hand in a wave as they slid on the bench below her and another woman with platinum-blonde hair that made Brennan do a double take.

Holy shit, the woman from the drive-in.

"Mom, this is Brennan."

"Yes, of course," she said with a nod in his direction. "I remember."

"And this is our church secretary, Mrs. Smith," Josh said, and she offered a polite hand wave.

Brennan sat frozen, trying to remember exactly what he witnessed between the woman and Mr. Daly. She'd been upset and he was attempting to comfort her. She also appeared angry at one point before they left the premises.

"What's up?" Josh muttered in his direction, a concerned look on his face.

"Nothing, I uh..." he spluttered and stole a glance behind him, but the women were involved in a conversation while looking in the opposite direction. "It's just that Mrs. Smith looks familiar. Does she always attend your brother's games?"

"No, uh she's one of the people they're counseling," he whispered as he leaned forward, and Brennan could barely concentrate with his hot breath ghosting over his ear. "It's not my place to say, but I overheard some things about her husband's gambling debts."

Brennan was overcome with relief but also still a bit troubled because it was sort of strange. But ultimately none of his business. Still, he felt he needed to finally say something.

"I think I might've seen her in the passenger side of your father's car one night," he whispered low enough for Josh to hear. "She was crying and now I'm putting two and two together."

He sort of felt guilty for thinking ill of both of them. She must've been struggling and needed all the support she could get from friends—or whatever she considered them.

Josh blinked as if thinking it through. "Yeah, makes sense. She's been having a hard time apparently."

"I won't say anything," he whispered back as they knocked shoulders and settled in to watch the game. Though Brennan wished they could stay in that little bubble where they whispered and shared secrets—with the sun blazing on them this time—but any more of that and people might talk or wonder.

It was already the third inning, and when Jimmy saw his brother in the stands as he went up to bat, he beamed. Until his dad barked something at him about getting his head in the game and he felt Josh stiffen beside him.

The smile was wiped from Jimmy's face as he took a couple of practice swings before zeroing in on the pitcher. Brennan glanced in Mrs. Daly's direction to see her reaction, and she simply looked tired. But when Jimmy hit a line drive up the center, she clapped and smiled. His dad was already motioning wildly from the first base line and once Jimmy made it to the bag, he paced the length of the dugout. Mr. Daly set him on edge, and he didn't know how the players could stand it.

They barely squeaked by the other team with two runs on top, and after the game Josh patted his brother on the shoulder and told him he did great.

Jimmy begged to ride home with Josh and once he told his parents of their plans, all three of them walked back through the path in the woods. Brennan looked over to the creek at one point, recalling their laughter but also their serious conversation and when he felt Josh's eyes on him, he blushed.

Damn, had they really admitted their virgin status to each other?

Once they got to their cars, the lot was already filled again for the afternoon league games. After Jimmy slid into the passenger seat, Josh glanced over the hood of his car at Brennan, "Well... thanks for tagging along. That was fun."

"It was," Brennan agreed. "You work tonight?"

"Yeah, and you?"

"Same." There was a long pause where there seemed to be unspoken words passed between them before Josh tapped on his hood and pulled open the door. "Catch you later."

Dear Diary:

How would you describe a perfect day?

Mine would be spent skipping rocks in the creek with Brennan Fischer.

Sharing secrets and dreams and those intense looks that give me hope.

Or maybe just make me dream. And right now, I could use a dream or two.

-Josh

15

BRENNAN FELT like he was floating on air after that day in the park with Josh, and it lasted all the way through his shift at the drive-in. Not even his dad's annoying bell or Abbey cheating on her route back to the concession stand could dampen his mood.

He went over their conversation too many times to count and was beginning to question more things. Like what it might mean that Josh told him he was attractive. It wasn't like he was saying he was attracted *to* him, but it was enough to get his body ramped way up. So ramped up that he jacked off in the shower thinking of him. And when he finally got his release, it was essentially mind-bending because he'd finally let himself go there. To imagine being with another guy as a possibility. And even if his intuition was way off about Josh, it felt good to finally settle into something.

Something that felt right for him and who he was to become.

The first movie flew by with plenty of food and drink orders to fulfill. Thankfully, Abbey didn't bring up anything more about Josh. Though he almost wanted to ask her what she really saw that one night. He was afraid he was reading way too much into it and would be crushed on many different fronts.

When Brennan ran an order to slot number five, he was surprised to see Charlie in the bed of a pickup with one of Josh's ex-teammates named Nate and couple of other guys from their school. Brennan remembered that Charlie and Nate lived in the same cul-de-sac and knew each other better as kids, so maybe they spent recent time together that Brennan knew nothing about. "Uh, hey. How's it going?"

"Good. You?" Charlie asked with an undertone of smugness on his face.

"Busy," he replied. "Catch you later."

After the concession line surge between movies and once all the orders had been delivered, Brennan took a chill pill on the picnic table. He pulled out his phone and his fingers hovered over Josh's name. They had exchanged numbers a couple of weeks ago in case of a schedule change but neither had used them yet.

What would he even say? Besides, he'd see him again in a couple of days at their next game. More and more, it felt too long between breaks and that was a worrisome thought. In another few weeks he'd be back at Solomon U, and Brennan's life would probably get busier again with college-level courses added to his schedule.

When he glanced at the parking lot, Charlie was heading in his direction with a large gulp in his hand, so he was probably looking for a refill.

"Hey," he said, sitting beside Brennan, the tension thick between them as they both stared blankly at the movie screen, which was some action-adventure flick Brennan wasn't too interested in.

"Since when do you hang with those guys?" he asked, cutting to the chase.

"Since you've been too busy," Charlie scoffed.

"Nice," Brennan deadpanned. It wasn't like he hadn't seen Charlie all summer. *Jesus.* But it was probably the vibe swirling around them as well. "Okay, I get it—things have been strange between us."

"Yeah, pretty much." Charlie shrugged. "Besides, looks like you have a new best friend, so..."

"Really? That's how we're going to play it—like we're five?" Brennan tightened his fist and made an exasperated sound. "At least Josh doesn't talk about hooking up with hot girls all the damn time."

Charlie's jaw ticked and his eyes shot daggers. Fuck, Brennan knew he had said the exact wrong thing, but it just spilled from his mouth in frustration.

"I didn't mean to say that," Brennan backpedaled. "I'm just having a weird couple of—"

"Maybe Josh doesn't talk about hooking up with girls because he's—" the words died on his lips as he shook his head.

"He's what?" Brennan urged. If they were going to do—whatever this was—maybe they should just get it all out in the open.

"Let's just say I've heard rumors," Charlie muttered, glancing at Brennan in his side view.

Brennan's heart climbed up his throat. "What kind of rumors?"

"That he..." he took a deep breath and looked Brennan in the eye. "That maybe he bats for the other team."

Brennan felt simultaneous shock and angry. Josh? *Holy shit.*

Was that how they'd talk about him someday? No wonder people stayed in the closet. *Fuck this bullshit.*

"Bats for the other team? Are we in the twenty-first century?" Brennan rolled his eyes, feeling completely on edge. "What are you going say next—that he's light in the loafers? Just spit it out."

Charlie scowled. "Screw you, I was trying to be nice."

Brennan's chest was thumping so hard, he felt like he might pass out at any minute. "And who the hell told you this nonsense?"

"Nate," Charlie confessed tipping his head in the direction of his car. "Remember that end of the year incident I told you about that between Josh and Todd Parker?"

"Yeah," Brennan replied, barely above a whisper. He was having trouble inhaling a decent breath.

"Well, according to *Todd*," he began and Brennan scowled. "He was changing in the locker room for practice and Josh looked at his goods."

Brennan's gaze snapped to Charlie's. "That's the story? Ridiculous. How can you *not* look at each other's junk, it's right there out in the open?"

Charlie clucked his tongue. "Like really looked—all slow and stuff, in a suggestive way."

Brennan's throat closed up, and he nearly choked on his own saliva. What the hell? He was having trouble believing Todd's version. Josh eyeing up Todd in the locker room?

Except—was that why there was so much tension between them?

"If I recall, the story you told me last year was that Todd lobbed an insult at Josh, it got out of hand, and they came to blows."

"Todd probably did call Josh a name, after *that*," Charlie insisted.

"What name did he—" Brennan trailed off.

Faggot. It was Todd's favorite word. Fucking homophobe.

Holy shit, Brennan's head was spinning now.

Had Todd caught Josh checking him out while he changed, so he accused Josh of being a faggot and they fought about it? If he recalled, it was Todd who came away worse for wear with a bloody nose.

"Except Nate said he didn't know if it was true because Josh and his family are pretty religious, and he goes to that Christian college and all so..."

And? So you can't be gay if you're religious? What was it that

Josh had confided in him that one day? *Lately I've been questioning everything. Even my beliefs.*

Was Josh gay?

Maybe Brennan felt hopeful about it at one time—but not like this. Josh's so-called friends gossiping behind his back. Had Josh heard the rumors? Did he know what Todd was saying about him?

He looked down at his cell again, wanting to reach out to him, but what would he say?

"So has Josh ever like..." Charlie nudged his shoulder conspiratorially. "*You know.*"

"What?" Brennan asked absently as he thought about the looks between them, the tender touch in the darkened closet. Brennan figured it was wishful thinking on his part and it probably still was. Todd was an asshole.

"Has Josh ever given you any clue that he—"

"Seriously?" Brennan bit out. "You think gay dudes go around hitting on every guy they meet?"

Charlie's eyes widened. "Don't get so bent out of shape. I was only asking if he *told* you since you're close and all—"

"Even if he did, I wouldn't go spreading it around." He huffed out a breath. "What if you found out a family member or a...a friend was gay, what would you do? Tell everyone you know?"

Charlie's eyebrows scrunched together. "Damn, you're really upset about this."

"I just don't like the idea of spreading rumors about something so important," he explained. "Josh is a good guy."

"It's not like his team doesn't hang with him anymore," Charlie countered. "Nate just said some stuff about Josh started adding up."

Brennan cocked an eyebrow. "Like what exactly?"

Charlie slurped the end of his drink and smacked his lips together. "Like the fact that he's never been with many girls."

"So what?" Brennan huffed. "Neither have I or you for that matter."

"Not for lack of trying," Charlie grumbled with flushed cheeks.

"What's going on?" Abbey asked glancing between them. They'd been so deep in conversation, they hadn't heard her walk up. "You look upset."

"It's nothing," Brennan replied, straightening himself before turning to Charlie. "You better get back to your friends before you miss the movie."

Charlie looked sullen, his gaze apologetic, before stalking off toward Nate's car.

Abbey slung an arm around him. "Hey, what's happening?"

Brennan sagged against the bench. "Charlie's acting like he's jealous of Josh and me hanging out. And then he had to repeat a rumor about him."

Abbey winced. "What kind of rumor?"

He looked pointedly at her. "Based on your comment from the other night, I'm sure you can guess."

"Oh, I see," she replied in a somber voice.

"Don't people have a right to their privacy?" Brennan threw up his hands. "Until they figure shit out?"

Brennan was definitely talking about himself, and he was probably being transparent enough that Abbey would figure it out, but he couldn't help himself. He was a mess.

"Of course, they do." When she squeezed his shoulder in a soothing manner, his eyes began stinging. *Fuck.* "People always freak about what they don't understand—and in time, the rumors will die down and they'll move on to something else."

"Yeah, I guess." He stood up, afraid hot tears would begin rolling down his cheeks. His feelings felt right at the surface, and he didn't know what to do with them—except stuff them for the time being. "Thanks. Better get inside before my dad rings the damned bell."

As he delivered more food, he'd decided that Josh deserved to know what people were saying about him. He'd want to know if the tables were turned. Josh would set the record straight—or not. It was none of his business anyway. But he considered him a friend and that was what friends did.

On his way back to the concession building, he noticed Abbey talking to Charlie outside of Nate's car, but he totally ignored them. He didn't think anything more troubling could fit in his brain.

Dear Diary:

Tonight, my parents invited some church friends over who just happened to have a daughter around my age. The only saving grace was that she looked as uncomfortable as I felt about the prospect of a setup.

When we sat outside on the porch together with some beverages, she confessed that she was secretly dating a guy who happened to be an atheist and then swore me to secrecy.

Once that tension between us was finally defused, I almost told her my secret. Thankfully, I kept my mouth shut.

It wouldn't even matter if I brought home a guy who just happened to be a devout Christian. The gay factor would always make him deviant in the church's eyes.

What a damned shame.

-Josh

16

AT PRACTICE THAT MORNING, Brennan tried to strike up a conversation with Josh, but his dad and brother had shown up to their game and sat in the dugout, which essentially squashed any hope he had of getting a discreet moment with him. He didn't want to upset him, but he thought Josh should know what his friends were saying about him.

So his plan was to text him before his shift and ask to talk in person or by phone.

But Josh beat him to the punch by messaging him first.

Hey, forgot to tell you I'll be at the drive-in tonight to catch the newest Fast and Furious movie.

Cool! See you later then.

Brennan was relieved and uneasy at the same time—especially since Josh would most likely be with the same friends who were gossiping about him.

Brennan watched as Josh arrived with a few of his old teammates, then spread out at the picnic tables up front. Josh's gaze sought out Brennan a couple of times as he and Sydney took turns with deliveries. He could've easily approached him to shoot the breeze, but it wasn't like Brennan knew his jock friends that well. Besides, Todd Parker had shown up with the group, which made it even more awkward. On one of his routes back to the concession stand, Todd glared at him and he returned the gesture. He didn't know how Josh could stand being around him. And that was exactly why he needed to tell Josh what he'd heard.

He was glad Abbey wasn't on shift tonight. She might've tried to intervene like she did last time. Not that Brennan was complaining—he got to talk to Josh that night, but he wasn't ready to have any heart-to-hearts with Abbey, or his sister for that matter. Since that morning he drove Sydney to cheer camp, he tried extra hard not to rock the boat at home and worry her unnecessarily again.

The good news was that Mom and Dad were actually laughing the last time he'd gone in to pick up an order, and his dad had winked at him as if to reassure him that things were indeed looking up.

"Told you it would be fine," he'd whispered in Sydney's ear on his way out the door.

During the second movie, which was another action flick, Brennan sank down on the picnic table nearest the concession stand. He told himself he needed to stay close even though he had his walkie on his hip. He felt on edge and wondered if there was some way to get Josh alone without calling too much attention to it. On the other hand, he wasn't all that certain this was the right place to talk to him about the very friends he'd shown up with.

He looked down at his phone when he saw a message blink across his screen.

It was from Josh.

On a break?

His gaze rose to seek him out, but Josh was facing the big screen, so it was impossible to read his expression.

Sort of—now that things have slowed down.

As Josh typed a reply his pulse spiked.

Is this a good time for you to *pay up*?

Brennan couldn't help grinning at the screen. Josh was referring to the bet they'd made, and he thought it was perfect timing.

Sure! I'll put the order in with my dad.

He hopped off the table and dipped his head inside the concession area.

"Hey Dad, can I get a cheeseburger?" he asked. "Actually, make it two."

His dad smiled from behind the grill. "Hungry?"

"No...well, yes." He sounded ridiculous. "I uh—I told Josh how good your burgers were and said I'd treat him."

"That was nice of you," he replied, and Brennan averted his gaze before he blushed furiously. "I'll let you know when the order's up."

"Perfect." He shut the door behind him, also avoiding the scrutiny of his mom and sister.

When he spotted Josh approaching, the butterflies kicked up in his stomach something fierce, and he had to pretend to be interested in the big screen, or he might've given himself away.

"Hey," Josh said, sinking down beside me.

"Hey yourself," Brennan replied, giving him a quick once-over. He was wearing dark-wash jeans and a deep-green shirt that brought out his eyes. "Having a good night?"

"Could be better," he replied with a shrug. He seemed nervous and if Brennan was reading him right, a bit melancholy.

"Is it the company?" Brennan asked with a raised eyebrow.

"Not anymore," Josh replied, meeting his gaze and Brennan's cheeks grew hot. "But yeah, probably has something to do with it. Not even sure why I agreed to hang out but guess it's better than the alternative."

Brennan studied him trying to guess what alternatives he

meant—he assumed church and home and what he said about feeling stuck.

"Plus, you're working, so now I can get some free food," he said, playfully knocking shoulders.

"Your order will be up soon." Brennan cracked a smile before he sobered. "But first, I need to tell you something."

"Okay." Josh furrowed his brows. "Is everything all right?"

"It will be as soon as I get this out." Brennan grimaced. "At least I hope so."

Josh nodded with wariness in his eyes. "Go for it."

Brennan glanced to the picnic tables up front to make sure no one was headed their way. "Charlie told me some of your friends have been talking shit about you."

Josh gnawed on his lip as he thought it over. He didn't seem upset or surprised—more *resigned*. "What are they saying?"

"It's about that incident that happened between you and Todd end of senior year."

Josh's face fell and he looked away. Brennan nearly changed his mind, but he'd said enough that Josh probably wouldn't want to drop it. And besides, the truth would definitely continue to eat away at him.

"Todd said you two got in a fight because..." he cringed. "Because you were blatantly checking him out."

"As if." Josh scowled in the direction of his friends. "*Asshole.*"

Brennan released the breath he'd been holding. "So that's not how it went down?"

"Hell, no." When Josh met his gaze, his eyes sparked with anger and determination. "He deliberately dropped his towel and stepped in front of me, practically daring me to look."

Brennan's eyes went wide. "Why would he do that?"

He forked his fingers through his hair in frustration. "Guess I wasn't giving him the attention he wanted."

Attention. Wait a minute, what in the world was he saying?

"It was a dick move and ended up backfiring on him."

"Backfiring?" Brennan asked.

"For one, I avoided him altogether after that," he replied. "Still want nothing to do with him. And second, I gave him a nice bloody nose."

"I heard," he replied. Brennan's brain was working overtime trying to put the pieces of the puzzle together. "So how did the incident turn physical?"

Josh momentarily shut his eyes as if to compose himself.

"When he heard the guys walking in, he pushed away from me and called me a faggot." He balled his hands into fists. "I just reacted. But it felt like a long time coming."

"Holy shit." Brennan glanced at the picnic tables up front, then back to Josh. "What about when you two were arguing the other night?"

"Empty threats. Making sure I still hadn't told anyone how it really went down," he replied through clenched teeth. "Obviously he didn't keep his end of the bargain."

Brennan shook his head. "Damn, I'm sorry."

"I'm still not going to out him to those guys." Josh made a frustrated sound. "I'm hoping what they say about karma is true. Because he deserves a good asskicking."

"Just so I have this right. What you're saying about Todd is that he's...."

He cocked an eyebrow. "A closeted jackass?"

Brennan could barely breathe. It totally didn't make any sense. But yet, it did. What was that saying about the biggest homophobes?

It would explain why he was seeing Kylie—he obviously considered her safe. His secret could be kept under wraps. So as it turned out, Brennan had more in common with Todd than he would have ever imagined. At the same time, they were worlds apart. Except, how far would Brennan go to keep his own secret?

He felt bile crawl up his throat. No way. No matter what, he'd just accept the consequences and live with it.

"So he wanted to what...hook up with you?" Brennan asked in a hesitant voice.

"Dunno. Or just see if he could get a reaction from me," he huffed out. "Regardless, I wouldn't touch him with a ten-foot pole. I've got standards, go figure...and a *type*, apparently."

He could feel Josh's gaze on him, but he wasn't brave enough to look in his direction. He felt hot all over like he was flushed from the inside.

Was Josh admitting that he...that Brennan...

You're certainly not hard to look at...

So many different emotions were coursing through Brennan at once that his fingers started trembling. He felt so close to his own truth that he didn't know what to do with any of it.

He tried to hide his reaction by sitting on his hands, but it was no use.

"Hey, are you okay?" Josh asked, concern in his tone.

"Yes...no...I don't even know. It's just that you...what you said..." Brennan sputtered unable to organize his thoughts. "Josh, I—"

"Brennan, your order's up," his dad's voice crackled through the walkie, startling him.

He sprang up on shaky legs and went inside to grab the order, barely looking his parents in the eye. He felt like they could see right through him even though he hadn't even admitted anything. Not yet.

Rejoining Josh, he held his burger out to him, wrapped in butcher paper with the drive-in logo on it.

"I ordered one too," he mumbled. "Thought I'd eat with you."

"Cool. I'd like that," Josh replied in a wary voice, still apparently concerned about the way Brennan was acting.

When Brennan sat back down, he placed a little distance

between them so he could freaking *think*. His brain was a hot mess, somewhere between relief and complete terror.

They sat in silence, watching the big screen and eating their food, meaningful words hanging off Brennan's lips, but he was unable to say any of them.

"You're right," Josh said around a mouthful. "These burgers are awesome."

"I'll let my dad know." Brennan offered a lopsided smile. "He'll be glad to hear it."

After another minute of uncomfortable silence, Brennan couldn't take it any longer. He was about to crawl out of his skin. "I'm sorry if I ruined your night. But I thought you needed to know."

"It's okay." Josh balled up his empty wrapper. "It's a relief to finally talk about it, actually."

"I get it," Brennan replied, pitching both of their trash in the can beside the table.

"And now that you know about me..." Josh cleared his throat. "It's okay if you don't want to hang anymore."

Brennan gasped, his eyes snapping to Josh's, and that was when he finally saw it so plainly. The relief, the hint of fear, the visceral longing that matched his own.

"No, I want to..." he murmured. "I want to very much."

"*Fuck,*" Josh whispered under his breath as his chest heaved and his shoulders sagged.

Brennan's cheeks colored and he stared at the screen again, feeling like he was a five-year-old with a crush. *Holy shit.* Was this really happening? Had they just admitted stuff to each other, in an indirect but mostly satisfying way?

Their hands were resting so close to each other on the table that he could almost take that leap—just one more inch and he could make himself clearer. But did he have enough courage?

If Josh had been brave enough to confess some things, then he needed to meet him halfway.

Mind made up, Brennan casually slid his hand over so that their pinky fingers rested flush together. And as soon as their skin made contact, he felt a zap of electric energy. His heart rose to his throat and when he glanced at Josh in his side view, his lips were parted as he softly panted.

Here they were out in the open, their fingers barely grazing and yet...touching him in this completely innocent way meant every fucking thing. And Brennan was so overwhelmed with emotion, he felt the hot sting of tears behind his eyes. Pure joy coursed through the marrow of his bones and the idea that Josh was affected by it as well, felt *profound*.

They stayed that way, neither making the effort to move, simply pretending to watch the screen but in Brennan's case, seeing nothing but a blur of action sequences.

When Sydney walked out of the concession stand, he ripped his hand away and hopped off the bench as if he'd been caught with his pants down or something.

"Dad wanted me to—" she glanced over his shoulder. "Oh, hello, Josh."

"Hi, Sydney," Josh replied in a throaty voice, and Brennan dared not look at him. "I uh, better get back to my friends."

"Yeah, see you," Brennan said, finally looking at him.

When Josh smiled at him in what felt like a new and secret way, Brennan wanted to melt into a puddle right there where he stood.

Holy shit, Diary.

My fingers are still tingling.

Such a small gesture but it made my stomach tilt like I was on some carnival ride.

I swear if Brennan Fischer would've turned to me right then, I would've kissed him under the stars—in front of God and everyone.

Todd might've had a heart attack.

Serves him right after what he pulled.

Not very Christian of me but he's the worst sort of person.

Besides, as it turns out, my God doesn't accept people like me anyway.

But maybe there's another God that does.

-Josh

17

BRENNAN COULDN'T SLEEP, not since he'd gotten home from the drive-in after sharing a cheeseburger and a hell of a lot more with Josh. His brain was spinning as he went over their conversation for the hundredth time.

It was a hot summer night and to take advantage of the cool breeze, Brennan did what he'd made a habit of since he'd moved to his room above the garage. He climbed out his window and sat on the flattest part of the roof.

He drew the evening sky but couldn't stop thinking about Josh as he gazed at the starry landscape.

Lifting his phone, he noted the time. After midnight. All the lights in his house were out, so he knew his family was in bed—unless his mom had fallen asleep on the love seat again. But he hadn't found her like that in the last couple of weeks, which must've meant she was resting more soundly. And even though he caught her smiling a hell of a lot more, he still wasn't sure what her reaction would be if she knew all the thoughts running through his head about a certain someone. Nonetheless, summer wasn't going to last forever, and before he knew it, Josh would be at college and he'd be left with nothing but regrets.

On that note, he took a chance and typed a text.

Ignore me if you're sleeping.

Josh's response came immediately.

I'm not.

His stomach fluttered over those two words. *Jesus.*

Sorry, I know it's late.

No problem. I can't sleep either.

Brennan could feel himself smiling. Damn, he was pathetic.

Everything go okay after you went back to your friends?

Brennan winced. He still wasn't sure how to feel about it all.

I didn't confront anyone if that's what you mean. Not sure it's worth it. I've got too much of my own shit to figure out, you know?

Brennan huffed out a breath.

Yeah, I know. Believe me.

Does your family know? Josh asked.

Brennan's pulse kicked up immediately, signaling his fight-or-flight reflexes. But maybe Josh was only asking something innocuous and Brennan was making assumptions.

Know what?

You know what I'm asking.

Brennan sagged against the roof tiles, which were beginning to feel stiff and unforgiving. So he stood and climbed inside to his room.

Sorry, it's easy to play dumb. Been doing it for so long, he texted as a response before undressing down to his boxer briefs and lying down in bed.

Tell me about it.

As he stared up at the ceiling, he decided to go for it. It would feel good to talk to someone about all the noise inside his head. Someone who understood.

No, they don't know and I was hoping to keep it that way until I'm finally on my own.

That was my plan too. But it's hard to hide the truest part of yourself.

It's pretty much torture, Brennan admitted.

Do you think they won't accept you? Because your parents seem pretty cool. You can imagine the position I'm in—my church and college both revolve around the Bible's teachings and they don't look favorably on people like us.

Now Brennan felt like a chump.

I'm sorry. You must think in comparison it's a piece of cake for me. But I...it's like I finally belong to a family, and I'm scared of what their reaction might be. Plus, my uncle is gay, my mom hasn't talked to him in months and though I've never gotten a straight answer, I'm afraid it might be because of his sexuality. So I've been trying to keep under the radar.

It was so much easier to admit these things by text than in person, but he was still nervous what Josh would think of him. How lame did he sound?

No, I actually get it. I want to belong too, you know...to people who'd actually accept all of me. Does that make sense?

Damn, Brennan hadn't considered that.

It does. So maybe we can form our own little group where we definitely belong.

Brennan thought of Todd again and how he might be feeling pretty lost too, but he had done some shitty things and needed to figure it out for himself.

That actually sounds amazing. Are we going to name this group of ours?

Brennan smiled as he considered it.

Hmmm, let me think on it. Maybe something as a throwback to our camp days?

Those were the best. You got a favorite part?

If I say being a stand-in for a performance, would that sound too corny?

Holy shit, had Brennan just admitted that?

Not unless you think getting locked in a closet is.

His stomach dipped. *Damn.*

Well, that's included in my answer, so no fair.

A long minute passed as Brennan watched the dots move from Josh's side of the conversation.

What about the closet makes it a favorite?

Such a simple question yet so complicated.

Are we really going there? He asked with a teasing emoji.

No pressure, sorry. It's just...I think about that day a lot.

He sighed. **Me too.**

And sometimes I think about...what might've happened next.

Brennan squirmed in his sheets, pushing them off because his skin was flushed.

I have too...plenty of times.

You have? Joshed asked using a shocked emoji.

Brennan's stomach was buzzing. **I have.**

Fuck. The one-word answer from Josh said it all.

No kidding.

A long silence between them and Brennan wondered what Josh was thinking.

You're gonna make it hard to fall asleep and we've got an early morning game. Brennan's cock filled with blood instantly.

So...sweet dark closet dreams, Josh typed with a wicked emoji.

I think I hate you.

No you don't. See you tomorrow.

Brennan fell back against his pillow and huffed out a laugh. No, he didn't hate Josh.

He didn't hate him in the slightest.

The next day at practice was definitely torture. It was all blushing and awkward glances when they first got to the field like they were a couple of seventh graders. But as soon as the kids and parents showed up, it was back to business.

After the game, Josh asked if Brennan was interested in seeing his brother's game again.

"After a walk along the creek?" Brennan asked as they stored the equipment in Josh's trunk.

"Naturally," Josh replied with a wink that he felt to his core as they took off toward the path, rehashing their winning game and seeming to avoid their discussion from last night. As they walked along the water and skipped rocks, Brennan noted their form had improved as compared to last time.

Once they'd soaked their feet, they stepped into their sneakers and started up the small incline to the paved path.

When Josh motioned toward a large maple, they stopped to marvel at the names and hearts carved into the trunk.

"Alex and Kyle," Josh pointed out. "That could be two guys. You never know."

"Wouldn't that be something?" Brennan replied, transfixed as much by the names as by the idea of being brave enough to admit such a thing out loud.

They were completely alone, with only the sound of the rustling leaves above their heads, and as Josh leaned his shoulder against the tree and sighed, Brennan couldn't take his eyes off him. How his bangs flopped over one eye and his lips looked full and soft.

The air between them grew charged and almost *commanding* as their gazes connected. Brennan's knees quivered as the urge to touch Josh intensified. To feel his silky hair against his fingers and press his nose in the crook of his neck to smell him.

Josh was biting his lip so hard, Brennan wondered if he'd draw blood.

Staring into his dazzling green irises, Brennan noticed new things about him. Like the freckles that dotted his nose, the rose color splashed across his cheeks, his dark and thick lashes, and the nearly desperate look in his eyes that probably matched his own.

Both clenching their fists, it was as if time stood still. Waiting on something to happen. For one of them to make a move. It was as if an invisible string of longing was tethering them together.

Brennan's breaths were rough and jagged, and all at once Josh squeezed his eyes closed and inhaled sharply, squirming but staying rooted against the trunk.

"Josh..." Brennan was the one to move first, narrowing the distance between them and curling his fingers against his wrist. "Last night...we...I..."

He didn't even know what he was trying to say—only wanted some affirmation. But it was as if Josh had lost the ability to respond.

"Do you want..." Brennan was lost in Josh's sweaty spearmint scent, his soft skin beneath Brennan's touch, and his lips, moist after running his tongue across them. Josh gazed into Brennan's eyes and took firm breaths through his nose.

Feeling braver, Brennan skimmed his hand up his arm to his shoulder and Josh shivered against Brennan's touch.

If Josh hadn't had a clue how much he'd affected Brennan, he would now—if only he glanced down at the front of his shorts.

"Say something, Josh," he mumbled. "Am I wrong about all this?"

Josh shook his head, then slid his hand to Brennan's waist. He had the momentary urge to back away, to pull his shirt down. But Josh wouldn't let him as he tightened his hold to keep him firmly in place.

His fingers felt like they were on fire, and Brennan's skin prickled like it might burst into flames. The anticipation of the moment coiled tight in his stomach as he sagged against Josh, his hip essentially pinning him to the trunk.

5

A moan tumbled from Josh's mouth and his head tipped against the tree.

Brennan leaned forward and dragged his nose along Josh's jawline, resisting the urge to taste his skin. When he drew away, the burning desire in Josh's eyes told him everything he needed to know.

Just as Josh's fingers twisted the material of his T-shirt to yank him forward, they heard voices on the path. Brennan stepped aside and rounded the trunk, breathing hard. He smiled and waved as two females crossed their path toward the creek.

They made it to his brother's game by the fourth inning, then back to their cars with Jimmy in tow, making only small talk along the way. As if admitting anything that happened aloud would ruin the sanctity of the moment.

I don't know what came over me, Diary.

It was like I couldn't speak. He was so close...a breath away again.

It felt like a dream was playing out in front of me and I was afraid to ruin it by talking or making any sudden moves. Brennan was braver than me...so, so brave.

He made me feel alive with need and want and hope.

It's time to stop being so afraid.

-Josh

18

AFTER HE HELPED his dad lock up at the drive-in for the night, Brennan was on his roof again, feeling restless and wondering what might've happened had they not been interrupted near the creek yesterday morning. Or if Josh had told him exactly what he wanted—with his words, but he supposed his hand was just as good. How his fingers had dug into his waist with such intensity.

Brennan wasn't sure what had come over him. He'd just felt so drawn to the guy and after being brave enough to touch him at the drive-in and then share so much over text, he didn't want to lose out on a chance to get closer to him. He had never felt so drawn to another human being in his life, and he now knew with utter certainty the very thing he had been fighting for years. Talking it over with Josh had felt amazing. Had made him feel not so alone. But he'd admit it was also a terrifying realization— even worse as an admission. He almost wanted to delete their conversation until he read through it again and it made him feel *free.*

Speaking of Josh, his phone buzzed with a text.

What are you up to?

He blew out a breath. He hadn't wanted to get in the habit of texting him this late.

I'm on my roof. I come out here sometimes to think.

That actually sounds perfect.

Want to join me?

Holy shit, did he just suggest that?

Wouldn't I wake your family? Josh asked.

Not if you're quiet. What about yours?

They're in bed, so pretty sure they won't miss me.

Same actually.

I can be there in five minutes.

Brennan's heart beat out of his chest.

I'll meet you at the side door of the garage.

Holy shit, were they really doing this?

His pulse was going crazy as he padded downstairs to greet Josh.

He quietly opened the door as soon as he saw him approach.

Josh's grin was shy as he stepped inside the garage. "What the hell are we doing?"

"Hanging out?" Brennan replied sheepishly. "What friends do, right?"

When their eyes connected for a drawn-out moment, Brennan held out his hand. As soon as Josh clasped it, he led him upstairs past his pile of laundry and this time he didn't feel embarrassed, he just felt...clandestine yet thrilled to have Josh's company.

Once they got themselves situated side by side on the roof, the air grew thick and there was a buzzing between them.

"The stars look amazing up here," Josh remarked with his head tilted upward.

"If you lie down, you can see them better." Brennan demonstrated the action.

When Josh reclined beside him and their elbows brushed, his stomach flipped.

They stared at the night sky for a while, pointing out constellations and discussing their work shifts. When Brennan asked Josh to tell him about college, he talked about his classes, his requirements for attending chapel—which was a total surprise to Brennan—and this really cool professor he claimed was more progressive in his beliefs. If he didn't know any better, he'd guess that Josh was hoping to find more people like himself and he hoped he did, but the idea made Brennan feel melancholy as well. What he was describing felt a world away and Brennan wondered what it might be like to visit him on campus. *One day at a time, dude.*

Brennan would have to figure a bunch out for himself starting that fall. Abbey always made it sound like there was a multitude of liberal-minded people at her college, and he didn't doubt it— he had only recently allowed himself to believe he could make it on his own someday. He didn't know if Josh would remain in his life in one way or another, or if he was just some sort of catalyst for him to get his ass in gear. Guess he'd find out soon enough.

"Why couldn't you sleep tonight?" Josh asked after a pause in the conversation.

"Dunno," he replied with a sigh. "Everything just feels so different."

Josh tilted his head toward Brennan. "What do you mean?"

"I've been going through the motions for so long. You know?" he admitted, rubbing his eyes. The idea of it exhausted him.

"Is that what you're doing now?" Josh murmured.

"Absolutely not..." Brennan shook his head vigorously. "This feels so real and true that I almost can't...catch my breath."

Josh quietly cursed, his fingers suddenly brushing against Brennan's, and now they were touching from shoulder to elbow.

"Have you ever done this before?" Brennan whispered, his fingers trembling.

"What, touched another guy?"

"Yeah," he replied as though somehow he was afraid of the answer.

What if Josh was more experienced than him?

"No. I've thought about it, but nobody has made me feel like this except for you."

"Me?" Brennan asked, completely overwhelmed by that reply. How could he make anyone feel much of anything?

"Fuck, Brennan, do you even know how amazingly cool and adorable you are?" Josh sat up and looked at him. "I guess you really don't."

"No, I..." Brennan's breath caught in his throat and he felt a flush crawl across his cheeks.

Something had shifted in the air between them. Something heavy and heated and so commanding, he felt it down to his toes. His pulse was throbbing so loudly, he was sure Josh could hear it.

After another moment Josh stood up and glanced at his window.

"You need to get going?" Brennan tried not to sound disappointed.

"I...." he reached out his hand and Josh helped pull him up. "Just don't want anyone to see us out here."

"Yeah, okay." They climbed through the window to his room, and Brennan figured he'd be walking him to the door. His head was spinning, trying to make sense of Josh's shift in mood.

But in the next moment he got it—the reason Josh wanted to go inside. Because he stepped closer than any two friends should rightfully stand, pinning him against the wall, and Brennan lost all manner of breathing.

His lips were a whisper away and Brennan momentarily shut his eyes to gain control of his erratic pulse.

Goddamn, if he didn't get a taste of those full lips, he would die in this very spot.

Right this fucking instant. He couldn't stand it anymore. The hesitation and guessing made his chest ache with too much longing.

When he looked into Josh's eyes, they'd turned darker and hooded.

Words were shouting inside Brennan's skull, working their way to his lips. Just hanging there, dangling for dear life. *Please fucking touch me.*

But Josh had been the one to hold back yesterday morning, so he didn't dare break the spell.

"It's not just me who feels this, right?" Josh murmured. His fingers curved against Brennan's neck, his thumb mapping patterns against the hollow of his throat.

The words that had been so readily available just moments before had flitted away on the wind. *Josh is actually touching me.* The way he'd dreamt of for days. Weeks. Maybe even *years.*

"There's something between us," Josh whispered. "And it's been there since that summer at camp."

Still, Brennan couldn't move or even speak. He was motion-less—spellbound by Josh's penetrating eyes, his rosy lips, his powerful words as he inhaled gallons of air through his nose.

"I feel like everything is about to change and I'm...scared," he said, rubbing his finger along the edge of Brennan's earlobe. "But I also want it so fucking much."

Finally, Brennan's hand became unstuck and he slid it to Josh's waist, feeling him tremble against his touch.

"If I don't put my mouth against yours, I might regret it— probably forever," Josh said with so much conviction, it felt like a pile of feathers had been let loose in Brennan's stomach. "Do you want that too?"

Josh's gaze held Brennan prisoner so all he could do was nod and mouth one word. *Please.*

Josh slanted his head forward, looking into his eyes one final time before his lips closed over Brennan's. One hand shifted upward to clutch at his nape, essentially holding him captive. Not that Brennan was planning on going anywhere. *Hell, no.*

And it was as if the world had stopped spinning as Josh's soft lips branded his own. Their gazes remained locked, and Brennan's breath felt stolen as he committed Josh's mouth, eyes, and hands to memory. *For later.*

Josh's tongue flattened against his mouth, licking his top then bottom lip before brushing across the seam. And Brennan was swept away—entirely in over his head—lost to this boy turned man turned mesmerizing creature.

Brennan groaned as Josh's tongue slid past his lips and met his own with velvety flicks that he felt to his core. It was as if he'd never been kissed before and essentially, that was the truth. Not like this. *Never like this.*

And Josh tasted...*God*, he tasted minty and earthy and quintessentially exactly the way he imagined Josh would taste. He couldn't possibly get enough as he gripped his waist, tugging Josh firmly against him. He needed to get closer, closer still, in case this was the first and last time he'd have this opportunity.

Josh drew away, panting hard, and his eyes were dark. So damned dark. He felt Josh's hot tongue against his jawline as he licked his way to Brennan's ear. He couldn't help the deep groan that erupted from his throat.

"Fuck, Brennan. I just knew it would be good." He hauled Brennan even tighter against him and his entire body thrummed. They fit so snugly together, he could feel Josh's arousal pulsing against his own. "You're so hot."

No one had ever made him feel that desirable, and Brennan didn't know what to do with any of it. Some reckless part of him wanted to be unleashed. He wanted to throw all caution to the wind, to shout from the rooftops that he was gone for a *guy.*

Not just any guy. This guy.

He crashed his lips against Josh's, hard and insistent, as his fingers dug into the small of his back. His tongue probed the seam of Josh's lips, and he parted them so Brennan could deepen the kiss. As he caressed his tongue, his teeth, the roof of his mouth, and dragged a satisfied groan from Josh, he had never felt so powerful, so on top of the world.

Josh's hands tightened in his hair as he pulled Brennan's bottom lip into his mouth and sucked it greedily. "Do you even know what you're doing to me?"

Brennan shook his head and whimpered.

"Damn it, Brennan." This time when their mouths met, Josh's tongue and lips and hands slowed down to a drugging rhythm. The way his thumbs caressed Brennan's cheekbones made him shiver.

And this kiss made him melt so completely that he nearly slid onto the floor into a heap. He knew everything from this point forward would forever be changed, but he welcomed it no matter the outcome.

Because for this singular moment, as the stars twinkled in the nighttime sky behind them, he wanted—no, *needed*—Josh's mouth on his.

Dear Diary,

I feel like I'm floating on air.

My first time kissing a guy and it was Brennan. The guy I've dreamed about for so long.

That kiss was everything. The first one and then the hundredth one after that.

I didn't want it to end.

And even though I left with a boner to end all boners, I wouldn't take it back.

Not for one minute.

-Josh

19

IT WAS PROBABLY good that Brennan had a busy week of work and Josh had family obligations, so Brennan had time to calm down and think. He even met Charlie at the beach on the Fourth of July and hung with his family at fireworks that night like he always did. And though things still remained awkward between them, he felt like he was looking at the world through new eyes. He was still terrified of people figuring things out, but Brennan also quickly realized what a support he and Josh had become to each other.

Their constant texting was a comfort as well.

I just wanted to blurt it all out at church group, Josh had texted last night.

I felt the same way at dinner with my family.

At least we can be free with each other.

It's the one thing helping me through my days.

Fuck, Brennan—I just can't wait...

For what? To be together? To be freer? A combination of both?

Me neither. Soon...

When he heard the doorbell ring, he put away his phone. Ms. Hurst was here for their family session.

Brennan joined his family in the living room where Ms. Hurst was already seated with a mug of coffee from the pot Mom had put on. She knew exactly how Ms. Hurst took it by now. Brennan remembered those early days when his parents would be nervous about their visits from Social Services and warned them to be on their best behavior. Brennan, of course, never had to be asked. If he could've turned into a statue, he would've so as not to call too much attention to himself.

Sydney was glancing at her cell, feet tucked under her in the corner of the couch. She had always been on the periphery of these meetings since Ms. Hurst was essentially Brennan's counselor, but thankfully she never complained unless she had pressing plans. But one stern look from Mom got her in line.

"How is everything going?" Ms. Hurst asked once everyone was seated.

"Good," his dad said. "At least I think so. What does everyone else think?"

Both his dad and his social worker glanced in his direction.

"I think...pretty well," he replied in a neutral voice, tamping down the giddy feeling bubbling inside. He just couldn't seem to help himself—every thought of a certain someone made him feel hopeful. But he needed to think of the bigger picture. His mom had come around more, and his parents seemed to be working through their stuff just like his dad had promised. In fact, they went off together every Monday afternoon, almost like they were keeping an appointment of sorts, and he supposed that was their business, but he certainly was curious.

"Sydney and Brennan have been keeping themselves busy this summer," Mom said.

After Sydney explained cheer camp, Ms. Hurst turned to him.

"How's coaching going with your friend?"

Brennan could feel the blush slash across his cheeks as he cleared his throat. "Good. Really good."

"That's great to hear. Glad you've reconnected with an old friend."

Holy crap, if someone didn't change the subject, he might hide behind the couch.

"Er, thanks." These family meetings were always slightly awkward, and he definitely felt more comfortable with Ms. Hurst one-on-one. But he understood that she thought it important to check in. And they'd agreed that after this year, their appointments would be weaned and Brennan would eventually be on his own—unless she was needed again.

The idea still made him feel off-kilter, but it was time to suck it up and embrace adulthood. And one of the most important responsibilities he had was to himself. It was up to him to live his best life and to figure out what that meant. And now that things had progressed between him and Josh, he couldn't help wondering if he would be able to share his life with someone he cared about someday. His Uncle Scott had done it, after all.

Refusing to glance in his mother's direction, he winced, remembering the consequences of that—that not everyone would approve. But he felt more like himself and more comfortable in his own skin than ever before, so maybe that made it worth the risk. Still...imagining sitting here without his family's support made his stomach revolt. He wished he could have some sort of guarantee, but that was not real life. He'd had to live with the same sort of uncertainty his entire life so why would he be granted that leniency now?

"So how about family life?" Ms. Hurst asked. "I know you all keep busy with your business, but do you still take time to do other things together—away from work?"

His mom explained how they made sure Mondays were reserved for family dinners and how they planned to go camping at Big Bear next month.

"That sounds good," she replied. "It's so important for all of you to stay connected."

And for Brennan to feel part of your family, was what she was trying to say between the lines. It had been a running theme in Brennan's life for so long, and his parents had heard it plenty. But Ms. Hurst was good at not making Brennan feel too on the spot—most likely because she didn't want him to retreat further into his shell.

"Maybe we can invite Uncle Scott over sometime soon," Sydney said, finally putting her phone down and Brennan froze, recalling their conversation the other day in the car.

"He travels a lot for his job," Mom replied in a flippant tone, and it made Brennan's stomach tighten into a fist.

"We'll see," his dad added as if trying to appease Sydney. And maybe in his own way encouraging his mom to extend an olive branch to her brother. Or maybe that was just what he hoped would happen.

Sydney gave Brennan a bewildered look, then shrugged as if to say she tried.

Ms. Hurst followed up the conversation by asking Mom what Uncle Scott did for a living, before moving on to other topics. Soon their time was up, and she informed them she would be running late for her next appointment if she didn't head out.

Brennan walked Ms. Hurst outside like he always did, so they could get a few minutes alone to chat. She was there for him after all—the case number was reserved for his name alone, so she always wanted to check in afterward to ask follow-up questions.

"Things do seem better with your mom," she remarked as they walked to the end of the driveway.

"Yeah," he responded. "They haven't shared anything specific, but I think they might be seeing a doctor or something. She and dad spend every Monday afternoon together now."

"Aha. Well, if it's some sort of therapy or who knows what—it's their business." She patted his shoulder. "But just remember, it'll help make your family stronger. Maybe they'll share it with you someday. For now, give them time."

Brennan nodded and looked away, that strange stitch in his chest again.

"What is it?" she asked.

Brennan sighed. "It's about Uncle Scott. It's just that Mom doesn't even talk to him anymore."

She looked over his shoulder to the house. "Is that why Sydney asked about him?"

"We had a conversation about it recently," he explained. "The last time we saw him was at Christmas when he brought his...*friend* and it was so tense between him and Mom. When I asked Dad about it after, he said the falling-out was private and only between them."

She arched an eyebrow. "Are you close to your uncle?"

"Well, no...not really. I mean it's nice to see him around the holidays. He's cool and funny and...he and Mom have always kind of bickered but in a friendly sort of way...I guess." He trailed off feeling ridiculous for even bringing the subject up. Plenty of families had squabbles, so he needed to just let it go.

She studied him closely as if putting some pieces together in her brain.

"This is really bothering you," she said, and he shrugged.

"Nah, forget I even—"

"What did you mean about Uncle Scott bringing a friend?"

Brennan swallowed. "His um, *boyfriend* or whatever."

He looked away as his cheeks flushed.

"And you think that has something to do with them falling out? That doesn't seem—"

"Maybe..." he replied. "I mean it would suck if that were the case, because you know...that would be hard on him if he wasn't accepted and stuff."

"Do we need to—" she looked over his shoulder to the porch.

"No!" Now he just wanted to send her off and never bring it

up again. But she had grown silent, which was the thing she did when she was attempting to figure stuff out. She was never one to push him though, to share anything, unless he was ready.

"They love you, Brennan, no matter what—remember that. You are their family," she said in a reassuring tone. Why had the conversation suddenly shifted back to him when they were talking about his uncle? "I'm only a phone call away. Your uncle is too."

He waved as he watched her drive away.

He'd considered reaching out to his uncle a time or two but worried it would feel like a betrayal to his mom. Besides, what would he say?

Hey, I heard you were gay and turns out so am I. Will Mom disown me too?

Dear Diary:

My favorite part of this busy week was when I brought Brennan an Oreo Tornado between my work and church schedule. I was sort of nervous, walking up the driveway to the garage. When he answered the door, and I handed it to him, he was stunned.

I got one kiss in too before his dad came outside to load up the wheelbarrow so they could mulch the flowerbeds.

I can't stop thinking about his flushed cheeks, that dreamy look in his eyes when our lips parted, and that smile that lights me up from the inside.

-Josh

20

BRENNAN WAS SURPRISED to notice his dad in the stands at their game on Monday. He lifted his hand in a wave, and Brennan tipped his chin in acknowledgment, strangely proud that his dad would take enough interest to show up. Not that he hadn't made an appearance at most of his games as a kid but it'd been a while since Brennan had much of anything for him to attend anyway.

Soon enough he got lost in the mechanics of the game, coaching third base, comforting Sean when he struck out and offering a pep talk in the dugout when they were behind three runs.

After the game, in which they squeaked out a win by one run, they got into a tight huddle to discuss some of the highlights—as well as things they needed to improve. When he glanced across the circle at Josh, he smiled at him in that way that made his stomach flutter.

Once they broke apart, he looked into the stands and noticed his dad involved in what looked like a casual conversation with Mr. Daly about the team—if his pointing at the dugout was any indication. He immediately tensed, remembering how he'd told his father about seeing Mr. Daly with another woman—not that he'd named him. Now Brennan knew he was with the church secretary who was having marital troubles, but he still felt uncomfortable about the situation even though there was a reasonable enough explanation.

"Great game," his dad said once he approached. He slung his arm around his shoulder and when he whispered, "I'm proud of you," Brennan felt like that kid all over again, begging for his acceptance. Would he still be proud if he knew the smiles he reserved only for Josh were something altogether different than coaching or friendship?

His dad stuck around a bit after the stands emptied and they retrieved the bases. He said his good-byes and before he headed toward the parking lot, his dad extended an invitation for Josh to join their backyard cookout that afternoon. Brennan held his breath, but this time Josh accepted.

After they officially cleared the dugout and headed to their cars, Josh promised to walk over after he showered and changed, and Brennan felt as if he was on pins and needles all the way home, anticipating spending more time with him, especially in front of his family. But he'd take it any way he could get it. It was near torture being around him and not being able to touch him.

Once he showered and changed into clean clothes, he headed outside to see if his mom needed any help. She was in the process of lighting the grill while his dad finished mowing the front lawn, something he enjoyed doing. It used to be Brennan's job until his dad admitted how much he liked tending to the yard, and Josh suspected it was nice for him to get out from behind the grill for a change.

"Dad said your team won." Mom smiled as she reached out to push a stray hair behind his ear. The warm gesture surprised him, and Brennan hoped it was a sign of things to come. She had never been as affectionate as his dad, but she'd always had little ways of letting him know he was loved. He had missed it the last few months. "He also mentioned that you're a good coach."

Brennan mumbled thanks as he blushed.

Sydney sprang out the back door carrying a plate of marinated chicken breasts and handed them off to Brennan.

"I invited Kylie," she called over her shoulder as she returned to the kitchen to retrieve the condiments her mother requested.

"The more the merrier," his mom said as he began loading the meat on the bottom rack of the grill. "You're free to invite Charlie too."

"I think he's busy." The lie came too easily, and he knew his mom caught on. He didn't know why he was trying to keep Josh and Charlie as separate parts of his life, but most likely it was because he didn't know how to mesh them together. Not when his friendship with Charlie had turned weird and his relationship with Josh turned to...*more. Way more.*

She patted his shoulder. "I understand. Sometimes we grow away from people."

"The way you and Uncle Scott have grown apart?" His hands were trembling as he shut the cover, shocked at himself for going there. His mom got busy loading the buns on a plate as she looked away guiltily. "Sorry, I shouldn't have said anything."

"It's complicated." She sighed. "A lot of things are."

"Tell me about it," Brennan muttered as he reached for the tongs.

"But it's nice to see you happier," she said.

He held in a gasp. "Wh...what do you mean?"

"Not sure I can put my finger on it." She studied him. "Maybe graduating and becoming an adult was exactly what you needed."

"Yeah, maybe," he mumbled. Or maybe it was him finally being his true self. "Still got a lot to figure out, though."

"Of course," she replied in a singsong voice.

"How about you, Mom?" he asked, gathering courage. "Are you feeling better?"

"I'm working on it," she admitted with a sad smile. "And I'm sorry if I've worried you. I've been seeing a therapist to work through some of my feelings after the miscarriage. And I think I'm finally rounding the corner."

"Oh, I...I didn't know," he stammered. That explained a few things. "I'm glad you're getting help."

When Josh and Kylie arrived, they all sat at the picnic table in the backyard and ate grilled chicken with Mom's macaroni salad. Brennan found himself blushing a couple of times as he caught Josh's eyes across the salt and pepper shakers and cursed himself for being too responsive to the guy.

Dad asked Josh about college and work; then Kylie and Sydney talked about the upcoming school year, and Brennan realized how glad he was to be done with all that. He was ready to pave a new path of his own—whatever that meant.

Once the meal was over, Brennan helped clear the table.

"Thanks for inviting me," Josh said, heading toward the drive-way. "The food was delicious."

Anytime," his mom replied.

Kylie and Sydney were sitting in a couple of deck chairs, involved in a conversation about cheer camp as he and Josh lingered awkwardly on the sidewalk.

"Do you have to get home already?" Brennan knew he was reaching for something to say, and he suddenly remembered their video game conversation at practice last week while warming up the team with grounders. "I have the newest Madden, so I thought maybe you'd want to—"

"Sounds good to me." The look Josh gave him said it all. He'd hoped to be asked to stay.

"Hey uh, we're gonna head up to play video games...." Brennan announced to Kylie and Sydney. "You're welcome to join us."

Sydney looked at him like he'd grown two heads, probably because he never asked before when she had a friend over. They'd played plenty when they were the only two home but now, he felt like an idiot. Like he actually had something to hide and was acting all strange about it.

"Do you have Sonic Mania?" Kylie asked and Brennan nodded.

"I'm in," she replied, and Brennan groaned inwardly. He tried not to look Josh in the eye as the four of them went up to Brennan's room to play.

"This is really cool up here," Kylie said as they got situated on the floor in front of the unit. He realized that since he'd moved above the garage, she'd never seen the space despite the amount of time she spent at their house.

They played a few rounds, sharing the controllers and switching players, and when it was his turn against his sister, he overheard Kylie asking Josh questions about college, which set him on edge. Not because he thought she might be flirting with him but because he suddenly realized how short their time was. Now he just wanted his sister and her best friend to clear out of the room.

When they switched to Madden, Sydney and Kylie seemed to lose interest and excused themselves to head back outside. Once he heard the door to the garage close, he put down the controller.

"I thought they would never leave," he said in a strained voice. "Sorry, I just felt strange not asking them and—"

"Shhh..." Josh's fingers brushed against the shell of his ear, which made him shiver. "Just come here."

Brennan didn't know who moved first, but it didn't matter. They were a clash of lips and tongues, teeth and hands, and Josh groaned into the kiss, flooding Brennan's stomach with warmth.

"I can't even think straight anymore," Brennan said when he drew away to catch his breath.

"That's because you're *not* straight," Josh replied, and Brennan rolled his eyes.

And then they were kissing again, Brennan's hands winding in Josh's hair, pulling on the strands like he needed more, more,

more. He wanted his mouth and hands to roam all over Josh's skin so he could touch every part of him. Before it was too late.

Josh rose up on his knees forcing Brennan backward and hemming him to the floor. Finally, their bodies were aligned, and Brennan sighed into the kiss.

"I feel like I can't get enough," Josh said against his lips. "Like I'm feverish for you."

"Ditto," Brennan replied as he thrust upward, and his hips were met with the same pressure. He thought he might combust from pure longing because he'd wanted this guy for so long, and now he finally had him all to himself.

"I'll admit I'm sort of nervous. but I don't want to stop," Brennan confessed. "You feel too good."

Josh stopped moving and looked down at him with concern in his eyes. "It's okay to make each other feel good. We're not doing anything wrong. Unless it feels wrong to you?"

He tried to pull away, disappointment painted evenly on his face.

"No, please." Brennan stopped him with his hands on his waist. "It doesn't feel wrong, it feels perfect. But I just...don't know how to...I've never..."

He motioned between them trying to express how inexperienced he was.

"I've never done this either—with *anyone*," Josh replied. "But it's just you and me and it feels so good. And I want—"

"I want too," Brennan replied, raising up to kiss his lips. "So much."

Brennan connected their lips, then pushed his tongue in Josh's mouth to deepen the kiss. When Josh groaned, it went straight to his groin. He could feel that Josh was hard as well, but he resisted rutting against him like an animal.

When Josh curled his fingers beneath the hem of his shirt, Brennan stilled, his pulse pounding in panic. "Is this okay? We don't have to—"

"I...want you to, but," Brennan pulled down the hem of his shirt, he couldn't even help himself. "I'm just not very confident about my—"

"I love your body, Brennan." Josh reached for his chin and his breath caught. "But it's okay, we can go as slow as you need. I only want to be with you."

Brennan didn't know why he felt such instantaneous relief. All the emotions and sensations swirling around him were all too much and not enough at the same time.

"I still want..." Brennan trailed off as Josh looked down at him. "Please, kiss me."

Wish granted, Josh kissed him soft and hard, fast and slow, all while feathering his fingers through his hair, making Brennan tremble.

When Brennan's thumb slid across the sliver of exposed skin on Josh's back, he moaned. "I don't mind if you touch me. I'm dying for it, Brennan."

Looking into Josh's eyes, he skimmed his fingers beneath the hem of his T-shirt and watched him shiver as Brennan raked his fingernails against his muscles. He had never touched another man like this before, and he couldn't help but be curious. Josh's skin was smooth and warm and as Josh propped himself on his forearms, Brennan's fingers trailed beneath the front of the fabric. When he brushed across to the fine hairs that lined his stomach, Josh panted softly.

Sliding his hand upward his knuckles drifted over his pecs and across his collarbones as Josh watched him intently.

When his thumb brushed over a nipple, Josh shuddered. "Oh, God. Do that again."

So he did and watched as Josh squirmed, and his eyes widened in wonder. "I might explode if you keep doing that."

"Do you want me to?" Brennan asked, feeling so powerfully aroused, he'd do anything to make him feel good.

"Yes. *No.* I'd rather feel you against me again." He rose above

Brennan and fit their mouths together before their bodies realigned. When their stiff cocks bumped together, both of them groaned.

"Oh, fuck, I've never felt this way before," Brennan said in a strained voice.

"Me neither," Josh whispered against his neck.

Brennan pulled Josh's head down to align their mouths again, and he got lost in Josh's lips and tongue and hands. When Josh ground his hips against him, Brennan met him thrust for thrust until the only sound in the room was a combination of groans and heavy pants. Brennan briefly panicked, wondering if anyone could hear them. But that thought quickly fled his brain as his balls tightened and pinpricks lined his nerve endings.

"I'm gonna come, Josh," Brennan breathed out. "Holy Christ, I can't hold back."

"Do it." Josh thrust against him. "I'm close too."

Mouths joined, they absorbed each other's moans as Brennan came first and Josh soon after. Josh kept thrusting until Brennan became too sensitive, and he stilled his hips with his hands. "Oh God, I can't take anymore."

Josh pulled away. "Fuck. Sorry."

When he smiled down at him with a lightness in his eyes he hadn't seen since the night they first kissed, Brennan felt so fucking happy, he could barely contain the feeling in his chest.

"I haven't come that hard ever," he admitted.

"Same." Josh gave him a final peck on the lips. "And we have a mess to prove it."

"Seriously," Brennan said with a groan and made the motion to get up.

"Let me do it." Josh looked around the room, then motioned toward the sink. "Can I use that towel?"

"Yeah," Brennan said, his muscles suddenly feeling heavy. That orgasm had wrung him out. He felt sticky and sweaty, but he didn't even care because damn, that had been incredible.

He watched as Josh dampened the rag and shoved it beneath his shorts to wipe his abdomen. After he wet it a second time, he carried it over to him.

Brennan cleaned up as well, straightened his clothes, and threw the rag in the hamper.

"Feel like playing another round?" Brennan asked as he reached for the controller.

"I'd love to," Josh replied, sinking down beside him on the floor. Brennan bumped his shoulder playfully, feeling completely giddy inside.

Dear Diary:

I can still smell him on my clothes.

I was sticky when I got home so I changed my underwear, but I left my T-shirt on so I can pretend he's still next to me. Lame or not, I can't wipe the smile off my face.

It was the best night of my life.

-Josh

21

Have any regrets? Josh had texted Brennan the next morning.

Brennan didn't even have to think twice about his response.

None. You?

No. I want to do it again.

Brennan shivered just thinking about it.

Me too.

And that was what they did whenever they got the chance the next several days. Josh would head over to Brennan's after their games with the idea of shooting hoops or playing video games, and then they'd make out and rub against each other until both of them came.

Most times it was a rush job because they were too aroused and too green to have any sort of stamina. Other times it was because his dad would need garden tools from the garage or Sydney would pop in to retrieve her bike for a ride over to Kylie's. Brennan was sure they were going to get caught, and it made him even more panicky. He felt like they were skating on the sharp edge of risky behavior that would be normal behind closed doors for anyone else. And that made him more disheartened that they couldn't openly show each other affection because they were of the same sex. *So bogus.*

Tonight was Elm Grove's summer carnival, and his family rented out the drive-in lot for the event every year. His family still ran the concession stand during the festival and though Brennan and Sydney always helped, they were also given free rein to join their friends and have fun if they chose to.

By dusk, it seemed the entire town had shown up, and the concession area was much busier than regular nights. Josh had mentioned he'd be attending the fair with his church group and while Brennan anticipated laying eyes on him, Charlie got in line with Nate and some other friends. Brennan immediately tensed. Things remained pretty uncomfortable between them.

"Hey," Charlie said, looking just as uncomfortable as he reached the counter. "What's up?"

"Not much," Brennan replied. "Just working."

He rang up their orders of hot dogs and drinks and once Sydney handed the food off to them and Brennan bid them good-bye, Charlie turned back to him.

"Can you hang for a bit?" he asked and just as he was about to beg off, his mom's hand landed on his shoulder.

"Go ahead, we got it handled here for now."

He initially felt irritated that she would meddle when she refused to broach other sensitive subjects with him, but he understood her intentions were coming from a pure place. She knew that Charlie had been his first friend and even though things had changed, maybe she held out hope that they could find some common ground again.

"Sure," he said, hanging his apron on the hook.

He walked around with the group as they played some carnival games and ate the funnel cakes he looked forward to every year along with the way-too-tart old-fashioned lemonade.

When he spotted a familiar head of wavy brown hair in a group of men and women, his stomach dipped.

After their groups intersected, there were some introductions made, but it was a bit awkward. Brennan wished they could just be themselves, but he felt scrutinized by Charlie and even Nate when he tried to talk to Josh in a more casual way.

Charlie never brought up the Todd rumor again, and he was tempted to tell him what an asshole the guy was, but he was following Josh's lead on it. Karma and all that shit.

And speaking of karma, Todd had indeed shown up with some girl he recognized from their graduating class, and he wanted to roll his eyes so hard. Except, he couldn't pretend to understand what his real story was. He could be bisexual for all Brennan knew, but it was still so shitty of him to throw Josh under the bus.

For Josh's part, he seemed miserable and on edge, and Brennan wanted to comfort him and tell him to hang in there. The stakes for him were higher after all. He definitely didn't want to lose sight of that.

After they parted ways and he went off with Charlie to wait in line for a carnival ride, his phone buzzed with a text.

Wish I could've held your hand.

He looked around him but didn't see Josh anywhere.

He typed a reply as discreetly as he could and kept his expression neutral. **Same.**

Have fun tonight.

You too.

He tried not to feel glum the rest of the night and actually had a bit of fun with Charlie when just the two of them wandered off to try their hand at the ring-tossing game.

"So how come Abbey's not working tonight?" Charlie asked, trying to act casual but Brennan could tell he'd been working up to it because of how fidgety he was acting.

"She was going to a concert with friends," he replied.

"Cool," he said but looked a bit glum.

"If you like her, maybe you should ask her out," he suggested.

"No, I..." Charlie's cheeks colored. "She'd turn me down flat. No way she'd be interested in me."

Brennan actually felt a certain solidarity with him in that moment. He preferred when Charlie let his insecurities show instead of trying to act all macho. It made him feel more human, more relatable.

"You don't know that." Brennan thumped his shoulder. "Try being a friend first and see where it goes?"

"Yeah, probably a good idea," he said, then brightened. "Besides, hanging out with these guys gets my foot in the door of some good parties."

Brennan wanted to roll his eyes but instead, he smiled. "Perfect. Exactly what you've always wanted." Truer words had probably never been spoken.

They moved to the next booth, which was a shooting game, and Charlie won a prize.

"So how about you?" he asked. "Interested in anyone?"

Fuck, he wished he could say something.

Yes, I am completely interested in someone, and I am totally aching to see him and touch him right now.

"Nah," he replied instead. "Been too busy."

Charlie looked disappointed, which only stirred those frustrated feelings between them again. "I figured."

He glanced toward the concession building which had a line out the door. "Well, I better get back to work."

"Yeah, looks like they're still slammed. Catch you later."

After he helped his parents close up the concession stand and they arrived home well after midnight, he pulled out his phone, his fingers hovering over his previous text exchange with Josh.

Still out?

Yeah. Stuck in a conversation with someone at the pizza place.

Should I be jealous?

He meant it tongue in cheek, but there was a touch of truth behind it as well. He couldn't help it—he would be jealous of anyone who could openly spend time with him.

Never. Can't stop daydreaming about you.

Brennan's entire body blushed.

You're welcome to stop by on your way home. He added a wink emoji.

Yeah? I just might. See you soon.

Brennan tried to stay awake and wait for Josh, but he fell asleep watching a movie.

When he felt a hand in his hair and Josh's soft voice calling his name, he blinked opened his eyes, warmth spreading through his chest.

"Didn't mean to fall asleep," he said in a groggy voice.

"S'okay." Josh's fingers brushed his jaw. "Tried to get here as fast as I could." He glanced over his shoulder. "I made sure to be quiet."

He didn't even know what excuse he could possibly use if his parents caught Josh visiting at this hour, but he could definitely come up with something on the fly. *He hoped.*

But now he couldn't wait to be next to him again as he held open the covers.

Once Josh toed off his sneakers and slipped inside the sheets, their bodies connected and Brennan felt a crackle of electricity.

"Thank you." Josh's eyes fastened on Brennan's with such concentration that he couldn't look away. His expression morphed into something tender, something that eased all the doubts Brennan had locked inside of himself.

"For what?"

Josh's lips were only a whisper away, and his gaze was so penetrating, it seemed to devour Brennan whole. He bent forward, connecting their foreheads, and they breathed the same air for a few intense seconds. "For being my safe place."

Brennan gasped at the sanctity of the words. So powerful they left him defenseless, threatening to steal the last pieces of Brennan's heart, which Josh already owned.

When Josh's fingers grazed his ear, he could barely catch his breath. He closed his eyes against the vulnerability he felt right then. "You're mine too."

His lips brushed Brennan's so gently, in such contrast to the way he'd moved his mouth against him the times before—when they were frantic and needy or had to rush—that his chest ached and his skin tingled.

He felt something profound in this kiss. Like his lips were trying to communicate something they couldn't—wouldn't—before. And as Josh hummed in a satisfied way, Brennan felt like he could see beneath Josh's layers to his very soul.

Something so honest and real, that it stripped him bare.

And Brennan wished this time with Josh would never end.

They kissed for hours it seemed, until their mouths were swollen and words were only whispered between yawns.

Even when their lips slowed, they kept holding each other, eventually falling asleep in each other's arms.

He didn't know how many minutes or hours went by before he felt Josh's body jolt and he sprang up. "Shit, I only meant to shut my eyes for a few minutes."

Brennan rolled over and rubbed at his eyes. He looked at his alarm clock and saw that it was five in the morning. "Crap, I'm sorry."

"Don't be sorry." Josh bent over and kissed his forehead. "Thanks for being amazing."

He tried to get up, but Josh steadied him with a hand. "Shhhh, go back to sleep."

He watched as he tiptoed down the stairs and out the door.

For some reason, Brennan reached toward his shelf and plucked his stuffed elephant from his perch. He hugged Peanut to his chest as his eyes shut and he dreamed of Josh.

Dear Diary:

Of course I didn't catch much flak for staying out late with the church group. Most likely my dad thought I was with a female member of our congregation.

If he only knew I was lying in Brennan's bed holding him in my arms.

Each time with him feels better than the last.

I wish I could stay holed up in his room forever.

-Josh

22

CAN I **take you on a date?** Josh texted and Brennan's heart galloped.

Seriously? I'd love it. But how?

I have an idea. Are you free tomorrow night?

It's my day off so I'm very available.

Cool. Just leave it up to me.

"Where are we going?" he asked as he slid into Josh's car after he pulled up to the curb. He ignored the curious glances from his sister as he swept by her on the front porch mumbling something about "getting food."

An amused grin played along Josh's lips. "You'll see."

After he turned the music up, he reached for his hand on the seat between them, and Brennan held in a gasp. Once their fingers were intertwined, they sang along to an old rock song, Brennan feeling excited and content. He didn't question Josh when he noticed them leaving Elm Grove and traveling to the next county, which was more rural.

He pulled in front of an Italian place in a strip mall and before they got out, Josh kissed his fingers. "Hope this is okay. I just wanted to get away from any prying eyes."

"It looks good to me," Brennan replied, eyeing the red-and-green striped awning.

Josh sighed. "I wish we could date for real."

"So, let's make it real tonight," Brennan replied around a parched throat.

Damn, Josh was adorable for even trying.

Josh briefly placed his hand on the small of Brennan's back when he pulled open the restaurant door and Brennan shivered, craving his touch.

They were led to a booth in the quaint but no-frills restaurant that was only half-full. When their knees brushed beneath the table, neither moved away and Brennan soaked in the warmth of his skin. They were touching in public but in a totally surreptitious way again, and Brennan was reveling in it. He had never felt this sort of fluttering in his chest—this raw and profound need to be in another person's orbit at all times.

They ordered pizza and a plate of ravioli to share, and nobody paid them any attention as they talked freely. When Brennan asked about his friends from the carnival, Josh told him he'd known most of them his whole life. That led to a discussion about him growing up in the church and how it shaped his world view—much like being raised in foster care had shaped Brennan's, he noted. And it was the exact reason both of them were frightened of making any sudden wrong moves that would leave them vulnerable.

"What do you do at your church group?"

"Most meetings center around reading a specific Bible passage and how it applies to real life. And more and more I realize that 'apply' is the key word."

"What do you mean?"

"Not sure. The church is supposed to be about love and acceptance, but some teachings feel cherry-picked and geared toward...I don't know. Intolerance, maybe? Sometimes what's said inside those four walls doesn't always apply to how people act on the outside." Josh made a frustrated noise. "And I'll be honest, hearing people my age planning for their futures—like marriage and a family—makes me feel left out. Why am I not allowed to aspire to those same things? It doesn't feel like tolerance at all, and I just don't know if I can do it anymore."

Brennan felt for him—really felt for him. For all Brennan's doubts about his life, he didn't have as many gatekeepers as Josh did, so he just listened and let him get it out. Brennan didn't know what any of the right answers were anyway.

"Sorry," Josh said. "I didn't mean to dampen the mood."

"No," Brennan replied in a fervent tone. "This stuff is important, and I want you to feel like you can talk to me."

"Thanks. You're the only one who makes me feel sane."

Right then, their food was served and as they dug into their plates in companionable silence, they smiled at each other across the booth, their knees brushing together. Brennan didn't realize how famished he was until he was on his third slice of pepperoni.

"Are you afraid the rumor Todd spread will come back to hurt you?" Brennan asked as they fished out their cash and split the bill. It was a subject that continued to bother him and felt unresolved.

"Besides having my ex-teammates question my sexuality?" he countered with an eye roll. "It happened a whole year ago and we're heading back to college soon, so people will believe what they want—and hopefully forget about it. I haven't done anything to prove him right or wrong, anyway."

"You are on a date with a guy right now," Brennan pointed out with a wink.

Josh captured one of his ankles beneath the table with his feet, and Brennan could feel the coarse hairs on his legs rubbing against his own. "A completely adorable guy, I might add."

Brennan's whole body flushed and he looked down at the table, moving his leftover crust around the plate with his fork.

"I just...have to take things as they come." Josh sighed. "As it stands, I have three more years until I graduate college—if I can only figure out a major. Then I'm free to make my own decisions. A college degree will definitely help, and I'm going to try and save money so I can be more independent."

"That's a good plan. I'm not sure what to expect until I've got at least my first semester behind me." Brennan replied.

Josh leaned forward. "Let's get out of here. Our date isn't over yet."

"What about your dessert?" Brennan asked looking at the plate of tiramisu he'd ordered and hadn't touched yet.

"I'll ask for it to be boxed with two forks so we can share."

Once in the car, they pulled out of the lot and made a couple of left turns. As they passed an inconspicuous church, Brennan saw a sign that read, It's Never Too Late to Find Jesus, and he noticed how Josh scowled at it.

Brennan was surprised when Josh went down a deserted road that wasn't paved.

"You know where you're going, right?" he asked as he took in the heavy thicket of trees as dusk descended upon them.

"There's a pond I fished in with my gramps before he passed away," Josh replied. "And I brought blankets...and there's no one around, but if you—"

"Sounds perfect."

They parked near a trail along the edge of a copse of trees, Josh reached for the blankets and they got out of the car.

The trail was only a short distance from the pond, the sound of crickets and frogs sounding loud in Brennan's ears. It brought forth a memory of camping at Big Bear with his family. "It's pretty here."

"I think so," Josh agreed as he spread out a blanket.

Once they had looked for rocks to skip at the water's edge, and Josh told him more about fishing with his grandfather in the summers, they sank down on the blanket. Josh fed him bites of the dessert and kissed the frosting off his lips as dusk descended.

"You sure no one else will show up?" Brennan asked, looking behind him to the trees.

Lifting the second blanket, Josh wrapped it around their shoulders. "I think we're good."

Josh's eyes turned dark and positively on fire for him. When he trailed a tingly hand across his thigh, Brennan's stomach bunched in anticipation, and all he wanted to do was fit their mouths together and breath him in again.

Brennan shifted sideways to get closer and ran his hand along Josh's biceps up to his neck. Josh bent his head against Brennan's fingers as he huffed out a breath. "Brennan."

Brennan leaned forward to trace his tongue against Josh's bottom lip, then pulled it into his mouth. Josh groaned and dug his fingers into his waist, tugging him closer.

The noise tumbling out of Josh's mouth was enough to make Brennan's shaft stiffen. He crushed his lips against Josh's in a greedy kiss. When Josh yanked Brennan against him, he straddled his hips.

Josh reached around his waist to pull Brennan tighter while lightly tugging back his hair with the other hand to deepen the kiss.

"You're driving me nuts."

Brennan combed his fingers over his cheekbones and through the strands of his hair as his lips captured Josh's again. As the sky grew darker, the stars made their striking debut. Their mouths were joined beneath the full moon until they felt bruised, but Brennan couldn't stop kissing him if he tried.

Josh's hardness was like a steel rod through his shorts. The heavy material separating them created a raw friction that was driving Brennan out of his skull. Keeping in mind that they were out in public and only hidden by oak trees and a blanket, Brennan brushed his fingers against Josh's zipper and he hissed through his teeth. "That feels good."

Brennan brought the second blanket up higher around their shoulders as he made his decision. "Concentrate on being quiet."

Josh let out a low growl before devouring Brennan's mouth again. His tongue probed deep, telling him just how desperate he was for release, and Brennan couldn't wait to give it to him.

He unbuttoned Josh's shorts and lowered his boxer briefs until he poked out. Even in the shadow of the blanket, he could see his cock was engorged and leaking. Brennan ran his thumb along the moisture that beaded his tip, and Josh's breath hitched.

"Relax," he whispered.

Josh leaned back, positioning his arms on the blanket behind him. With his hands out of the way, he was in easy reach. He felt warm and solid in his palm and Brennan gave his cock an upward stroke, testing the same technique he used on himself.

"Damn." Josh screwed his eyes shut and tried to control his breathing.

"Watch me." Brennan surprised himself with his boldness. Having the power to make Josh putty in his hands was so completely heady.

As he pumped his cock, Josh's head tilted to the side. His eyes softened and his gaze never left Brennan's. With his other hand, Brennan reached below his shaft and grasped his balls, teasing the area with his fingers. "Does that feel good?"

"Fuck, yes." Josh's voice was strained. "I'm gonna come."

"Kiss me. Wanna feel you when you fall apart."

Josh sealed his lips over Brennan's, and their tongues tangled in time with the up-and-down motion of his fingers.

When he groaned his release into Brennan's mouth, his lips quivered with the effort and it was the sexiest damn thing Brennan had ever experienced in his life.

Once he used the dessert napkins to clean himself up, he reached for Brennan.

"Please, I wanna touch you too."

Brennan wasn't going to argue. He was nearly ready to burst from just watching him.

He quickly unfastened Brennan's shorts and took him in hand with the perfect pressure. Brennan whimpered and arched his back. He gritted his teeth, attempting to control his urge to shoot his seed all over Josh's hand.

"Oh, God you feel so good." Josh's eyes were widened in awe. "I've wanted to touch you for so long."

Brennan buried his face in his neck, his cheeks heating, as all his nerve endings felt like they were on fire. "Don't ever feel embarrassed in front of me," Josh said into his ear before he licked the shell and sucked on the lobe.

That was all Brennan needed to come undone. He grabbed on to Josh's shoulder as he came. *Hard.* Josh kept pumping until the last of his seed spurted out.

"Holy shit," Brennan groaned as he lightly panted.

Josh laughed. "I know, right?"

Once he cleaned up, they lay side by side on the blanket and watched the stars.

The connection between them felt deeper somehow—like vines rooted between them and twining themselves more tightly around Brennan's heart.

Dear Diary:

Is this what it feels like to fall for someone?

Like this tender spot in your stomach from all the trembling and a deep ache in your chest from all the daydreaming?

Oh God, I think I'm in trouble.

-Josh

23

JOSH SHOWED up for Disney night with his brother again.

Brennan was so busy running food, he apparently missed him pulling into a slot in the far end of the lot. It wasn't until the middle of the second movie, as Brennan was taking a break on the picnic table with Abbey, that they came walking up.

His entire body turned warm when Josh gave him a heated look, and Brennan's mind immediately traveled to what'd transpired in his loft between them last night.

All the lights were out, and they were under the sheets and Brennan finally got brave enough to take off his shirt and soon after... everything else.

Josh's hands explored his body, and his nipples were especially sensitive. Brennan hissed when his fingers brushed over them and his cock filled with so much blood as he squirmed beneath him.

Then Josh trailed his fingers down to his sensitive rib cage and across to his stomach, where he was most vulnerable. His hands shot up to cover himself, but Josh was quicker. He entwined their fingers and held his arms over Brennan's head as he kissed his ear, sucked on his neck, and whispered everything Brennan longed to hear.

"Don't you dare try to hide from me," Josh said. *"I love everything about your body. Your lips, and your smell, and your skin."*

"Hey, Jimmy," Brennan said, springing up from his perch and trying to thrust the thoughts from his head before he became rock hard. "You guys getting some food?"

Jimmy nodded. "I wanted some popcorn with extra butter."

"And I love your dad's cheeseburgers so...you know," Josh added with a hint of amusement in his voice before he glanced at his coworker. "Hey, Abbey."

"Hey yourself," she replied in an indulgent voice, and Brennan didn't dare look in her direction, afraid of what she might say or poke fun at. He knew he was acting out of sorts, but it was becoming almost impossible to hide his reactions where Josh was concerned. The guy had always made him a bit nervous, but this was a different kind of tension between them altogether.

Brennan watched them walk inside the concession area, and he couldn't stop staring at Josh's ass in those tight jeans, remembering the firm shape completely bare.

Josh got completely naked for him as well and let Brennan look his fill as the moonlight filtered through the window. Jesus, it was so arousing, he almost came on the spot.

After Josh flopped on the bed, he pulled Brennan down, so he was on top and as soon as they were skin to skin, it was mind-meltingly good. To feel all that smooth skin, except on his legs and of course, his groin. When their dicks lined up—holy fuck—it was like a come to Jesus moment. He could feel how hard Josh was and as they thrust together, his coarse hair tickled his abdomen.

Brennan reached down to touch the unruly patch below his abdomen, running his fingers through it, surprising himself as Josh trembled beneath him.

"Do you think this is how most guys have sex?"

"You mean facing each other?"

"Yeah...instead of from behind." His cheeks heated. *"I would want it this way—so I could see you...not that I'm ready for that, I..."* he stam-

mered, hoping Josh didn't get the wrong idea. He wanted that someday, but right now he was so overwhelmed by everything.

"Shhhh," Josh said, placing his finger against his mouth. "I'm not ready either. But what we're doing right now is so fucking perfect."

He smoothed Brennan's hair off his forehead, then pulled him down to fit their mouths together. "I need you, Brennan. I need you so much."

When he curled his hand around both of their cocks and they got a rhythm going, he came so hard his teeth clattered.

Then they kissed and touched and fell asleep for a bit while the come dried on their skin.

But this time Josh had set his alarm so he could head home at a reasonable hour.

Brennan's bed felt so empty after he was gone.

"What?" Brennan asked when he felt Abbey's gaze burning a hole in the side of his head. At the same time, his dad's voice piped in on the walkie that an order was up.

"I know you're going to deny it, so I won't ask," she replied with a smirk. "But...you're both adorable and I totally ship you."

Before he could protest or make fun of her fandom term, she kissed him on the cheek and sped inside to retrieve the order.

Fuck, he totally needed to stop being so obvious or other people might pick up on it too, and that would be a terrible idea right now. There was too much at stake and besides, this was just the two of them figuring out who they were, what they wanted, and how that might translate into the future. And that needed to stay private and sacred for the time being.

He saw Josh and Jimmy skirt by him as he pointed out the restrooms for a mother with a screaming infant in her arms. He took out the next order and hurried back, trying to beat Abbey's time.

"That's the spirit," she said, poking fun of him when she made it to the picnic table first. "Hey, forgot to tell you that I saw Charlie out last night."

"Glad he finally found people to party with," he remarked,

still feeling strangely funny that he wasn't asked, but it was just as well. He'd always resisted the idea anyway. "I've never been much fun to hang out with."

She nudged his shoulder. "You're totally fun once you get going. So what if parties and drinking aren't your thing? At least you have less to be embarrassed about than me."

"Truth." He barked out a laugh remembering the night of the game and their kiss. It seemed eons ago now.

"So...does it seem like he's having a good time with his new friends?" Brennan asked and then silently berated himself for the inquisition.

"The both of you are funny. He asked about you too," she replied. "He might be a bit misguided, but he's sweet and cares about you."

"Yeah, I know. Things are just sort of strange right now."

"I understand." She patted his shoulder.

"So...did you guys hang out or anything?" Brennan could imagine Charlie freaking out about being in the same space as a girl he drooled over.

"*Maybe,*" she responded in a coy voice. Was she messing with him or did she mean....?

"Don't hurt him," he said, suddenly feeling protective of his friend.

"Yep, just like I thought. You still care about him too." She rolled her eyes. "You guys will figure it out eventually."

When his phone buzzed, he half expected it to be from Charlie telling him he'd hooked up—or almost did, if that was the case—with Abbey. More than likely she was pulling his leg.

But it was a text from Josh and when he read it, his breath hitched.

Can't stop thinking about last night.

Tell me about it. If you don't quit I'll be walking around with a boner.

It would be a nice one, that's for sure.

Holy shit! Stop!

LOL!

"I do enjoy seeing that goofy grin on your face," Abbey pointed out as she walked back inside the concession building.

Diary,

Brennan was so sweet and sexy and vulnerable last night. The way he let me touch him—like he was offering me a sliver of his heart.

I don't think we're ready for anything more, but it doesn't even matter. The only thing that does is being with him.

-Josh

24

"You sure your parents aren't gonna be home for a while?" Brennan asked as Josh led him through the kitchen with the blue floral wallpaper to the stairs.

"Stop worrying so much," Josh replied, squeezing his hand. "We're not doing anything wrong, remember?"

Brennan took a deep breath and blew it out. He had never been inside this house before, and he didn't know why it freaked him out so much. Maybe because he knew how strict Mr. Daly was...and it wasn't like Josh had a separate space like Brennan did above his garage. Wasn't like they still couldn't get caught there, but Brennan's family was more likely to be heard before being seen.

"Yeah, okay," Brennan replied with a coy smile as he noted the pristine living room with the tonal couches and walls. "Because this is what friends do, right?"

"That's right," Josh pulled him closer. "Friends kiss like this."

Josh crashed their mouths together and kissed him deeply.

"And touch like this," he added, running his hands over Brennan's hips and pulling him flush.

"Fuck, you're making me hard," Brennan whined in his ear. "We need to stop before we get too carried away."

Josh sucked on his ear. "But maybe I want my friend way too much—"

Brennan chuckled, then drew back to give him a warning look. He might've been brave at a dark lake or beneath the sheets in his room, but it would take him a bit longer to find that sort of courage in Josh's house.

"Okay, I get it." Josh gave him one final peck. "You're probably right. My parents would have a cow if they knew I was kissing a guy under their roof."

"What if it was a girl?" Brennan asked as he followed him up the stairs.

"They'd ask when we were getting married and having babies."

The answer left his stomach unsettled. It just didn't seem fair. He wanted the same thing as anyone else. Why did there have to be double standards?

Josh's room was like a time warp of his sixteen-year-old self. He had Major League ballplayers posted on adjacent walls and a bookshelf with a mix of schoolbooks and Bible-study type paperbacks, from what Brennan could gather from the spines. He wondered if any passages in them talked about homosexuality being wrong.

But you didn't have to be religious to believe that.

The room didn't exactly feel like Josh, but he couldn't put his finger on why. The Josh he'd come to know had many layers beneath the surface levels of baseball and religion. He was smart, thoughtful, funny, and as it turned out, pretty damned romantic.

His kisses alone made his knees weak.

Josh watched as he checked out all the photos on his dresser and ran his hand over the younger pictures of Josh like they were a precious commodity. Probably because they represented the kid he'd always felt some sort of connection with, never comprehending what his feelings even meant.

And now here they were.

When he spotted Josh's violin on a shelf, he smoothed away some of the dust collected on the delicate mahogany neck.

"I remember you on the stage that summer," Brennan remarked, his face heating up as a newer revelation came front and center. "I could not keep my eyes off you. I thought you were beautiful."

"Fuck Brennan, the things you say." Josh stepped up behind him and ran his fingers through his hair. "You make me feel—"

"What?" Brennan asked, his heart thundering.

"Like I can be myself," he whispered against his neck. "Like I can tell you anything."

"You can," Brennan said, twisting to face him. "Don't forget that."

"I won't," he replied, kissing his temple.

"So why did you give it up?" Brennan asked, tracing his fingers over the bow.

"I lost my passion for it," he replied with a shrug. "I lost a lot of myself over the years, I think."

"Have you ever considered doing something with all that talent?" he asked in a hesitant voice. It was something he'd wondered while staring at the ceiling one night.

"Like what?" Josh's voice held a tone of curiosity.

Brennan whirled around. "What about teaching music?"

He cocked an eyebrow. "Like—in a school or something?"

"I can totally see it—you're really good with kids," Brennan said, unable to rein in his enthusiasm. Kids seemed to be drawn to him, on the field and off. "Coaching is sort of like teaching, and you said you're having trouble deciding on a major."

His shoulders deflated. "I don't think Solomon U has that kind of program."

"Let's look it up," Brennan said, pointing to the laptop sitting on his desk.

So they sank down against the headboard and clicked around on his computer, checking out different music education programs.

"What do you think?" Brennan asked after Josh finished reading a longer article about what kind of jobs were available for that type of degree.

"It's the first time I feel interested in something," he replied with a glazed sort of look in his eyes. "Except it's not offered at Solomon U."

"Maybe ask around their teaching department—they might know more about it or if credits could transfer or something." Brennan trailed off, brainstorming more. "Or, *ooh*, I know! Make an appointment with the academic counselor."

"Good idea." Josh bumped his shoulder. "So how about you?"

He sighed. "Not sure I have many options with art either. I'm pretty good at it. I love it. But..."

"Let's look it up," Josh said as he typed "careers in art" in the search engine. Several options popped up. "Oooh, speaking of someone who works well with kids...what about art therapy?"

Brennan's eyebrows scrunched together. "What's that?"

He studied the screen. "You'd do therapy with kids—adults are an option too—through art."

"Holy crap, that never even occurred to me," Brennan said, turning the screen toward him. He clicked on a photo of the therapist painting something with a young kid. "I wonder if Ms. Hurst would know anything more about it."

"Who's that?" Josh asked.

Brennan cringed. "My um, clinical social worker."

He rubbed his hand over his face, realizing there were parts of him Josh didn't know. Josh shifted the computer off his lap and reached for his fingers.

"Hey, don't be self-conscious." He clasped their hands together. "Tell me more?"

"Yeah, okay." He breathed out. "Ms. Hurst has been my counselor the longest. I went into foster care when I was five. My mom...she died of a drug overdose, and I only remember certain things about her—like her blonde hair."

Her cooing voice, her delicate fingers that he suddenly realized trembled a lot. Damn, he hadn't remembered that before. Melancholy sliced at his chest like a sharp knife.

"Damn, I'm sorry," Josh squeezed their palms together and it made him feel less alone.

"Nah, it's okay. It feels good to talk about it."

"So that summer when you told me how you hoped to stay with the Fischers..."

"It's because I've always wanted to belong to a family," he confessed. "It's why I'm afraid to tell them that I...I'm gay."

It was the first time he said it aloud, he realized, and it made his head spin. Liberating and frightening all at once.

"They seem like totally reasonable people. I don't think—"

"But what if I'm wrong? What if that's why she doesn't talk to my uncle anymore?" he covered his face with his hand. "God, I suck. I'm so afraid of everything."

"Come here." Josh pulled at his arm, then wrapped Brennan up in a giant hug. "It's okay, I get it."

Brennan felt the hot sting of tears behind his eyes and swallowed them down. He felt cared for and understood when he was with Josh.

"You belong right here," Josh murmured into his hair and Brennan's breath hitched. "Don't ever feel afraid when you're with me."

They kissed tenderly for several long moments before Brennan drew away to catch his breath. When his eyes were drawn to the violin again, he had an idea. "Play for me?"

Josh scrunched up his nose. "I'm rusty. It's been awhile."

"Doesn't matter." He shook his head. "Still want to hear you."

He sighed. "Okay, but don't say I didn't warn you."

Brennan rolled off the bed to retrieve the instrument and bow for him.

Brennan faced him on the bed while Josh carefully tuned the violin.

Then he lifted it to his shoulder, positioned his arms...and played. He found his rhythm by the middle point of the unfamiliar song, but it didn't matter if Brennan didn't recognize it. Josh was stunning as he shut his eyes and became one with the music.

His instinct had been right—Josh missed playing and he looked more comfortable this way than he ever did on a baseball field. Not that he couldn't do both—that was for him to figure out, and Brennan would support him no matter what.

After another minute, Brennan lay down and stared up at the ceiling as he listened to the music fill him up. When Josh moved to a second rendition of something that sounded vaguely familiar, he rolled to his side and rested his head on Josh's knee so he could watch him play.

Brennan could feel the music vibrating through Josh's skin. He shut his eyes and let it rush through him as his fingertips tattooed a pattern over the downy hair on Josh's thigh.

Suddenly the door to Josh's room slammed open, startling both of them out of their reverie. Josh's final note came to a screeching halt. Brennan's eyes sprang open and he bolted upright.

Mr. Daly stood in the doorway, wearing a venomous scowl.

"What the devil is going on here?" Josh's father came barreling into the room pointing at the both of them accusingly.

"Dad, what the hell? Don't you knock?" Josh thundered back. "You need to respect my privacy."

"I tried to knock, but you obviously didn't hear me. And now I know why the door was closed." He pointed at Brennan.

"I should've known something was going on right under my nose!"

Brennan sprang off the bed, shame washing over him as warm bile crawled up his throat. *Fuck. Fuck. Fuck.*

When he saw Josh's mom standing behind Mr. Daly with her hand clamped over her mouth, his mortification was complete. It all played out like some horrible nightmare come to life.

He'd been nervous coming over to Josh's house and now he knew why. His parents stood against everything he and Josh represented. They would never be accepted. He cursed himself for ever believing it possible. He wished he hadn't allowed himself to *dream* with Josh.

For Josh's part, he was furious. His hands were clenched, and his face was beet red.

"Get out of my room, Dad." He motioned toward the door. "I'd like some privacy to say good-bye to my friend. We can talk afterward. You're being very rude right now."

"Rude?" Mr. Daly bellowed. "What's rude is having homosexual relations under my roof!"

Josh looked as gobsmacked as Brennan felt. "There were no— I was only playing the violin."

"You were lying in bed together and I saw how he was touching you. Did he talk you into this?" He turned to Brennan, his eyes bulging. Brennan was frozen in place mulling that question over in his brain. Was Mr. Daly suggesting that Brennan had turned Josh gay?

"You need to leave right this instant, young man!"

Brennan snapped to attention and immediately bolted for the door.

"Wait, Brennan. I'll walk you out," Josh called after him.

"No!" He waved him off. "It's okay."

He sped down the stairs and practically ran Jimmy over in the kitchen, where he was pouring himself a large glass of milk at the counter. *Goddamn it!*

As soon as he got outside, tears flooded his eyes. He felt gross, dirty, like a damned fool, as he ran all the way home. He passed Kylie and Sydney practicing cheers in their backyard.

Just fucking great.

"Brennan, what's wrong?" Sydney asked in an alarmed voice. "Did something happen?"

His hand flung around his stomach. "No, it's okay. I don't feel good. Gonna lie down."

It wasn't too far from the truth. He felt like puking his guts out.

Thankfully he made it to the sink where he dry-heaved and coughed up a lung.

Brennan stayed in his room all evening long, reliving the moments in Josh's room. As well as the look on his parents' faces. Were they really that vile? And if Josh's parents thought that, what in the world would his own parents say?

When his dad called up to check on him he begged him off, explaining he was feeling better and just needed to sleep. No way he wanted to be seen right then. His face was a blotchy, snotty mess.

He kept looking at his phone to check for a message from Josh, but none ever came.

———

Dear Diary,

What a fucking mess.

I wanted to punch my father in the face. Especially for the way he'd embarrassed Brennan. Damn it all to hell.

I stayed in my room after my father questioned me like I was in front of a firing squad or something. How long? How long have you been choosing the homosexual lifestyle?

I was so angry I responded since birth *and he almost popped a blood vessel.*

Serves him right.

When Mom asked, What happened to you? Where did we go wrong? *I came close to bursting into tears, she looked so sad. It's not that I don't love my parents and I'm not grateful for everything they provided me. I told Mom that as she stared at me from the doorway— as if she'd catch something if she crossed over the threshold into my room—still with that horrified look on her face.*

But they don't know me anymore, and I'm not free to show them who I've become.

And that just makes me fucking sad. And angry. And then shame began seeping in.

After my father warned me I would be thrown out of the house with no help for college if I didn't toe the line and stop seeing Brennan immediately, I sat on my bed with my laptop, trying to calculate things. Could I make it on my own? Would my job at Dairy Whip help?

Could I make it three more years by pretending—and come out with a degree in hand?

Three years. Three years. I think I can do three years.

When there was a knock on my door a couple of hours later and Reverend Coleman stepped inside, I knew what he'd say even before he opened his mouth.

You cannot act on your urges. We have special counseling for people just like you who've engaged in a deviant lifestyle. *And as he went on and on and threw in some scripture passages to back up what he was saying, want to know the most fucked up part?*

I started getting confused and scared all over again.

What if they were right? What if I could cast it all from my body like it's a demon?

Get out, get out, get out. Let me be normal again.

After a while I tuned them out because my brain was going to split wide open.

Instead I pictured Brennan and how he was looking at me when I was playing the violin. Like I hung the moon.

I don't know what to do anymore, Diary. My brain is a wreck.
Please make it all go away.
Or at least have it make sense.
Make sense, make sense, make sense.
Please let everything make sense again.
-Josh

25

BRENNAN WOKE up with a stuffed nose and puffy eyes and as soon as the reality of what happened yesterday slammed into him again, his gut churned.

Fuck, why hadn't they been more careful?

He wanted to cry and curse and scream, but if he was honest with himself, he'd always known there might be this sort of outcome. They were hiding their affection after all and playing with fire.

But damn it, why couldn't they have more time to figure stuff out?

He glanced at his phone. Still no messages from Josh but he wondered if that was because they had their final game this morning, and Josh expected him to show up like usual.

Except this was anything but usual. Would his attendance be too awkward after what happened, and what if Mr. Daly embarrassed him again or kicked him out?

He'd have to decide if it was a chance he was willing to take.

Brennan washed up and changed into the team shirt that read Coach on the front and Holy Cross on the back. It felt wrong to wear it now—but no two ways about it, their church was the sponsor after all.

He paced the floor in his room, unsure of what the hell to do.

But it was his team too, goddamn it. He had helped those kids have a halfway decent season, and he wanted to see it through. He needed to face his fears head on and deal with the consequences. Besides, if he didn't get to see what condition Josh was in, he might not last all day. He'd have to take some other drastic measure to make sure he was okay.

Mind made up, Brennan threw on his baseball cap, headed to his car, and drove to the field. His hands shook on the steering wheel as he pulled into the lot. When he noticed the lone figure carrying a bag of bats to the field, he exhaled in relief that it would only be the two of them. For now.

Josh seemed to cave in on himself when he spotted Brennan walking toward him. He didn't know if it was in relief or protection, but he was still tempted to throw his arms around him and breathe in his scent. He was sure it would calm his own jittering pulse.

But as he got nearer, he saw something else in his eyes, something that looked like caution, restraint. Maybe even regret. And it made a frisson of fear steal up his spine.

Were they wrong to be their true selves? It made his doubts increase tenfold.

Suddenly everything felt different between them. Like overnight a chasm had broken open, pushing them further apart. And Josh was doing all he could to safeguard his feelings.

"I'm sorry," he said as soon as he reached Josh in the dugout. "I should've done things differently. Maybe I shouldn't have laid down on your bed. If your parents think I was the one to—"

"No, it's my fault," he replied, barely making eye contact with Brennan. "I should've known better. I'm sorry I put you through that."

Josh looked so downtrodden and remorseful, so unlike himself that he lifted his hand to reach for him, then thought better of it. What if he rejected him? It would feel much worse.

Instead he grabbed the bases and they worked in tandem, setting the field up, like they always did.

"Will your dad be here?" Brennan asked as he stole a glance toward the parking lot, unable to shake that image of the pure scorn on Mr. Daly's face when he'd walked into the bedroom.

Josh shook his head. "My brother's game is at the same time."

Something shuttered in Josh's gaze, like he was attempting to wall himself off from Brennan, and his heart positively ached.

Maybe showing up wasn't such a good idea after all.

"Do you want me to leave?"

"No, of course, not," Josh replied, but it was in a distant voice that gave Brennan pause. "This is your team too, and the kids would be bummed if you weren't here."

He wanted to hear different stuff from Josh—that he was glad to see him, but Josh was almost careful with his words when he hadn't been before, and the stitch in his chest poked and jabbed where it was most sensitive.

"What happened after I left?" Brennan asked around a tight throat.

Josh's shoulders drooped. "I was drilled by my parents of course, and then our reverend made a special visit to the house to talk to me about my deviant behavior."

"Fuck." Brennan balled his fists as he looked at Josh. Really looked at him. He seemed worn-out and almost cagey.

"I thought I had time to figure stuff out, and that was probably my first mistake," Josh added. "But maybe it's for the best."

"What do you mean?" That statement made an alarm bell sound off in his brain. "What's going to happen now?"

"Well, if I don't immediately cut off contact with you right after this game and begin attending the church's special sessions for people like me, then I'll be homeless and college will no longer be paid for."

A gasp escaped Brennan's lips. *Holy shit.* All for being attracted to someone of the same sex? "Are you kidding me?"

"Nope, that's how the church operates," he replied, looking somewhat resigned now. "According to Reverend Coleman, some members have been able to rid themselves of their urges with enough counseling."

Brennan's mouth opened in shock.

"Is that what you really think? That this—what we are, can be like, I don't know—prayed away?"

He dipped his head. "I don't know anymore. Does it even matter?"

Anger flashed hot in his stomach. "Just listen to yourself—you sound like—"

"Like what?" Josh rounded on him, anger flashing in his eyes. There was that energy he'd seen in the past, but this time it was firing bullets at him.

He didn't want to push Josh. He definitely looked confused and more than conflicted. He only wanted to light a fire inside him again. Maybe it would help him fight through this and find himself again. After all, it had been Josh who'd first convinced Brennan that who he was wasn't wrong.

So he backed down and softened his voice, hoping to tread more carefully. "I don't know—not like yourself, I guess."

"What the hell do you want me to do? I'm stuck—I just need to listen to whatever the hell they want until it's time for me to return to Solomon U."

"No! That doesn't sound very—" Brennan was pacing now. "You can, I don't know—come stay with me and we can figure—"

"And what—quit school? Be kicked out? Have ties severed with my baby brother?" He clenched his teeth. "Then what? Ask for more hours at Dairy Whip?"

"Isn't it better than the alternative?"

"I don't know. I just need time to think—damn it!"

"You can always talk things through with me, remember?" He clenched his jaw. "We said we were each other's—"

"No, I...you...you're too tempting. You confuse things for me."

He waved his hand between them and Brennan's stomach bottomed out.

Lead me not into temptation?

Goddamn it!

"So, for right now I just need to..."

Break away from you.

"Don't say it. Please don't fucking say it." He stormed off to place the bases down and swallow the warm bile inching up his throat.

As their team began showing up, Brennan was completely miserable but tried not to show it by putting on a brave face. He greeted the parents and got the kids going on their final practice. Soon he got lost in the basics of the game, and the pain in his stomach retreated for a little while.

After they ended the season on a high note and won their last game...they got into their final huddle to congratulate the kids and discuss how they'd grown individually and as a team. Surprisingly Sean took the lead by having the other kids go around and thank the coaches and Brennan felt proud of how assertive he'd grown over the season. Many of the kids looked up to him now, and even though he'd still more than likely get teased because kids could be asshats, he at least had better skills to arm himself with now.

When his eyes met Josh's across the circle, Brennan found melancholy in Josh's gaze, and he needed to look away before he did something stupid like grab his shoulder and plaster their lips together.

Once they took a group photo as a keepsake for the parents and kids and said their good-byes, Josh and Brennan cleared the field in virtual silence. Dread climbed up his throat that this was it, that he might never lay eyes on him again the rest of the summer, so he slowed his steps a bit on his way to the parking lot.

When Josh placed the bag of bats in the trunk and slammed it shut, the sound rattled his bones like they might shatter at any moment.

"I hope this isn't good-bye," Brennan said, forcing the words out of his mouth and facing the truth head on. "I'll always be here if you need—"

"I'm sorry for everything—" Josh suddenly blurted out.

Brennan squared his shoulders. "Well, *I'm* not—"

Fuck, Josh shut his eyes and swore under his breath.

One moment they were standing with a narrow sliver of space between them and the next, Josh was pulling Brennan into his arms, their bodies flush, Josh's scruff rubbing against Brennan's ear, making him all shivery and then the embrace was over, as if it never happened at all.

Throwing Brennan one final glance, he got in the car and fisted the steering wheel so hard his knuckles turned white before finally driving away without a glance back.

Brennan stood frozen, watching the wheels kick up dirt until he finally gripped his door handle, feeling utterly bereft.

When he noticed Mr. Daly approaching through the path from the other field, he braced himself and stood his ground. He was tired of feeling ashamed. He could fall apart later.

"Heard you won your final game," the tall and hulking man said as he approached.

Brennan nodded, a bit baffled by the comment, but the vitriol followed soon after.

"It was good of you to help coach, but now I see what your intentions were." There was disgust in his eyes. "Stay away from my son!"

Brennan had the urge to rip off his shirt with the church logo and throw it in his face. Along with his fist. Instead he took a couple of grounding breaths.

"The connection Josh and I share is not wrong," he said through clenched teeth. "Being gay is not a choice. Not like adultery is."

Mr. Daly narrowed his eyes. "What in the devil are you going on about?"

Interesting that he used the word devil.

"You know exactly what I'm talking about. My family owns the drive-in...remember?"

He waited until the idea settled in the man's brain, and then his reaction said it all.

He raised his chin. "I have no idea what you're referring to."

Brennan had never been certain about the man's supposed *counseling* of the church secretary and maybe he never would be, but he sure looked away guiltily now.

"You should attend those counseling sessions or whatever fancy word you call them for being a hypocrite." Brennan pointed in his face as he said it. "For not loving your son for who he is."

"How dare you!" he sputtered and when Brennan glanced over his shoulder, he saw Jimmy and Mrs. Daly coming toward them from the path. Sick to his stomach, he yanked open his car door, slid inside, and skidded out of the parking lot, hoping he kicked up enough dirt to choke the bigoted asshole.

Dear Diary:

I feel like I'm drowning and nothing makes any bit of sense anymore.

Or maybe it's just that the light has gone out of me.

Along with the fight.

-Josh

26

"Honey? Can I come up?"

Shit, it was his mom. Brennan tried to rally himself out of bed, where he lay staring at the ceiling for what seemed like hours, but he didn't know if he had the emotional energy. He'd considered calling Abbey, but instead he sank beneath his covers like they were a refuge from his conflicting thoughts. "Yeah, sure."

He glanced over as his mom cautiously entered his room.

"Oh, honey." She strode over to the bed and hunched over him, feeling his forehead like she used to do when he was younger. "Syd said you weren't feeling good last night, and you didn't even come down to breakfast—or lunch for that matter."

Is that what it took to get her to notice him? He knew he wasn't being fair and now that he had her full attention, he had the urge to cry into her shoulder. Things had been off between them for some time, but he needed her. He needed someone in his corner.

Could he be brave enough? What if his mom wanted to send him packing too?

Fuck, his heart pounded out of his chest as he sat up against the headboard.

"I'm okay...I just...." And then he just couldn't hold back the dam of emotions spilling out of him—they had nowhere to go but out. He slumped forward. "I don't know what to do."

"Talk to me, Brennan." She sat on the edge of his bed. "You're scaring me."

"You've been scaring me too." He couldn't believe he actually said it out loud, but his emotions were raw and right at the surface. And besides, what the hell did he have to lose?

Plenty, but he felt so empty already.

"I'm sorry," she replied in a softened voice. "But I got help and I'm feeling better. Do we need to call Ms. Hurst?"

"No." He panicked. He didn't want a third party; he just wanted his mom. "I just need...I need someone to understand."

When she wrapped him up in a hug, it felt so fucking good. "I'm sorry I've been distant, but I'm here now. Please talk to me. Whatever it is, we can work through it together."

His pulse was going crazy. He needed to get it out, but he didn't know if he should.

So, he tried with a small kernel of truth.

"It's about Josh," he said into her shoulder. "I'm nervous for him."

She drew back to look him in the eye. "What happened?"

"He...uh..." Fuck why did he even open his mouth? This wasn't going to be a simple explanation. "He did something that went against his religion. His parents threatened to kick him out and take away his college funding if he didn't fall in line with the church."

There, that was most of it, anyway.

She gasped. "Was it alcohol or drugs?"

Oh, shit, he hadn't been expecting that off-base interpretation.

He shook his head and made a frustrated sound. "No, Mom."

"Did he get someone pregnant?" she said in a hushed tone.

"Heck no! That would never happen because—you know what?" He shook his head. "Never mind, I should've never started this conversation. I shouldn't be talking about him when he's not—"

"Hey, sometimes it's okay if you're trying to protect or help someone." She squeezed his shoulder. "I promise to honor that. But if he needs help maybe we can come up with some sort of—"

"His church doesn't accept that sort of behavior," he blurted out.

Her eyebrows knit together. "Did he hurt someone?"

"No, they're the ones hurting him." He ground his teeth together. "So hypocritical."

She looked alarmed. "Is there someone we should call?"

"No. Shit, I'm messing all this up." Why the fuck did he say anything at all? Would Josh mind if he told? Maybe his mom would know what to do.

"Take a deep breath," she said, reminding him of Ms. Hurst's instructions for him when he'd fly into a panic about something.

So he did—several in fact—and it calmed him down.

"His parents found out he's...attracted to guys, and now the church is *counseling* him about it."

She gaped at him and he tried to read the emotions in her gaze. She didn't seem disgusted, only concerned. "I am sorry for your friend. How did they find out?"

"He...uh..." Damn it. His entire body felt hot. He sputtered unable to come up with a good enough excuse.

"Were you with him?" she asked in a hesitant voice. "Were you *together*?"

When his eyes sprang to hers, she brushed his hair from his forehead in a loving gesture. He nearly sagged against her. In that moment, he decided he couldn't sit with his truth one moment longer. Not one fucking moment. No matter the consequences.

"Yes. But, we weren't *doing* anything. I was only lying on his bed, listening to him play the violin." The tears readily sprang out of his eyes, and he couldn't wipe them away fast enough. "I'm so sorry."

His voice broke on a sob, and he buried his head in his pillow, unable to meet her eyes. What did she think of him now? Would she ever look at him the same again?

"My sweet boy." He felt her hand on his back. "Never apologize for who you are."

His heart was beating so fast, he thought he might pass out as he raised his head, afraid he'd heard her wrong.

"I think I always knew." She reached out and cupped his cheek. "Well, at least for the past couple of years. But I couldn't be sure, and I needed to wait for you to—"

"*How?*" The question sprang from his lips. "How did you know?"

"Uncle Scott is gay." She shrugged. "And I probably knew since childhood. I can't explain it really—just call it intuition."

Brennan shut his eyes, trying to find the courage to ask the one question he'd been dreading. "Does this mean you'll need me to leave?"

"What? No!" The words jumped from her throat. "Unless you want to go?"

He shook his head almost violently, his pulse pounding at his throat.

"So why would you ask that?"

"You don't talk to him anymore, so this whole time, I figured... maybe it was because..."

"Oh, my God!" She put her hand to her mouth, and he could see her throat working to swallow as tears filled her eyes. "We don't talk because...because siblings sometimes have lots of history between them, and Scott and I—well, we've always ruffled each other's feathers." Brennan nodded because it was true. They'd always bickered about this or that, but it had never lasted, not like this. "And when I told him I might be pregnant, he made a joke I didn't particularly appreciate. I took it the wrong way—because I was emotional—and we had words, and it's so silly now that I'm describing it to you."

He felt so much relief he nearly cried again. "It does sound silly."

"Too silly to hold a grudge for so long," she agreed and then looked at him pointedly. "Remember that when you and Sydney get older."

She wrapped him in her arms again, and he felt happy and reassured and absolutely wrecked at the same time. He wished that Josh had this, and his heart ached for him.

"I don't know what to do," he said into her shoulder.

"Do you have feelings for him?" she asked as she stroked his hair.

He nodded and bit back a whimper. "Yes." *So many feelings.*

"Oh, sweetie, this is so tough and unfair." She angled her head to look at him. "He must be so hurt and confused."

"I don't know what he is—he's almost like, resigned. And that scares me."

"Give him some time to figure out where he needs to land. Just always be here for him. And we will too. You let me know if there's anything you need."

"I will," he whispered around the lump in his throat. "Thanks, Mom."

When they heard a creak on the stairs, their gazes darted to Sydney nervously standing there. "You okay, Brennan?"

"I'll leave you two alone to talk." His mom kissed his head. "And I'll send your dad up later. Don't forget that we love you no matter what."

Dear Diary:

When Brennan got in my line at Dairy Whip, I felt a sharp stitch in my chest that grew the nearer he approached the counter. I'd been drowning in hours of church "counseling," which consisted of Bible passages and prayers and videos showing the end stages of the world and discussions about how I would not be called to stand with Jesus if I continued on this path.

That, along with piercing questions from my father, about exactly what I'd been up to with Brennan and whether he'd persuaded me—to which I continued to answer hell no *because even though that would've undoubtedly cast me in a better light, there was no way I could throw him under the bus.*

And seeing Brennan standing in my line all shy and worried brought my reality sharply back in focus for me.

They can wear me down, but I'm never going to give up any intimate details. Those belong to us and I won't share them—even if they sow doubt in me and nearly convince me that I can be set straight. It's like being in a police interrogation room where they eventually get a forced confession. Yes, I did the crime, now let me do the time.

But when I think about what Brennan and I shared, I'm only filled with light—but maybe that's because I refuse to let the darkness taint those memories. They're the only thing I have. Nothing else feels like my own.

When I asked Brennan if he wanted me to make him an Oreo Tornado with extra cookie pieces, his smile turned me inside out.

When he asked if I was okay, I lied and said yes. Then added, I will be.

Because I will. Won't I? Someday.

After he leaned over and told me his folks knew and they were being supportive, my heart leaped and cracked at the same time. If only I had parents like his.

When I told him I was confident they would be, his smile was so sad, I had to look away.

I almost broke down and cried when he said he was sorry again for the umpteenth time, but instead I asked if he wanted extra whipped cream.

Once I made his Tornado and handed him his cup, our fingers brushed, creating a path of electricity directly to my heart.

When our eyes met, he mouthed words that nearly killed me.

I miss you.

I miss you too, I replied. When I saw a flicker of hope in his eyes, I regretted it because I was pretty messed up and I didn't want to fuck him up too.

Instead, I took a step back and the fire in his eyes dimmed.

He told me he'd give me my space, then went out the door.

I noticed how he sat in his car for a full minute before he pulled out of the lot.

I considered hopping in the passenger side and asking him to drive —to just take me anywhere away from this shitty town, but I knew my thoughts would eventually circle back to the same stark reality.

It isn't that easy. Decisions need to be made, and sometimes those decisions will absolutely gut you.

-Josh

27

BRENNAN STARED at the big screen where the latest blockbuster thriller was playing. He'd gone through the last several days in a fog, hoping to stuff all his emotions into a tight box in a dark corner of his heart but it was nearly impossible. The good news was that he had his family's support now, and that meant literally everything. The only thing missing in his dream scenario was the guy he was crazy about.

Mom had even reached out to Uncle Scott and had invited him over for dinner once he returned from his latest trip. He'd have an earful for Ms. Hurst his next session with her. And maybe she'd have some words of wisdom for how to deal with heartbreak.

Some nights he'd lie awake, cursing himself for agreeing to show up at Josh's house that day and for getting so caught up in the moment that he didn't hear Mr. Daly knocking on the door.

The flip side was that being caught in a so-called compromising position had forced everything out in the open, but the after-effects had only worked in Brennan's favor. Josh was the one suffering the consequences, and Brennan felt absolutely helpless to do anything about it.

"Charlie's up front," Abbey said as she passed by him with a delivery.

"Thanks for the warning," he replied, tongue in cheek.

Abbey had been supportive as well after he finally confessed that she'd been right about him and Josh. But she was furious about how his parents and church had responded. Brennan admitted he'd been driving up to the Dairy Whip every couple of days to check on Josh. Sometimes he'd just sit in the parking lot, satisfied when Josh's gaze found his through the large front window. He was reassured by the small look of relief that always crossed his features. Like Brennan was his lifeline and if that was what he could be to him right now, he'd take it.

Brennan hoped to convey to him that he could come out at any time and leave it all behind. Yeah it would be tough, and he'd be estranged from his family—and especially his brother—and that would be hard to take. He understood why Josh was choosing to see it through and wondered if he wouldn't do the same. Brennan's only fear was that Josh would lose himself completely again.

When Brennan's gaze swung toward the picnic tables and he spotted Charlie sitting beside Nate and a few other guys, he felt uncomfortable. They'd barely spoken since the carnival and he wished they were still the kind of friends that could talk about anything. But somehow things had changed overnight, and they had lost their way.

Unfortunately, his next delivery was to Todd's beater of a car and he swallowed back the bitter taste in his mouth. He was with a girl he didn't recognize and again, Brennan questioned exactly what the hell he thought he was trying to accomplish.

Oh yeah, being a homophobic asshat. Good luck with that.

He lowered his window with a snarl. "It's about damn time."

Brennan narrowed his eyes, a frisson of frustration rolling through him. "What are you gonna do, call me a faggot? Go for it. You're the biggest of them all."

There was flicker of panic in Todd's eyes before he tried to wave Brennan off. "What the hell are you even talking about?"

He cocked an eyebrow, satisfied that he'd rattled him. It was the least he deserved.

"You know exactly what I'm talking about," he said in a lower voice, checking to make sure his date was still absorbed in the movie. "And for the record, it's pretty cathartic once you can admit it to yourself. Scary as fuck but liberating. Maybe you'll get there someday."

Todd scoffed as he attempted to grab the large gulp out of his hand, but Brennan refused to let it go. There was more he wanted to say. As they wrestled for it, the drink tipped over and spilled in Todd's lap. He'd take that ending to their conversation. Perfect, actually.

Todd narrowly missed hitting Brennan in the gut as he pushed open the door. Swearing, he got out of the car to clean off his clothes, and Brennan hid a smug smile.

"Don't just stand there, get me something to clean this up," he snarled at Brennan as his hands frantically swiped down the front of his pants.

"Sorry, too busy," he replied with a grin as his date tried handing him some napkins from inside the car. "Besides, you brought all that on yourself."

His hands were shaking as he strode toward the concession stand but damn, that had felt good. Thankfully, his parents had seen none of it and wouldn't complain about his rude customer service. If they did, he'd have to give them an earful.

A few minutes later, Todd left the lot, most likely because it was uncomfortable sitting through a movie with wet pants. Served him right.

During the middle of the second movie he saw Charlie strolling toward him on the picnic table and he braced himself.

"Nice," Charlie said, sitting down beside. "I saw what happened between you and Todd."

Brennan shrugged. "He deserved it."

"Probably," Charlie agreed.

"Definitely." Brennan clenched his teeth. "He started that rumor about Josh. You know what they say about people in glass houses or however that goes."

Charlie cocked an eyebrow. "What do you mean?"

"Just take my word for it," he replied with a sigh. "He's a douchebag."

There was a long beat of silence as if Charlie was measuring his words. "Nate said he hasn't seen Josh around lately."

Brennan winced, remembering how fast rumors spread around a small town. He may have shared stuff about Josh with his family, but he wasn't sure Charlie would keep his confidence, and that made him sad. Regardless, it was time for him to face some hard truths of his own.

"Thing is, Charlie..." He took a deep breath. Fuck, this was hard. He clamped his shaking fingers beneath his legs. "That rumor could've just as well been about me."

"You?" Charlie asked as his eyebrows knit together.

"I'm attracted to guys, and I've been fighting with myself about it for a long time," he admitted unable to meet Charlie's eyes until he got it all out. "And it's probably the reason why I sort of pushed you away. But I was just so confused about everything."

Charlie looked completely dumbstruck. "You saying you're gay?"

"That's what I'm saying," he confessed, and the weight of his admission sat heavy on his chest. He swallowed past the boulder in his throat and soldiered on. "I'm sorry I haven't been a good friend, but I've been struggling with accepting my sexuality and so fucking afraid of what everyone would think, including you."

Charlie's face went through a series of emotions, from shock to regret to sadness. "I haven't been that great of a friend either. Think I was sort of pissed that you were acting so weird."

"Makes sense." Brennan's fingers ran along the wood grain on the table.

"You weren't interested in even talking about hooking up or girls in general—and now I know why." Brennan snort-laughed at that and it felt good. "Then you started hanging out with Josh, and I couldn't figure out what I'd done to tick you off. I mean, besides the obvious."

"It's sort of hard to admit you're, like, crushing on a dude when your best friend is trying to hook you up with girls."

"So...*Josh*?"

"Not ready to talk about it with you. At least not yet."

"That's cool," he said in a small voice. "I'm sorry you were silently suffering while I've been carrying on like some...some..."

"Dude on Viagra?" Brennan supplied and Charlie laughed.

"Touché."

They grinned at each other, and somehow Brennan knew things would probably be okay. It reminded him of times they'd argue over the rules in some backyard game, and all it took was for one of them to laugh and everything would be okay. They didn't always see eye to eye, but they could at least mostly talk things through.

After a beat of silence, Charlie glanced toward the concession stand hesitantly. "Your family?"

"They've been great," Brennan replied as a breath whooshed out of him. "And fuck, I'm so relieved."

"Damn, Brennan." Charlie thumped his knee. "I wish I could've...would've..."

"S'okay," Brennan replied, and a comfortable silence fell between them.

"Thanks for telling me." Charlie glanced at him through his lashes. "I won't betray your confidence."

Brennan cocked a brow. "Can you help yourself?"

"On this I can," Charlie replied with a smirk before he sobered. "I don't want anyone messing with my best friend."

"Appreciate that." They watched the movie for a minute or two before Brennan turned to his friend. "Gonna be freaked around me now? Like I'm going to try and look at your junk?"

Charlie scrunched up his nose. "Are you?"

"For fuck's sake—"

Charlie's hands shot up. "I'm kidding! Though I'm sure I'll mess up from time to time. I obviously have a lot to learn about, like, stereotypes and all that. That's what Abbey says—"

"Abbey?" Brennan asked. They made eye contact. "Yeah?"

"Yeah," Charlie replied in a hushed voice as his cheeks flushed.

And speak of the devil, Abbey came bouncing outside from the concession building. "Oooh, is this a reunion of sorts?"

"I hope so," Charlie said, bumping shoulders. "I missed this pain in the ass."

"Yeah...yeah, me too."

Diary,

So many confusing and contradictory things.

If these homosexual feelings are a choice, then why can't anyone turn gay on a dime?

But fuck that, why would anyone actually choose to be this vilified?

It's like I have leprosy or something.

-Josh

28

BRENNAN WAS LYING on his bed, staring at the ceiling well past midnight when he heard a noise from down below in the garage.

He sprang out of bed, wondering if he needed to grab something to defend himself with when a familiar voice drifted upward. "Brennan?"

"You scared me." Brennan's chest throbbed as Josh climbed the stairs to his room. He felt like he was in some sort of a dream sequence, having the guy who'd been on constant rotation in his brain standing across the room again.

Ribbons of dim light from the small lamp on his nightstand cast shadows in the room that seemed to draw attention to the ones beneath Josh's eyes. His hair was mussed, and his shirt was rumpled, as if he'd been tossing and turning as well.

"What are you doing here?" Brennan asked through a parched throat.

"Sorry, I..." Josh dipped his head looking so lost and forlorn. "I just needed..."

"Come here," Brennan said and held out his hand. When Josh willingly closed the space between them, he knew it would be okay to wrap him up in a tight hug. "Are you okay?"

"I am now," Josh whispered and Brennan pulled him tighter, burying his nose in his neck. It had only been a couple of weeks, but he missed his touch and smell and especially his smile.

Though as he drew back and looked into his troubled eyes, he was certain he wouldn't get a glimpse of one tonight.

"I had to come see you. I couldn't leave without—"

"Leave?" Brennan's stomach dropped.

Josh leaned in and brushed his lips across the corner of his mouth, and Brennan felt the sting of it down to his toes.

"I agreed to return to school a couple of weeks early," he explained. "There's apparently this program for students who... have 'strayed off the path.' The reverend contacted the head of the ministry department to arrange it."

"For fuck's sake." Frustration flooded him. "That's their solution? Why can't they just leave well enough alone?"

"Suppose I wasn't praying hard enough or whatever," he said in a glum voice.

"*Josh*," Brennan replied. "You've done everything they've asked and now—"

"It's okay. I can handle it." He offered a small smile that didn't reach his eyes. "Plus, three years from now, I'll have my degree sorted out and hopefully a job lined up. This is the best way. I won't lose my brother and everything else—not until I'm on more solid ground."

"But what if you lose other things in the process?" Brennan countered. *Like your sanity.* That thought sat like a boulder in Brennan's stomach.

"Nah..." He squared his shoulders as if to rally. "It'll be okay."

"Fuck, Josh. I'm afraid for you—been afraid for days. What if they change you—change who you are or were meant to be?"

A frisson of fear danced through Josh's eyes before he backed Brennan against the wall. "Then show me, Brennan. Show me who I was meant to be."

Brennan didn't know who moved first before their mouths

crashed in a deep and searching kiss. There were frantic moans as possessive hands clutched and desperate mouths devoured.

"Lie with me," Brennan pleaded as he led him to the bed. "Like we did before so I can hold you and feel you again."

Brennan was only in his boxers and a T-shirt, but Josh made quick work of pushing down his jeans and tugging off his shirt before they slid between Brennan's sheets and curled up together in a tight embrace.

"I'll miss you," Brennan said between kisses.

"Me too." Josh murmured against his throat. "But you have your parents' support and you can live your life, Brennan."

"I don't want—"

"Shhhh...I don't think we should make any promises to each other. Not yet."

He remembered what Josh had said about him being too much of a temptation. He thrust it from his mind. This—whatever this was between them—was more than that.

It was special and sacred. Fragile and forbidden.

And perfect. So fucking perfect.

If only there was time...they were always running out of time.

"I wanted to be your first," Brennan whispered into the quiet. "Someday, when we were ready, I wanted to..."

Josh made a noise like a whimper and reached for his jaw. "You've already been my first. Everything we've done has been a first for me."

Holy shit. If that wasn't the most amazing thing anyone had ever said to him.

"I wasn't your first kiss," Brennan refuted, trying to lighten the intensity cloaking them like a heavy blanket.

"Sure felt like it," Josh replied, looking into his eyes and Brennan's heart vaulted to his throat. "Kissing you that first time was like...the best thing that ever happened to me."

"I was terrified," Brennan admitted. "Afraid I wanted it more than you. But then...holy fuck. Please, kiss me like that again."

So Josh did, leaning forward and sucking on his lip, then painting his tongue across the seam of Brennan's mouth until he opened for him. And as they took their time exploring with lips and teeth and tongues, Brennan didn't think anyone else's mouth or taste would ever do.

Josh had ruined kisses for him.

They tangled hands in hair and moaned into each other's mouths until they were both hard as fence posts. Suddenly Josh reached for the waistband of Brennan's boxers and looked down at him. "I need you, Brennan. Please...I need you so much."

And as Josh rolled off Brennan and slid to the floor in front of him, it became apparent what he'd considered doing.

Brennan lifted his hips to give him better access as he slid his underwear to the floor, his shirt following directly after. This time Brennan wasn't embarrassed. He didn't try to hide himself, not with that reverent look in Josh's eyes bordering on needy.

"Just look at you." Josh stared at Brennan's cock, which was standing tall and proud from his groin. "You're beautiful."

Brennan whimpered, his legs trembling. He needed Josh's hands on him so badly, but he also didn't want him to feel conflicted—not with all the bullshit that was probably on a rotating script in his head. He balled his fists, angry all over again that he couldn't just be accepted for who he was—not where his family and church were concerned.

Josh's fiery gaze was filled with something that looked a lot like determination as he leaned over and buried his nose in the patch of hair at Brennan's groin, like his smell was some sort of elixir, and Brennan had to admit seeing him like that did something to him. He grew even harder at the look of desperation in his eyes. "Please let me put my mouth on you."

"I've never...." Brennan gasped when he felt his warm breath wash over his cock. "Oh God, yes."

Josh hesitantly licked a tender path around the head of his

shaft before wetting a stripe down a vein to the root. Brennan moaned, unable to take in all the sensations at once.

"Oh, fuck. I don't think I can...nobody's ever..." he whimpered as his entire body thrummed.

"You taste...*damn*." Josh fit the tip of Brennan's dick in his mouth and seeing how his stiff cock obscenely stretched Josh's lips almost made him shoot right then and there. He shut his eyes and groaned, trying to stay present.

"I can't get enough, Brennan. Of how you taste and smell." He fit more of his length between his lips and tried to take him all the way down until he gagged. Taking a small breath, he doubled his efforts with his lips and tongue, stuffing Brennan back in his mouth as if he would never get the opportunity again. Brennan avoided thrusting his hips as he moaned shamelessly.

Josh's eyes positively blazed. "This is what I've been missing, what I've been craving...and I can't...I can't imagine...."

"Shhh...it's okay." Brennan reached for Josh's hair, tangling his fingers in the dark locks. "This is just us now. Take your time... you don't have to—"

"Yes, I do." His fiery gaze met Brennan's as his fist tightened on his shaft. "I need this, Brennan. I fucking need *you*."

Brennan stroked his thumb across his jaw and then his ear, attempting to calm him, but he seemed desperate and over-whelmingly needy as he rubbed his chin across Brennan's groin and buried his nose in the wiry patch of hair.

When Brennan shifted his thighs to allow him more room, Josh took his shaft in hand again and licked the underside of the crown. Pinpricks lined Brennan's thighs as his tongue fluttered into the slit and the action was so sensual, it was all he could do to hold himself back.

Josh sucked the swollen tip into his mouth, keeping his hand low on his shaft and stroking upward. Brennan trembled and groaned as he fisted the sheets for leverage. "It feels so good."

Josh gagged a couple more times as he tried to take his shaft deeper into his mouth, and with Brennan's cooing words of encouragement, they awkwardly fumbled their way through their first blowjob on a night he wouldn't soon forget.

Josh's fingers played across his sac as if feeling the weight of his balls in his hand, then lower to his taint as electricity shot up Brennan's spine. "*Oh...Oh God...I'm gonna come.*"

When Josh's fingertips grazed his crease, his entire world was rocked to its core. He'd never felt anything like it, and when the pad of his thumb brushed over his hole, Brennan came apart at the seams. Thick spurts of come hit the roof of Josh's mouth as Brennan shuddered his way through the most intense orgasm he'd ever experienced.

Josh made a noise of surprise as he hollowed his cheeks and sucked in earnest. But for all his effort, Brennan's seed leaked out the sides of his mouth and when he pulled off to draw a breath, a white stream of come gushed over his hand and leaked to his abdomen.

"Oh, my God. That was...*wow*," Brennan exclaimed in a raw voice as Josh seemed to marvel at his softening cock and the come it had produced. His fingers played across his thigh and into the hair at his groin, his eyes wide with wonder.

"It was definitely that." The whole room smelled like sex, and Brennan could do nothing but lie flat and take gulping breaths, attempting to bring his heart rate back to normal as Josh used his shirt to swipe at the mess.

When Josh scooted farther on the bed to rest his head on Brennan's stomach, he ran his fingers through Josh's hair in a lazy pattern, his eyes closing on a sated sigh.

Josh's soft pants fanned across his torso sending shivery fingers along his skin.

"I was born this way," Josh whispered into the quiet of the room.

"Yeah, you were." Brennan's fingers stilled a moment. "We both were."

There was a drawn-out pause as their eyes met and held.

"They want me to believe it's a choice. But not this. Never this." He burrowed his cheek into Brennan's skin. "The way I'm drawn to you is real and almost primal and...and..."

"And valid," Brennan murmured. "And it should be enough. What we feel should be enough. We are meant to be who we are."

When he felt wetness slide across his belly button, Brennan's fingers stilled in alarm.

When Josh's gaze lifted he saw the tear tracks down his cheeks. "Hey, it's okay—come here."

Josh raised himself on his knees, his face hovering closer. "I'm sorry. I don't know why I'm so emo—"

"Shhhh..." Brennan stretched upward to kiss the tears from his cheeks. "It'll be okay—everything will be okay."

He said the words but didn't know if he could believe them. All he could do was hope.

Josh's eyes held fear and sadness and pain, and he wanted to wrap him up again. So that was what he did. They cut the lights and held each other as they drifted in and out of sleep.

When Brennan shifted and felt Josh's hardness against his thigh, their eyes met against the backdrop of moonlight. Brennan rose up on his knees and bent his head to kiss Josh's trembling stomach. Then downward, his mouth feathering over the head of his cock, savoring the warmth and saltiness of his skin.

Positioning his shoulders between Josh's thighs, he took his time kissing and licking the length of his shaft and nuzzling the swollen crown. He tested how far he could take him into his mouth which wasn't far at all, but it didn't even matter, not if Josh's shivers and sobs were any indication.

He wanted to memorize everything about the way Josh tasted and smelled as Josh rocked and shuddered, losing himself in the feel of Brennan's hands and mouth on him. Frighteningly beautiful sounds erupted from Josh's throat and tears leaked from his eyes as he unraveled completely beneath Brennan's tongue.

He tasted salty and musky and though they'd made another mess, Brennan licked his softened cock clean until he was too tender to handle any more. They kissed, tangled limbs together, and whispered against swollen lips until sleep took them again.

Brennan felt the exact moment Josh's feet shifted toward the floor and he knew their stolen time was coming to an end. He was too wrecked to open his eyes and watch him go.

His heart clenched so tight that tears sprang to his eyes. But he couldn't let him leave without...something. Something that would keep them connected.

"Wait." Brennan sat up and wiped his eyes before reaching toward his shelf. "Peanut will always keep you company."

Josh clutched the stuffed elephant to his chest and leaned down to kiss his lips a final time. "Brennan..."

Brennan shook his head. "I can't hear any good-byes."

As soon as he left, Brennan's fingers stroked across his lips, chasing the remaining traces of his kiss until he fell into a restless sleep.

Dear Diary:

How can being with Brennan be wrong when it feels so fucking right?

-Josh

29

Doodled in Brennan's Psych 101 notebook:

Written while sitting on a bench outside the Solomon University chapel:

Dear Diary,

The leaves are changing, there's a chill in the air, and just now I could've sworn I felt the ghost of his fingertips against my skin. But it was probably only the breeze.

It made me ache with need. And also sowed some doubt.

As if what we shared had been a figment of my imagination.

But screw that. There's no way I'll ever forget how he tasted like sunshine and smelled like summer.

-Josh

Dear Diary:

The leaves are changing, there's a chill in the air, and just now I could've sworn I felt the ghost of his fingertips against my skin. But it was probably only the breeze.

It made me ache with need.

And also sowed some doubt.

As if what we shared had been a figment of my imagination.

But screw that. There's no way I'll ever forget how he tasted like sunshine and smelled like summer.

-Josh

30

It was the Sunday before Thanksgiving, the weather was a balmy seventy degrees, and though his parents always wished for a pretty snowfall around the holidays, they were also grateful to keep the business running in milder temperatures.

There were more cars dotting the lot than the previous weekend but between him and Sydney, deliveries had been a piece of cake.

Some of the usual suspects were home on break from college —but the rest would filter in by midweek. Brennan forced himself not to think about what Josh might be up to even though he was never further than a stone's throw away from his thoughts. He couldn't help replaying their last conversation over in his head.

It's okay. I can handle it.

And then...

They want me to believe it's a choice. But not this. Never this.

Brennan sent a nearly daily wish into the wind that Josh was still exactly who he was meant to be—a vibrant, passionate, beautiful guy who, if given the opportunity, would totally rock the violin.

They hadn't laid eyes on each other in three months, but he didn't want to anticipate holiday or summer breaks, because he couldn't imagine what Josh's state of mind was at this point, and it would be too hard to say good-bye all over again.

Sydney told him of a rumor floating around that Mr. Daly had been caught sleeping on the couch overnight in the coach's office at the high school. It was near the weight room where the football players worked out in the early dawn hours during the season. Someone had apparently speculated that the Dalys were having marital trouble.

He considered reaching out to Josh, banking on the idea that maybe the rumor was true, but then he'd be in that same place again questioning Mr. Daly's motives.

Besides, Brennan had classes to focus on, which he enjoyed for the most part. He had become friendly with a couple of other students, and he and Charlie had begun hanging out again. Ms. Hurst had helped him solidify the idea of applying for the art therapy program at TSU once he got his general education classes out of the way at community college.

It was more cost-efficient that way too, which his parents appreciated, and TSU was in driving distance, so he could commute there every day. Mom seemed happier in general now that her brother was in her life again. With his mom's encouragement, he even met Uncle Scott for lunch a couple of times alone. It was sort of awkward at first until the one day he confided in him about Josh. It felt so good to talk to someone who got it.

Uncle Scott shared his own story about a guy he loved who went back into the closet because of his religion. It was the very thing Brennan feared, but his uncle assured him that not all stories had to end that way. In fact, his new boyfriend belonged to a very accepting church, which gave Brennan a measure of hope that Josh might eventually find his way.

Brennan spotted Charlie pulling into the lot just in time for the second movie and when he saw Abbey in the passenger seat, he grinned. She was home on break as well and for the first time in a long while, he and Charlie had something in common. They were both missing people who had left them behind. Charlie didn't talk much about what he and Abbey had gotten up to over the summer or even when he drove to visit her the one long weekend, which only solidified the idea that Abbey mattered to Charlie.

"Our little Charlie is finally growing up," he'd said to him and Charlie had flipped him the bird and called him gramps, which he totally deserved.

Tonight was '80s night with a double feature of *Flashdance* and *The Princess Bride*. He'd almost asked his dad to take the movie out of rotation but figured he'd have to suck it up.

Besides, almost everything in this town was a reminder of Josh Daly.

His dad would probably give him the same advice—to push through the heartbreak so he could come out the other side stronger. He'd been totally supportive of Brennan the last few weeks and he felt closer to his family than ever before.

That was one good thing about this whole mess.

He looked up at the screen just as the beginning credits were rolling.

As you wish.

As he sat on the picnic table with a soda filled with extra ice, he felt a hand grip his shoulder and a close breath in his ear.

"Just in time," the familiar voice said.

When Brennan whipped his head around, his heart practically stopped. He hadn't seen Josh in what felt like forever, but the impact was immediate. His bright eyes were crinkled in humor but also held a hint of wariness. His brown curls had grown out a bit, and his teeth held his plump bottom lip hostage.

Brennan's pulse was throbbing at his throat. "What are you doing here?"

"I couldn't miss the showing of *The Princess Bride*."

"You came home for this?" He motioned to the screen. "Or are you on break?"

"I'm home for a whole lot of different reasons, but I definitely couldn't pass this opportunity up."

When he sat down beside Brennan, their arms brushed, and that pile of feathers kicked up in his stomach again as if they had been blown in by a northern wind.

"Is everything okay?" Brennan asked in a hesitant voice.

"It will be," Josh replied, then winced. "With time, I *hope.*"

"I've always only been a phone call away. You could've—had you just—" he fumbled, trying to make the message clear that he'd been here all along.

He tamped down the frustration that had bubbled up in his throat—that was there most days since Josh left for college.

"I know." His voice was solemn. "But I needed to figure stuff out on my own."

Fair enough.

"Peanut's helped me through some tough times," Josh said with a smirk.

"He's good like that," he replied, and they playfully bumped shoulders.

As they watched the opening sequence of the movie, Josh leaned over. "Did you have suspicions about my dad?"

"The church secretary?" He asked in a hesitant voice.

Josh nodded, anger flitting through his gaze.

"No...I mean *yes*...I guess I wasn't sure," Brennan replied. "I'm sorry."

"I think I probably ignored some signs." His eyebrow rose. "How'd you hear?"

Brennan winced. "A rumor going around school that Syd told me about."

"He's living out of a motel while they seek church *counseling.*" He exaggerated the quotation marks around the word and rolled his eyes. "Guess that Daly family always makes a mess of things."

"Not you. Never you," Brennan countered, trying to make it clear that his father's infidelity was not the same as his sexuality. "Hope your parents figure it out."

"It's definitely complicated." He tightened his jaw, and Brennan could only imagine the varying emotions the family would go through in a situation like this. Poor Jimmy.

"You doing okay?" Josh asked.

"Yeah, pretty good. Just work and classes," he replied. "Gonna eventually transfer to TSU to get my degree in art—then on to an art therapy certification."

"Yeah?" It was the first genuine smile he'd seen from Josh in months and it was dazzling. "That's amazing."

Brennan's cheeks grew warm as he ducked his head. "Thanks."

Josh nudged his shoulder. "Guess I'll be seeing you around campus then..."

Brennan's eyes sprang up to meet his. "Huh?"

"I was already getting all my ducks in a row to transfer my credits to the TSU music program, when my mom called me and all hell broke loose."

Speechless wasn't even the word for what Brennan felt in that moment. Thunderstruck might have been more like it, or maybe just completely overwhelmed, because he could barely move his lips to form anything remotely coherent.

"No shit?" Brennan asked as his pulse quickened.

"Gonna finish the final three weeks of the semester, and then I'm home. I need to be there for Jimmy."

"I'll bet it's tough on him—on all of you," Brennan replied, still trying to wrap his brain around what Josh had confessed. "You're a good brother."

"I'm trying to be." He made a frustrated noise. "But that's as far as the prodigal son act is going to take me. I told my mom I'd only move back home on one condition."

Brennan's eyes widened. "What's that?"

His thumb pressed at a nail on the bench. "That I'm free to come and go as I please and live my life the way I want."

"I'm so happy for you!" Brennan grinned as relief coursed through him. He'd been so worried. "I mean, all things considered."

"Thanks." The corner of Josh's mouth lifted. "It feels good."

The air swirling around them suddenly changed to thick tension.

"And what about you?" Josh asked in a hoarse voice. "Have you been living your life?"

Brennan wasn't sure where the conversation was headed. "Yeah, sure."

"I mean..." He bit his lip and stared at the ground, his cheeks dotting red. "Have you been dating or—"

"No," Brennan replied with no hesitation. "I...I couldn't."

"Why not?" He asked in a throaty whisper.

"Guess some guy from Solomon U hijacked my heart—and my stuffed elephant too." When he glanced at Josh in his side view his eyes darkened as his lip quirked. "How about you?"

The look he gave Brennan left him breathless. "Only ever wanted to be with you."

When Josh inched his hand to rest alongside Brennan's on the bench, too many emotions pelted him at once—from relief to profound affection, as he felt winging in his chest.

He stared at the screen as his pulse pounded in his ears.

When Brennan met Josh halfway and laced their pinkie fingers together, his skin prickled like it did that very first time.

Josh leaned close to Brennan's ear. "You know this is another one of those firsts."

"What is?" Brennan asked as he softly panted.

"Watching a cult classic with my favorite person on earth." When their gazes clashed Josh's eyes softened. "Who also happens to be the guy I'm madly in love with."

"*Josh,*" he mumbled as a million pinpricks lined his skin.

Imprinting Brennan with his words. And their meaning. He cleared his throat. "Then it's a first for me too."

Josh swore under his breath as he interlaced their fingers.

"Not sure I'll be able to concentrate," he said, motioning to the screen. "With you sitting so close and not being able to touch you the way I want."

Brennan grinned and dipped his head as a blush heated his cheeks. *Damn.*

"So, does this mean—"

"That we're boyfriends?" Josh supplied. "Fuck, I hope so."

They watched the movie in silence for a couple of minutes, more than likely trying to let everything soak in. And as it turned out, the simple act of holding his boyfriend's hand in public felt more intimate—profoundly real—than one of his kisses.

Though he would have welcomed one right then.

Brennan shifted uncomfortably as a couple of locals walked by them to the concession stand, the woman eyeing them curiously. "You know everyone's going to talk, right?"

"Yep." Josh lifted their joined hands to his lips. "But this time it's you and me against the world."

"I love the sound of that." In fact, it was everything Brennan always dreamed of.

Josh quirked an eyebrow. "So maybe we should give them something to talk about."

And then his fingers cupped Brennan's jaw and he steered his face so that he was looking into dazzling green eyes. They were only a breath apart and as Josh angled his head, his heart throbbed.

The secret smile he gave Brennan was almost better than the slow and hesitant kiss he delivered.

It only lasted a couple of seconds but this first—*this one*—was the bravest and best moment of his life.

Dear Diary:

I know it's been awhile. Sorry, I've been busy.

It's winter break and Brennan and I have been making plans on his roof under the stars. And dreaming too. About all our firsts.

And maybe all our firsts will turn into all our forevers.

Because there's this feeling of rightness in my bones when I'm with him.

For now, we're taking our sweet old time. With everything. Wink wink.

I discover new things about him every day.

Like that dimple on his lower back that I like to circle with my tongue.

But there's no rush. There's just us forming a connection so deep it scares me sometimes. But warms me too, because when I look at him, I can see my future.

Things might be a wreck at home and I'm still not sure what's going to happen.

But for the first time in my life, everything finally makes sense.

-Josh

31

THE FOLLOWING SUMMER

Josh

"I'M READY," Brennan whined. "For God's sake, hurry."

"Shhh..." He concentrated on Brennan's face as he inserted a second lubed finger and curved it toward that place inside him that made him see stars. "I don't want to hurt you."

Brennan moaned when Josh brushed over his prostate. "No, you're just trying to torture me."

Josh grinned as Brennan rocked against his fingers, his stiff cock leaking against his stomach. Josh wasn't faring much better as he kneeled beside him on the thin sheet.

It was the official start of summer break, and after Sydney's graduation ceremony, they'd taken off to camp under the stars at Big Bear. To be precise, they were inside a tent, but there wasn't a soul in sight, and it was a much-needed break after lots of chaos the past few months.

Josh was officially attending TSU and living at home to be closer to his brother. His parents were still separated, and he had technically stepped into the role of patriarch in his family. He made sure his brother got plenty of attention and lent his mother any support she needed around the house. She still attended church services with Jimmy as well as counseling with his father, but she no longer pushed him to participate—it would only result in an ugly argument if she did. His relationship with his father was strained at best, but he visited Jimmy weekly and looked properly conciliatory for his "sins of the flesh"—or whatever the hell they were calling it. He had fucked up, plain and simple, and had definitely broken the family's trust—so as far as he was concerned, anything Josh had done against the church paled in comparison. Besides, it didn't matter anymore; he was no longer a member.

When Brennan writhed beneath him, Josh knew he was pushing his luck. Their stamina had improved over the past few months, but he wasn't sure what would happen once he was finally inside him.

They had been prepping for their first time for months, it seemed. Lots of stolen moments—mostly in Brennan's loft—licking and sucking and grinding. *Christ,* just thinking about it made him so hard.

Brennan especially loved Josh's tongue, and last night under the full moon he licked him from behind until he shouted his name and spurted all over his stomach. And Josh had been woken up that morning with a blowjob that curled his toes, so all in all, it was an amazing weekend. Best of all, they were free to make as much noise as they wanted out there.

Now that they were somewhere alone, how could they not make love with the pretty scenery as a backdrop?

"Can't wait any longer," Brennan groaned. "I want you so much."

Josh hovered over him. "It'll feel uncomfortable at first...so don't expect—"

"We know this already," Brennan complained. "Stop freaking about it."

Brennan cupped Josh's face, delivering such a desperate and needy kiss, Josh had to rearrange the airspace in his lungs.

When he pulled his fingers out, Brennan gasped at the sensation and seemed nearly bereft.

"God, Brennan, look at you," he whispered as he kneeled behind his lifted knees and lined up his cock with his entrance. He considered slathering on more lube, but Brennan would only accuse him of drawing the moment out longer. Neither had been with anyone else, and after both had gotten clean bills of health, they decided to forgo using a condom.

Truth was, Josh was afraid he'd lose it in one second flat. He wanted to make it good for him. More than good for their first time—if he could.

His thighs began trembling as he looked down at Brennan's tight hole. It was as if all the pleasure receptors in Josh's brain had sent messages directly to his groin, because he felt impossibly hard, his cock red and leaking pre-come.

But Brennan made an impatient noise and rocked upward just as Josh surged forward, his tip pressing inside. Making contact with his tight heat almost made Josh explode instantaneously. He couldn't even describe how fucking fantastic it felt.

Brennan's mouth opened but no sound came out. Josh watched his face as he gazed up at him in wonder. "Talk to me, Brennan."

He trembled all over. "It feels so...intense...*fuck*."

"I know, babe." He smoothed the hair from his forehead, carefully gauging his reaction.

"You okay, though?" Josh whispered, afraid even to move a muscle.

"Yeah...I just need to get past this first part," he grunted, his face and chest a bloom of red. "Don't you dare quit."

They both knew it would sting like hell. They had watched

enough scenes together on his laptop. And those had led to some fun nights of exploration.

"Goddamn," Josh choked out as he pressed forward. He lost his breath as spikes of pleasure rushed straight to his balls.

Seeing his cock buried halfway inside Brennan made him clench his muscles so he didn't spill inside him all too soon.

He gripped Brennan's thighs, his chest tight as sweat pooled along his hairline. A couple more inches and Josh was seated fully inside of him.

Moaning, Brennan's fingernails practically gouged the sheets. Josh stilled, the pressure almost too much to handle as he hissed through his teeth. Brennan was warm and soft and tight—holy Christ.

Josh leaned down to softly kiss his mouth. Brennan's cock pulsed and twitched between them and that, along with the sensation of their bodies connecting so intimately, made him groan out loud.

"I'm inside you, Brennan," he murmured against his lips. "And you feel amazing."

"Finally." Brennan was panting softly and his eyes were glassy. "I think you need to move, so I can really feel you."

Josh slid his fingers across his jaw as he looked down at him. "You sure?"

"Please." Brennan's needy moan brushed across all his nerve endings.

When he reached up to suck on Josh's lower lip, he snapped his hips forward, and Brennan's eyes darkened.

Brennan hooked his feet around the backs of his thighs as Josh thrust harder. Seeing his shaft buried to the hilt made a line of heat lick across his balls.

"God, yes." Brennan's eyes lit up. "I need you to keep moving."

Josh withdrew almost all the way, then drove inside. He pressed Brennan's knees to his shoulders, almost folding him in half. At that angle, Josh was able to plunge deeper.

"Oh God," Brennan said, gritting his teeth. "Right there."

Josh had no earthly idea what he was doing—he was running on pure instinct and barely hanging on. He needed to make it good for Brennan, whose head was thrown back, completely blissed-out—and it made Josh's heart trip over itself.

When he reached down to tighten his fist around Brennan's stiff cock, he bit out a curse and went sailing over the edge. Watching him get his release was mesmerizing. His chest heaved, his face flushed, and his lip parted as if relief.

Josh skated on the brink of his own orgasm as he pumped his hips haphazardly. There was a dull buzz at the base of his spine as his balls tightened and he came with a shout. "Fuuuuuuck."

He sank on top of Brennan, panting and shuddering, as his lips brushed his throat.

They were a mess of limbs and sloppy kisses as Josh's cock softened and slid from Brennan's hole.

Sitting on his knees, he glanced down to where they'd been connected and watched his come leak from Brennan's hole on to the sheets. He couldn't help but slide his finger through the mess, then slip it back inside him.

Brennan gasped. "What are you doing?"

He gave a sheepish grin. "I like having my come inside you."

Josh continued probing with his finger as he sucked a spot on his neck.

"I think we created a monster," Brennan said with a smirk.

His angled an eyebrow. "You like my monster."

Brennan pulled him down for a thorough kiss. "I really fucking do."

"And I really fucking love you," Josh murmured against his lips.

"I love you too," Brennan replied. "Also that we shared another first."

"That was the best part," Josh agreed as he sank down on top of him.

Brennan firmly wrapped his legs around him. "Let's do it again."

Josh laughed into his throat. "I think I need some recovery time."

"I can give you forever," Brennan replied.

Josh kissed his lips. "Does your forever come with s'mores and sexy smiles?"

"Of course," Brennan whispered. "I'll even throw Peanut in for a bargain."

Josh chuckled. "Sold!"

He still hadn't returned the stuffed toy. He felt a certain comfort in having a piece of Brennan in his room until they someday had a place of their own. Probably after graduation, if not sooner. Until then, they had a lot of growing and living to do.

"Me and you against the world, babe." He shifted to curl Brennan in his arms and they gazed out the tent to the canopy of stars.

BONUS SCENE

Brennan

"What are you up to?" Brennan toed off his shoes as soon as he entered the loft after work. Josh was resting against the headboard, staring at his computer screen. They had a dinner date planned for that weekend, so Josh was probably searching for a decent place within driving distance.

"Some research," he replied absently.

Brennan's eyebrows scrunched together. "What kind?"

"Come over here and look for yourself," he said with a wink.

When Brennan crawled onto the bed and settled beside him, his gaze snagged on the screen. It was frozen on an image of two men passionately kissing.

"Is this porn?"

He nodded. "It's amateur, and these two are a real couple," he explained, as if that might help settle Brennan's anxieties. Josh had more easily shrugged off the stigma surrounding such things. For Brennan, it was more the shock value than anything. People being free enough to allow a camera into their bedroom. He wasn't sure he would ever in his lifetime get to that comfortable a place. He was still getting used to Josh seeing him naked, for God's sake, let alone kissing him in public.

"Maybe we can watch it together?" Josh asked as he leaned over to kiss his ear.

Brennan was exhausted from his shift at the drive-in but having Josh waiting always gave him a burst of energy when he came through the door. Maybe their future would include a place of their own, and those green eyes would greet him every day.

Baby steps. That was how he'd define their relationship. They were going slow and figuring life out together. And he wouldn't have it any other way.

"Yeah, I'm down," Brennan replied even as a shiver raced through him, his cock already plumping in anticipation.

As soon as Josh clicked the screen, the make-out session resumed, and Brennan was rock solid in seconds. He watched with rapt attention as the sexy couple got naked, gave each other blowjobs and had sex with the one guy pounding the other from behind. The idea of a cock being stuffed inside him made his nerves feel raw, but he couldn't deny the anticipation of it either —especially with Josh.

When they heard his dad pulling into the driveway, Josh clicked off the screen and Brennan padded down the stairs to make sure the door was locked. Something he'd been doing recently so there were fewer surprise visits from the family. They'd had a couple of close calls, but his family was cool about their privacy in general.

When he returned, Josh was sitting in the chair in the corner of the room in only his boxer briefs, which meant he planned to stay a while longer. He wished there were more nights Josh could hold him until morning, but things were rough for him at home and he wanted to be there for his brother, which was completely understandable. And though his mom no longer questioned his whereabouts, he knew there was still plenty of leftover tension—because that was something neither of them could easily shake. They were a work in progress, together.

"Come'ere," Josh said, motioning with an outstretched arm. Brennan noticed the solid outline of his cock beneath the thin fabric of his underwear as he approached.

Josh delivered a kiss that radiated through his body as his fingers traced the waistband of his jeans. "Take them off? I want to make you feel good."

"You already do." Brennan eagerly pushed down his jeans and underwear and kicked out of them. His cock stood tall as he lifted off his shirt and let it fall to the floor.

"Gorgeous." Josh linked their fingers and pulled him nearer, looking his fill. Out of habit, Brennan's hand shielded his stomach, then dropped once he saw the desire in Josh's eyes.

Brennan moaned when Josh leaned forward to lick one of his nipples, then the other, and it felt so arousing that his knees nearly buckled.

Josh's hand clamped onto his hip to urge him forward. "Straddle me? I want to try something."

"Fuck," he whispered as he climbed onto his lap and felt the hair on Josh's legs tickle the backs of his thighs.

Josh reached for his face and planted a solid kiss on his lips. "Trust me?"

"Yes," Brennan replied without hesitation. If there was one thing he'd come to learn about their newfound relationship, it was that he could tell Josh practically anything and feel supported. And he hoped he brought Josh as much comfort.

"Can I put my finger inside you?" Josh asked, and a shudder quaked through Brennan.

That was when he noticed the lube on the side table. He must've bought it earlier in the day. They'd discussed experimenting and had done plenty over the last few weeks. Josh regularly circled his thumb around Brennan's hole during blowjobs and once used his tongue, which made him shoot like a geyser.

But this was the first time there would be any kind of pene-tration.

His cheeks heated as he buried his head against Josh's shoulder and nodded, trying to hide his reaction. "I never imag-ined anyone would touch me there, let alone..."

Josh drew back forcing Brennan to meet his gaze. "Making each other feel good is not dirty."

Brennan studied him, noting the hint of wariness. "Who are you trying to convince?"

"Maybe both of us," he admitted. "But I need this. I need to be inside you."

"I need it too," he admitted and this time Brennan didn't break eye contact.

Josh cracked opened the lube and dribbled it over his fingers. "This'll make it easier."

Brennan recalled the video and how the guy had responded to fingers inside him, and his cock grew harder despite his nerves.

"Kiss me," Josh whispered. "Wanna feel you."

When Brennan leaned forward and licked into his mouth, Josh wound his arms around his waist to his ass. He grabbed his cheeks and pulled them open. Brennan felt exposed but completely turned-on at the same time.

He moaned when he felt his slick fingers feather along the crease of his ass.

"This okay?" Josh asked with concern in his tone. He was always worried about how Brennan was feeling, which only endeared him more.

"Better than okay," he replied and sealed their mouths together again while shamelessly pushing against his fingers because he wanted this. He thought he might explode with only Josh's slippery hands on him.

When his thumb circled his hole, a shiver stole up his spine. He thought he might possibly lose it right then, so he stilled as his eyes rolled in the back of his head.

"Feel good?" Josh asked against his exposed throat.

"So much," he whispered.

When Josh's finger finally breached his hole, he winced from the initial discomfort.

Josh grew motionless watching him. "Give it more time. I heard it feels amazing after a while."

Brennan kissed his lips. "You've been doing your research without me."

Josh chuckled. "*Maybe.*"

When Brennan relaxed enough around the intrusion, Josh pushed farther, making Brennan gasp. He couldn't believe his boyfriend had his finger inside his ass.

He trembled all over from the sensation.

Josh bit his lip in concentration as he maneuvered inside him, and then Brennan saw fucking stars.

"Holy shit, do that again." So he did until Brennan's entire body was thrumming. All the blood seemed to rush straight to his groin; his cock felt engorged as it leaked against his stomach.

"That's your prostate," Josh said as he thumbed one of his nipples.

"I had no idea it would be so..." Brennan squirmed in his lap. "If you keep doing that...I don't think I can..."

When Josh's hand trailed down to his cock, he groaned and shuddered.

"Oh fuck...that's too good."

Slicking his fist up and down while simultaneous rubbing that magic place inside him, Brennan broke apart all over Josh's stomach.

He slumped against him, his limbs heavy as Josh carefully removed his finger and stroked his back. "That was beautiful."

Brennan could barely move his lips to kiss his neck; he felt completely spent.

"Give me a minute..." he panted. "I want to—"

"No, it's okay." Josh brushed his hair from his forehead. "Remember, we have all the time in the world."

And as he reached between them to pump his own cock, and their come mixed together on his stomach, he'd never felt more connected to another human being in his life.

"I love you," he murmured after watching his boyfriend chase his own release.

Josh pulled Brennan tightly against him, their seed slick between them, and whispered in his ear. "I love you too."

"Stay with me?" Brennan pleaded as he burrowed himself inside his arms.

Josh kissed the top of his head. "Always."

ABOUT CHRISTINA LEE

Once upon a time, **Christina Lee** lived in New York City and was a wardrobe stylist. She spent her days getting in cabs, shopping for photo shoots, eating amazing food, and drinking coffee at her favorite hangouts.

Now she lives in the Midwest with her husband and son—her two favorite guys. She's been a clinical social worker and a special education teacher. But it wasn't until she wrote a weekly column for the local newspaper that she realized she could turn the fairy tales inside her head into the reality of writing fiction.

She's addicted to lip balm, coffee, and kissing. Because everything is better with kissing.

She mainly writes MM Contemporary as well as Adult and New Adult Romance. She believes in happily-ever-afters for all, so reading and writing romance for everybody under the rainbow helps quench her soul.

OTHER BOOKS BY CHRISTINA LEE

First Light

Co-written with Nyrae Dawn (AKA Riley Hart):
Free Fall series:
Touch the Sky
Chase the Sun
Paint the Stars
Spinoff from Free Fall series:
Living Out Loud

Standalones with Riley Hart:
Ever After: A Gay Fairy Tale
Forever Moore: A Gay Fairy Tale
Of Sunlight and Stardust

M/F books that can all standalone:
All of You
Before You Break
Whisper to Me
Promise Me This
Two of Hearts
Three Sacred Words
Twelve Truths and a Lie
When We Met Anthology

EXCERPT FROM BEAUTIFUL DREAMER
GARRETT

"We're almost there," Mom exclaimed, and I barely held back my groan. Maya and I were in the back seat, Mom and Dad in the front, and there were enough suitcases and bags surrounding us to keep us packed in like sardines. It was certainly reminiscent of the ski trips from my childhood, except now I was well out of college and could've driven up by myself if Mom hadn't insisted we all arrive together at Crystal Creek near the Allegheny Mountains.

"Oh good, maybe I'll get some feeling back in my legs," I griped as I sat wedged between two packages Mom swore needed to be held precisely upright so the contents wouldn't be ruined. From the scent wafting up my nose, Mom had purchased some bakery to go along with the strong coffee she loved to serve.

When my stomach rumbled, Maya smirked. She was always the more cheerful and optimistic one of the family but also the baby, or should I say *babied*. We bickered daily as kids, but now that she was in college and called frequently for updates, she'd become one of my best friends.

"The Sweeneys probably beat us here," Maya said, looking past Dad's shoulder as he turned down the snow-covered street toward the chalet my best friend's family rented. Mom and Mrs. Sweeney had been thick as thieves since they were in grade school, and bonded even more when they got pregnant with me and Rory at the same time. We'd been invited to the charming cabin getaway every year during winter break for as long as I could remember. Then our lives changed about six years ago when Mom was diagnosed with stage three non-Hodgkin lymphoma. She ran a fever for weeks, and they had tested her for everything from TB to HIV, finally settling on the right diagnosis. One that rocked our world.

She got to ring the bell two years ago after officially completing chemotherapy, and then last month, when her annual test came back negative, we all breathed more easily.

I'd been in my senior year of high school when we first got the earth-shattering news that the cancer was aggressive and present not only in her lymph nodes, but also in her lungs. I had basically gone off the rails, vacillating between sorrow and anger. I considered deferring college a year, but she insisted I continue with my plans. The only shard of hope I held on to my freshman and sophomore years of college was that this cancer was one of the most treatable.

I knew how much this time together over the holidays meant to her, and I didn't plan to take it for granted. Even if I was feeling a bit uncomfortable about the circumstances.

Gotta bite the bullet sometime, Garrett.

Mom adjusted the knit hat with an embroidered flower on the front that covered her short, wispy hair, which had never quite grown in as thick after chemo. Dad complimented her every chance he got, and damn, I loved him for that. He and Mrs. Sweeney had also arranged a secret vow renewal on this trip, for nostalgia's sake — just a small private ceremony in a place my mom loved. Mrs. Sweeney had gotten ordained through an online program and would be performing the ritual in front of family and friends on Christmas night.

It'd been hard to keep it from Mom, but no question she was going to flip—her emotions were right at the surface these days. All of ours were, to be honest. It would be everything she'd want for Christmas.

And I'd be lying if I didn't say I was glad for the break from my whirlwind life. I was in between productions, and the dance studio where I taught classes was on winter break as well.

"I'm thrilled we'll all be together again," she said from the front seat. "Just like old times."

But it would be far from old times as far as I was concerned, and I felt the familiar tension as the large, wooden structure came into view with its floor-to-ceiling windows in the picturesque setting of a snowy Crystal Creek. I wasn't that naive teen anymore. The one who crushed so hard on my best friend's brother that I wore rose-colored glasses around him most of my life.

The last night we ever spoke ruined all that. The summer before college.

Mortification heated my cheeks as I recalled the incident. It made me slide even farther down in my seat.

My gut cramped as I remembered Mom's diagnosis for the hundredth time that week. The two beers I'd downed to try to forget threatened to crawl back up my throat. It was the weekend before my eighteenth birthday, and I'd dragged Rory to some baseball jock's party. And though we weren't technically invited, it was all cool because Rory was Finn's brother—former star wrestling captain. Please. I might've gone regardless because I was feeling reckless tonight. Nothing seemed to matter—not final grades or my dance scholarship. Nothing. I could tell Rory was worried about me, and he stuck near me all night, watching me like a hawk. I told him to cut it out, but he pretended not to hear me.

A dude I secretly hooked up with junior year gave me a hit of his joint, and I inhaled deeply, begging my brain to fade into oblivion.

When he offered me a ride to another party in a rougher part of town, I stumbled my way to the door behind him.

Rory pleaded with me not to go, but I wouldn't listen to reason. "Stop this, Gar. This is not you."

"It is tonight," I replied and pushed past him.

As soon as we got to the bridge, I knew I was in over my head. Someone had lit a fire in a barrel, and the gravel was littered with empty whiskey bottles. A couple of guys were passing out drugs like they were candy. After some dude handed me a pill to swallow, I pocketed it instead, the first rational thing I'd done that night.

I didn't even know how I was getting home, but no way would I be calling Rory to pick me up, only to have him lecture me some more. I loved him like a brother, but he didn't understand what the hell I was feeling. My mom had cancer, and it was very possible she would die. I reached for a cheap beer sitting in a crate, cracked the lid, and downed half of it.

When Finn Sweeney stepped out of his truck like some knight in shining armor, I wasn't impressed. Instead, I was pissed at Rory for calling his brother to rescue me. This might've not been my crowd, but no way would I be humiliated in front of them.

Finn made eye contact with me right before placing a firm grip on my arm, and I tried to shrug him off. I knew when I was being treated like a kid, and I didn't like it one damned bit. Didn't matter if it was Finn or not. He could go fuck himself.

But Finn was stronger, always had been, and his grasp tightened as he dragged me toward his truck.

"Think you're a tough guy?" he grunted. "I saw you pocket that Molly. Why not swallow it in front of me? I'll wait."

I hesitated, feeling the smooth pill in my hoodie pocket with the edge of my fingers. I'd planned to flush it as soon as I got home. He knew I wasn't into that shit. But I almost wanted to show him I could handle it. Be as much of a hard-ass as he always was, sliding through life with tons of friends and enough confidence to choke a horse.

"Just as I thought. Clueless." He spat on the ground. *"Do you even know where that stuff came from? It could be dangerous."*

"What do you care?" I glowered.

"I don't, you little shit," he replied, shrugging. *"I'm just doing this for Rory."*

Fuck, that had hurt.

"Why do you look nervous?" Maya whispered in my direction as Dad pulled into the long driveway leading to the chalet. She could always read me so well. "Is this because of the falling out between you and Finn? What happened back then, anyway?"

I groaned. "Nothing. Like I told you, he just embarrassed me in front of friends."

Okay, they weren't actually friends. But that wasn't the point.

"He probably doesn't even remember," she replied.

"Yeah, right," I mumbled. But *I* certainly did and had avoided him ever since.

Fortunately, I rarely saw Finn again. College made life busy, as did caring for my mom as she battled cancer. I'd also had enough hookups to help me get over my first real crush.

But you know what they say—you never truly forget.

As we exited the car and I was finally able to stretch my legs, the crisp winter air filled my lungs, making me feel instantly calmer. *I can do this.*

"You guys head inside. I can manage the luggage," I said, waving off my family as Mom reached for the bakery boxes and Dad grabbed one of the heavier bags from the back seat.

Squeals could be heard from the front stoop as Mom was greeted by her best friend. Seeing them together always warmed my heart.

Trunk opened, I began unloading the suitcases and placing them down in the snow-covered driveway.

"Let me give you a hand." Rory's voice drifted from the front porch.

"Hey, you," I said, patting his shoulder when he met me near the rear of the car to grab a heavy bag. Damn, I was glad to see him. His girlfriend would be joining him tomorrow, and while I really liked Kate as well, it would be cool to catch up with him before the house became too crowded. Not that we didn't text or email most days and live in the same area of town, but time and responsibilities had a funny way of getting in the way of meaningful connection.

My stomach tightened as I wondered if his brother, Finn, was here alone. Fuck, I wished I'd had someone to bring. But it was just my luck that it ended with the last guy over two months ago. Not that I was heartbroken about it. Still, he would've made a good buffer.

And just as I had the thought, the guy of my teenage wet dreams walked out of the house, wearing a flannel shirt hanging open over a gray Henley and snug jeans. He adjusted the beanie he wore over all that cinnamon-colored hair. Like some lumberjack, he was sure to still tower over me, which only served to refuel my fantasies about getting manhandled by him. Because despite him mortifying the shit out of me at the party that night, what happened afterward was what I remembered most.

Fuck me. The man was still gorgeous, and time had done nothing to dull that swooping sensation in my stomach that felt like I was bungee jumping off a bridge.

I pushed the unruly bangs out of my eyes and concentrated on my task of emptying the trunk. But it was impossible to look away after not laying eyes on him for so long, so my gaze sprang up to track him again.

After Rory swept past his brother to head inside the house, Finn looked momentarily stricken as he gawked in my direction. I wished I could read his mind as he furrowed his brow. Cursing inwardly, I hoped it wasn't going to be tense between us all week.

I swung a tote bag over my shoulder and lowered another suitcase to the ground just as he reached for the piece of luggage.

"Let me help," he said in a low register as his fingers fumbled over mine on the handle.

"Oh, um, thanks," I replied, trying to act as cool as possible without staring too hard at his hazel eyes or light scruff. "You can grab the last one."

"Cool." Once Finn took out the remaining suitcase, I pushed the button to close the trunk.

I could feel his scrutiny without even meeting his gaze, and I supposed it was natural. I was no longer the teen he once knew. "How long has it been?" he asked.

"Erm, not sure," I replied, playing it off, even though I could probably count it down to the minute. "Maybe six years?"

"Where does the time go?" he muttered, and we turned in the direction of the house.

"Tell me about it," I said, trying to act as unaffected by him as I could, except my pulse was skittering in my veins.

As he trailed behind me up the porch steps, I looked down at myself to double check what I was wearing. Jeans, sweater, ski jacket. Christ, what the hell did it matter? It was as if I had transformed into that lanky adolescent all over again. I needed to chill the fuck out.

"Good to see you, Gar," Finn remarked as I reached for the door handle. It was the name he'd sometimes called me as a kid. It made warmth travel through me at a rapid pace, heating my cheeks in the process.

"You too," I said over my shoulder, briefly catching his eye. Maybe that was our icebreaker and all would be okay.

And just as I breathed a sigh of relief, an unfamiliar voice drifted from the foyer as a very attractive man came into view. "There you are. How can I help?"

"I think we're all set," Finn answered, an edge to his voice. "Garrett, this is Blair. He's, uh, with me."

"This week, at least," Rory grumbled as he grabbed one of the cases to set near the stairs leading to the second floor. Vaguely, I caught Finn throwing his brother a sharp look, but I was too busy concentrating on my breathing. Besides, they were always bickering about something.

And of course Finn Sweeney had brought someone with him. He never seemed to hurt for willing partners. Still the same charismatic dickwad who had everything at his fingertips. I drew in a breath and locked my emotions down. I would not allow this trip to turn into a clusterfuck.